TRACK 61

TRACK 61

EVE KARLIN

cp

coffeetownpress

Kenmore, WA

coffeetownpress

A Coffeetown Press book published by Epicenter Press

Epicenter Press
6524 NE 181st St.
Suite 2
Kenmore, WA 98028

For more information go to:
www.Camelpress.com
www.Coffeetownpress.com
www.Epicenterpress.com
www.EveKarlinBooks.com

Cover design by Scott Book
Design by Melissa Vail Coffman

Track 61
Copyright © 2022 by Eve Karlin

ISBN: 978-1-94207-839-5 (Trade Paper)
ISBN: 978-1-94207-841-8 (eBook)

Printed in the United States of America

To Omi
Grete Baumann Sohn
May 23, 1920 – June 28, 2021

Forever – is composed of Nows –
'Tis not a different time –
Except for Infiniteness –
And Latitude of Home –

—Emily Dickinson, "Forever is Composed of Nows"

Inspired by true events.

ACKNOWLEDGMENTS

THANKS TO PHIL GARRETT, JENNIFER MCCORD and the team at Coffeetown Press. I also appreciate the support given to me by Carolyn Brody, Jesse Bartel and my colleagues at BookHampton. To Toni Fioriello, both colleague and early reader. Many thanks to Maryann Calendrille and my fellow writers at the Ashawagh Hall Writers' Workshop for their input. Special thanks to Christine Knapp Kim, friend and grammarian extraordinaire. Love and gratitude to my husband David who has read and edited the manuscript nearly as often as I have. I also want to thank my parents Sam and Peggy Weiss for adding depth to the characters through their own personal histories. Thanks to Ben for a memorable fieldtrip to Grant's Tomb and to Ally and Jason for their encouragement and inspiration.

PROLOGUE

12:40 a.m., June 13, 1942
Amagansett, New York

PETER SOUGHT SOLACE IN THE PITCH-BLACK SKY. The shore was shrouded in fog and his eyelashes were moist with sea spray, or was it tears? He had endured seventeen months in prison and seventeen days at sea only to have landed on a desolate beach with three misfits, none of whom could be trusted. Fifty yards past the breakers, a long, dark object lurked just below the ocean surface. If he did not know better, he might have thought it was a whale. The hull scraped sandy sea bottom and gravel washed against iron. There was a loud swish he recognized as the sound of the submarine blowing water from its tanks as it tried to lift itself off the ocean floor. The surf pounded like a war drum, urging him to run, while his feet sank into the wet sand, cementing him in place.

George stood beside him, frantically searching his pockets. "Dammit, Pete. I lost something." The silver streak in his hair glistened with salty mist as he dropped to hands and knees to comb the sand. "There was a little book I had. It's important."

Peter cringed at the thought of following such a bungling leader on this risky mission. George had a towering ego and an off-putting habit of holding his index finger to his nose while talking as if to prevent anyone else from getting a word in edgewise. Peter might have been amused if the situation were not so dire. They had come ashore less than an hour ago and had just finished unloading their deadly cargo when they experienced a terrifying close call: a tall figure striding toward them, swinging a flashlight. The beam illuminated the man's blue Coast Guard uniform. George gave a curt wave of his hand, motioning for the others to stay back. Peter reached into a duffel bag and pulled out a red sweater which he tossed to George, who slipped it over his wet fatigues. The other men snatched up the heavy crates and took cover while George went to intercept the guardsman. The encounter had been tense, but mercifully brief. George was convinced "the boy" had believed his story that they were fishermen who had lost their way. Peter was less sure. The fellow had fled quickly. Either he was frightened or he was planning to return with reinforcements; probably both. Peter squinted into the gray surf. The rubber dinghy and the sailors who had brought them here had been swallowed by darkness. His head shot up as an eerie mechanical hum cut through the fog; more trouble.

"Sub's stuck," he noted, deadpan. He pictured dozens of men desperately scrambling to raise the thousand-ton sub out of the ocean silt, but fear for his own safety surpassed any compassion he may have felt for the stranded crew.

"If they can't free themselves, Captain Linder has orders to blow it up." George sounded like a spectator betting on a boxing match, not a man on the ropes. "Come on, Pete. Let's scram."

Peter trailed George up a slope toward the dunes. He had not walked more than a few feet or stood straight in weeks. His calves ached and his body rocked as if he were still onboard the sub. They found the other men sitting on a large piece of driftwood, passing a bottle of Schnapps between them. Both had changed into wrinkled civilian clothing and their discarded uniforms lay in a sodden heap beside a scattering of wooden crates. Both sprang to their feet as a searchlight began scanning the sand.

The Schnapps slipped from the smaller man's hand. "The jig's up," he said. He had a cross-shaped scar in the center of his forehead that flashed in the darkness like a cyclops eye.

"Get a hold of yourself," the other man snapped. He stood to face George. "This is all your fault. You should have killed that boy while you had the chance, or I would have done it for you." He was a heavyset fellow and Peter had little trouble imagining him twisting the guardsman's neck and snapping it with his bare hands.

"Now, boys," George said evenly, "this is the time to be quiet and hold your nerves. Do exactly what I tell you. Each of you get some crates and follow me. Pete, throw those uniforms in the duffel and come on."

Peter curbed his worry by telling himself that, at the very least, George was taking charge. Maybe the circumstances were not as hopeless as he feared. One look at the other men told him otherwise. The thickset oaf was halfway toward George and might have lunged if not for a flare that exploded overhead. The danger seemed to sober him for now. Swearing under his breath, he hefted a pair of crates onto his shoulders and started toward the dunes. The man with the scar hoisted another set and followed. When their backs were turned, Peter stuffed the wet uniforms into the duffel, strung the bag over his shoulder, and picked up the remaining crate. The box held a sealed tin container to prevent water damage to the explosives inside and weighed close to thirty kilos. He had only taken a single step forward when the searchlight caught a glint of glass on the sand, the forgotten Schnapps. The light seemed to linger on the label: Jagdstolz, the Wehrmacht ration-brand. Disgusted that the others had left such an obvious trail, Peter stooped to pick it up. His fingers had just closed around the bottle's neck when he had another thought: Better to leave one small clue, a breadcrumb in the witches' forest, should things not go as planned.

Peter lagged purposely behind as George led the others inland. When he had fallen a safe distance back, he dug a shallow hole and dropped his ship cap inside it. Another crumb, and not much of a safeguard. If he was going to survive, he would have to find better means to protect himself. Peter dumped handfuls of sand over the cap, but could still see the insignia with its spread-winged eagle and blood-red swastika glimmering in the fog.

CHAPTER 1

2:00 p.m., June 13, 1942
New York City

BOMBERS ROARED OVERHEAD AS ARMORED TANKS with menacing names—*Bazooka, Custer, Hellzapoppin*—rumbled up Fifth Avenue. Paratroopers brandished Jump Wing badges and sailors in Dixie cup caps sang "Anchors Aweigh." But all the bugles, trumpets, and drums were drowned out by a wave of cheers in a sea of Stars and Stripes. Thousands of onlookers waved miniature flags; thousands more leaned out of windows, releasing a whirlwind of confetti.

Grete dove into the throng, eager to submerge herself in America's melting pot. Most people were speaking English, some more fluently than others. She heard Irish brogues and nasal French vowels, Spanish, Russian, a smattering of Italian; no German, yet she recognized her countrymen immediately. She could spot the women from behind, ten feet away. Their shoes were clunky and their stockings were made of heavy silk or cotton and did not have seams in the back like the American ones. She was tempted to approach them and ask if they shared her same jumble of emotions: pride in her new country, sorrow for the one she left behind, and weightless uncertainty, as if her feet were planted nowhere.

"Get your souvenir program!" a hawker cried. "You can't tell who's winning the war without a program."

A marching band struck the opening notes of Handel's "Dead March" and a sharp pain flared in Grete's gut. A German composer seemed like a disturbing selection for an American military parade; a funeral march outright macabre. A row of mounted police on spirited horses ushered in the floats. The first featured a cloaked skeleton astride a decrepit horse beating a red, swastika-bearing, drum. Grete sprang back as if that might allow her to escape the swastika's reach. Her heart pulsed in her ears, louder than the drum. With the exception of a few grainy newsprint photos, she had not laid eyes on a swastika since leaving Germany three years earlier. The more she looked, the more it churned round and round like an undertow threatening to drown anyone who dared swim against the tide. She closed her eyes and felt a fierce current surround her. She had earned shelves of trophies at the swim club on the Rhine, but the last time she had visited, on a warm June afternoon very like today, the club was overrun with strangers. One man in work boots and overalls spat *"Schmutziger Jude,"* dirty Jew, before snatching her off her feet and flinging her beyond the roped swim area into the raging river. The current dragged her down and she struggled for air. But the true shock was the venom in the man's eyes. That day she summoned the strength to swim to shore, and she did the same today, imagining strong, powerful strokes. *Ruhig,* she told herself, *steady.*

The man to her left jerked his head toward her and her throat knotted closed. Had she spoken out loud—in German? She never spoke in her native tongue. "How can you be German *and* Jewish?" a classmate had asked when she first arrived in the U.S. Now, when asked about her accent, she said she was Swiss. Trying not to be too obvious, Grete peered at the stranger. His hat rested on a slant like someone who did not want to be recognized. He wasn't tall, but his broad shoulders and solid build cast a shadow over her. Would he snatch her by the elbow, and then declare her an enemy in their midst?

On top of the bleachers, the flags of every Allied nation hung limp in the stagnant heat: symbolism that did little to inspire confidence, Grete thought. A red, white, and blue banner proclaimed, "I Need America, America Needs Me." She read it twice. The first part rang true enough; she was doing her best to fulfill the second. She saved cooking fat in cans, donating it to the local butcher, who poured it into a huge vat before turning it over to the Army, where the grease was improbably transformed into bombs. Twice a week, she visited the Salvage for Victory depot on Amsterdam Avenue where she and other girls passed hours cutting up old girdles, leaky hot water bottles, ripped bathing caps, and galoshes, whose rubbery remains would be melted into tires. And though she was only one among thousands cheering the troops on a stifling summer afternoon, she lent her voice with zeal.

The stranger watched her with wondering eyes and offered a half smile, difficult to interpret. As the mercury rose even patrolmen had removed their jackets, but this man still wore his. The buttons were fastened, his necktie was tightly knotted, a matching pocket square neatly folded. Most of the people around them were in old clothing, either out of necessity or as a show of support for the war, but his outfit looked brand new. His cufflinks winked in the sunlight. *Spiffy* was the American word she would use to describe him, maybe even slightly garish. The clothing didn't suit him. Grete held very still, frightened her silence revealed too much. Moments passed until she felt compelled to say something, anything, to ease the tension.

"Swell day," she said, careful to keep her lips in a tight circle and her cheeks drawn as she pronounced *swell*. She imagined it was the type of thing that might have been uttered by her favorite actress, Myrna Loy. She had seen *The Thin Man* her first week in New York and become an instant fan. Loy's character, Nora Charles, had brains as well as curves, a stylish finger-curl bob, and a winning attitude. Grete liked to think of America as a place where a woman could use stick-to-itiveness and ingenuity to save the day.

Grete stood spellbound as the stranger reached out to touch her forearm. The familiarity of the gesture startled her. There was something conspiratorial about the way he drew casually closer and spoke into her ear. *"Ich auch."* Me too. The words flowed over her, the guttural tone bringing a sense of relief. His whispered German suggested he was a fellow refugee, someone who understood the danger of speaking out loud in German. She looked closer and recognized the lines of strain between his brows, a perplexed expression she often wore. The grooves framing his mouth led her to believe he was a few years older than she, maybe mid-twenties. His complexion was olive, his nose long and straight. Their eyes met before she could avert her gaze. His hand slid down to where the top of her glove fastened with a single delicate pearl. She could feel his callouses as his fingers brushed against her tender skin. His touch was inappropriate, but she remained still, baffled by the intensity of her emotions. Rather than threatening, his touch felt like a cry for help, and she could not remember the last time she had been in the position to help anyone. Grete did not move, afraid that if she did, he might lose his balance and fall.

"Is something wrong?" The question escaped her lips before she considered the wisdom of asking it. Having asked about his well-being, she was aware that she was the one trembling.

"I'm Peter," he said in a voice so soft Grete found herself leaning in to hear. Peter smelled fresh, with a hint of something she couldn't place; not like the sticky Brylcreem the young men who stood uncomfortably close on crowded subways used to slick their hair. As if suddenly aware he was overstepping, Peter pulled away and tapped the brim of his hat, blinking in the sunlight. "Forgive me. I didn't mean to offend you." He smiled openly. His smile changed his features, brightening dark lines.

Grete could feel herself softening. At home, she had taken pride—*ridiculous*, she thought now—in her slim waist and glossy hair. Of course, that was before she had been scarred by the ugliness of war. "Grete," she said, attempting a smile as optimistic as his. It did not come naturally.

"Gretel. Like the fairytale?"

"Grete." She stressed the final vowel to distinguish herself from the hapless young girl lured into the witches' gingerbread house.

Peter picked up on her aversion. "Gretel was quick-witted. She and Hansel lived happily ever after."

Grete was not sure there was such a thing as happy endings. Heat shimmered over the asphalt as an enormous dragon-like creature rumbled into view: Hitler the Axis War Monster. Three scales jutted from the beast's spine. One displayed the Fascist flag, another the Japanese Rising Sun, a third a large black swastika. Above the dragon's withers, a larger than life, mustachioed figure clad in a Prussian helmet and body armor plunged a sword into a skeleton at his feet. As the hot sun glinted off the Prussian's blade, beads of sweat trickled down Grete's brow and she fumbled in her purse for a handkerchief, Papa's handkerchief. He had given it to her on the day of her departure so she could wipe away her tears, and it had become a cherished keepsake. A vestige from her former life embroidered with Papa's initials, it smelled faintly of steamed linen and home. She ran her finger over an elegantly stitched *J* and a rotund *B*. It was the kind of small luxury she used to take for granted. Now the stitching was beginning to fray and the fabric had faded from too many washings.

"Heil Hitler!" a loudspeaker bellowed, "Il Duce!"

A young boy standing in front of Grete burst into tears.

"Sweetie," his mother soothed. "Don't cry. It's not real."

Grete silently disagreed. While she had been lucky enough to escape, her home had already become a battleground. She followed her memory down a well-worn path. One morning, just a week before her departure, there was a commotion on her street. An area of the sidewalk had been roped off and there was a white sheet on the ground covering a crumpled heap. Grete could see the bulge of a leg brace, and knew it belonged to the boy next door who had polio. "He was a feebleminded child," the hag who ran the corner bakery hissed knowingly to anyone who would listen. Grete knew the opposite was true. He was a bright boy who simply required crutches. Later, she learned the Nazis had labeled the boy *feeble* and refused to grant his family travel papers. He had thrown himself out the window and left a note explaining that he could not burden his parents any longer.

Trying to still her whirling thoughts, Grete turned back to the parade. A group of men, women, and children, dressed in tattered clothes, pulled a cart of household goods along the white traffic line. Trailing them, starved and beaten people representing refugees lay behind barbed wire on a crêpe-hung float. To Grete, the ghastly procession seemed like a distressing way to bolster American troops. She stole another peek at Peter and was curious to see that he looked just as baffled. His head was cocked, his mouth agape. He turned to her and shrugged in confusion. Her cheeks flushed. Their otherness felt like a shared secret.

The crowd booed. A woman cupped gloved hands to the sides of her mouth like a bullhorn. "Roast the Krauts!" Grete marveled at the speed in which ordinary-looking people turned vicious.

The boy's sobs increased. "Darling?" the mother said, uneasily nudging the man beside her.

"They're showing the causes of the war," the man explained, craning his head to look down the street. "Don't worry, buddy." He patted the boy on his head. "The victory float's coming."

Grete clutched Papa's handkerchief. If only her father were by her side, reassuring her of pending victory. It made little difference that her family was not religious. Nor did it matter that Papa had fought bravely during the Great War and been awarded the Iron Cross. Now, a Jew, even one who died for Germany, was not a real German. Her family owned an industrial supply factory in Mannheim—or they used to, she had to keep reminding herself. The Reich had confiscated it. The factory manufactured asbestos, invaluable insulation for work gloves, military vehicles, and submarines. But nothing could protect her family from the scorch of anti-Semitism. As the violence escalated, her parents sent her to live with her Uncle Jacques in New York City.

Mama had insisted the madness in Germany would blow over and, if not, Papa would settle his business affairs and they would join her in New York. But months passed and years faded. The last letter from her parents was dated November 18, 1940. It explained that three policemen had arrived in their apartment at nine in the morning and given them an hour to pack a bag small enough to carry provisions for a day. Mama wrote that they had traveled three days and three nights by train before arriving at a camp near Lourdes. *There are about 15,000 people here,* the letter said. *All behind barbed wire. We sleep fifty-six to a barrack, arranged in alphabetical slots. Men and women are separated. Thank God our days are spent outside and I am able to see your papa. Papa is working to fix all this. He has reported to an officer and told him we have relatives in France. Please do everything you can for us. If we could put up 12,000 francs we could get out of the camp.* Uncle Jacques sent the money. There was no confirmation it ever arrived.

Grete watched the endless stream of khaki-clad troops filing uptown and did her best to single out one man in each group, to study his features and gait, and remind herself that he was someone's son, brother, or beau. A plaintive prayer arose in her throat, *Who shall live and who shall die, who in good time, and who by untimely death, who by water and who by fire, who by sword and who by beast . . .* The parade was meant to showcase America's military might, but only six months had passed since they had entered the fight and their strength remained untested.

"Those boys are off to kill or be killed," Peter said, echoing her thoughts. Her skin prickled. His voice was somber with a note of acknowledgment as if he too had experienced the cruelty of war first hand. He raised his chin toward a blonde majorette strutting in sailor shorts with a panel of shiny brass buttons adorning her waist. "War isn't about marching bands."

The more Peter spoke, the more she marveled at his American accent. Only another German could have detected the hint of mother tongue. "Have you been here long?" she asked.

"A few hours."

"America," she clarified. "Have you been in this country long?"

Peter stood pin straight. "I'm American."

"Oh?" Had she imagined everything? She used to consider herself a good judge of people, but all that had changed. Understanding Americans was more difficult than mastering English.

"A naturalized citizen." He delivered this news with a cautious formality that made it difficult to believe he'd lived here the five years it took to become naturalized. "I was born in Augsburg and my . . ." His eyes scanned the pavement. "My loved ones are still there." He nodded dismissively in a manner that struck her as distinctly German.

"My parents are also in Europe." She fought the quiver in her voice. Speaking about her parents was like rubbing salt into an open wound. She preferred to keep her pain hidden and could not explain why she was airing it now, openly, to a stranger. Her thoughts slipped backwards to her departure from the port in Bremen. Their family wasn't one to express emotions, but Papa had embraced her then, hugging her for a long moment during which she sensed his frailty. She wished she had told him how much she loved him. Grete still could not bear to even think about Mama. It had been physically painful to turn and walk away. Lot's wife had looked back and turned into a pillar of salt. *Don't look back, don't look back*, she coached herself. As it was, she was forever hardened, having left an essential part of herself behind. She shook those thoughts away and turned back to Peter. Recalling those goodbyes at the port helped her recognize what he reminded her of. Peter smelled like the sea.

A truck backfired as it came to a screeching halt. Troops leapt out, raced to the rear, and flung open the doors. Peter jumped, landing squarely on her toes. Grete stifled a cry. She expected Peter to apologize. Instead, he was backing away. There was a loud fluttering and a smattering of applause as dozens of pigeons took to the air. Peter removed his hat and wiped his brow with the back of his hand. "Excuse me," he said, self-consciously looking down at her foot. "I don't know what came over me. Did I hurt you?"

She wiggled her toes. Peter was needlessly embarrassed. "I understand," she said, and she did. Since Mannheim, stray bangs and sudden movements made her heart skip too. She was relieved she had not misjudged him. Peter may have lived here for a long time, but he was raised in Germany, like her.

"Homing pigeons." He shrugged. Her heart tugged as she registered the wistful timbre of his voice: Homesickness. The birds branched out in the open sky. Grete watched them scatter, set free their first instinct was to find their way home. A wave of heat washed over her. The crowd was suddenly confining.

"Time for me to fly," she said quietly. Peter tilted his head, confused. "Like the birds." She flapped an arm.

Peter's eyes crinkled, his shoulders dropped, and his entire being seemed to relax as he took a deep breath and laughed. His laughter was hearty and rich. They were standing among thousands, but his joy felt intimate. How long had it been since she had made anyone laugh? Grete had the impression that Peter saw her as more than a skinny girl with a funny accent. He seemed to see the lighthearted person she had been—the person she wanted to be again.

"You're very kind," he said. "Are you alone at this exhibition?"

"Parade," Grete quickly corrected. A holdover from school where she'd been a bit of a know-it-all. In Mannheim, her teachers had made Jewish students feel incompetent, rarely calling on them and snickering if they performed poorly. Resentful, Grete had begun speaking out of turn and had spent most of her days standing behind the blackboard as punishment.

"Parade." Peter nodded appreciatively. "Are you alone here?"

"I . . ." Grete stalled. She used to be outgoing and social, but as the crisis in Germany worsened she had become reclusive, withdrawing even from Jewish friends, as if a pair might invite twice the danger. Her separateness had only intensified in America. Lack of English made her shy and she didn't feel as if she had much to offer new friends.

"Before you go . . ." He nodded toward a vendor's cart and shrugged hopefully in a way that seemed to show he did not have any real expectations. "Can I buy you a frankfurter?"

"Hot dog." She held her hands up, pulled them apart, and wagged her pinky to indicate a dachshund's tail. "We're to call frankfurters hot dogs."

"Who would want to eat a *hot dog*?"

She did her best Nora Charles impression, scrunching her nose and assuming an air of breezy sophistication. "I know, and sauerkraut is now *victory cabbage*."

Peter laughed again. "Maybe it would be better to have an early dinner? Away from the crowd."

Grete wavered. Talking to Peter had made her feel less isolated, strangely invigorated—and famished. A favorite expression of Mama's came to mind: *forever is composed of nows*. The sentiment seemed especially appropriate because it was penned by an American woman. Mama, a voracious reader, always had a book in-hand. Her favorites were Thomas Mann and Goethe. Grete suspected Mama would frown at her new passion for drugstore romances, just as she would disapprove of Grete dining with a stranger. But the weather was warm, the evenings long, and loneliness clouded her judgment. Her days were a delicate balancing act as she tried to maintain hope for her parents while simultaneously preparing for the worst. She knew she should thank Peter for the invitation and politely excuse herself; she also knew what was waiting for her at home. Uncle Jacques would be absorbed in the latest headlines or some thick tome and she would be alone, caught in the endless cycle of her own churning thoughts.

"It'd be nice to talk," Peter said.

Grete was surprised to find herself nodding; talking would be nice. The desire crept up on her like hunger. All at once, she was starved for company.

CHAPTER 2

As Grete strolled away from the parade with Peter by her side, there was a spring in her step she had not felt in ages. She had almost forgotten this sense of buoyancy. While she knew she was being foolish, maybe even reckless, she was curiously detached. She was playing a role, that of a sophisticated New Yorker, walking beside a dashing man. She lifted her heel and flexed her calf as unflappable as Nora Charles. Peter's stride did not have the same bounce. He was lugging a bulky canvas satchel that did not match his snappy attire. Standing shoulder-to-shoulder in the crowd, she had not even noticed the bag. Now the cumbersome sack hung like a barrier between them. To Grete, it looked like a feedbag. The weathered leather strap cut into his shoulder and creased his suit. They were passing Grand Central Terminal when Peter came to an abrupt stop.

"Would you mind if we take a quick detour?" he asked.

Grete stood, pinned to the spot. Harried commuters coursed all around them. One man grunted, "Step aside," but she remained motionless, unwilling to turn and leave, unable to proceed. Peter had invited her to come with him and she had neglected to ask the only logical question: *Where?*

"I thought we were getting a bite to eat," she said. It was possible to dine at Grand Central, but they wouldn't be escaping the crowds.

"We are, but I promised to meet someone here and give him this." He shrugged, indicating the bag. "It won't take long."

She scrunched her nose at the misshapen sack which had a

musty odor. "What's in there anyway?"

The parenthesis around Peter's mouth deepened. "It belongs to the fellow I'm meeting." His hand hovered behind the small of her back. Its proximity had an almost magnetic pull. *Forever is composed of nows*, she told herself as she allowed Peter to guide her into the terminal. The drumbeat of hundreds of people in motion propelled her past flower carts, shoeshine chairs, and newsstands. Paperboys shouted the latest headlines, "Bombers Blast Japs!" "War Might of City on Display Today!"

She was aware of the steady click of her heels as the entrance ramp opened into the aptly named Great Hall and its acres of pink marble. Grand Central's beaux-arts splendor quelled any lingering trepidation. The oblong windows framing the hall had been blacked out as a precaution against nighttime bombing raids. In place of sunlight, gilded chandeliers threw off honey-colored light like the waning hours of a fall day. She had been here before with Uncle Jacques, during an introductory tour of New York that also included the Empire State Building and Chinatown. A thrill had shot through her as she imagined King Kong scaling the Empire State Building and she had savored all the exotic flavors of Chinatown, but Grand Central had been her favorite stop. The terminal reminded her of a European cathedral. With its underbelly of mysterious passages, it could easily have housed a recluse like Victor Hugo's hunchback. Better yet, it was a secular sanctuary. She had learned to fear religious discord and would have preferred a world where people shared the same morals without all the pomp, ceremony, and divisiveness of religion. After Jacque's introduction, she had returned to Grand Central several times on her own; once to seek shelter from the rain and twice more to simply sit. She liked the irony of being invisible in one of the busiest places in the world, watching what she imagined to be long lost lovers tangled in a passionate embrace, families parting due to hardship or war, and others joyfully reuniting.

Towering over them all was a massive advertisement for

defense bonds featuring photos of clean-cut servicemen and beaming children. *Government by the people shall not perish from the earth*, it proclaimed. The terminal was the last rail stop for troops going to Europe and the USO had set up a lounge on the East Balcony where GIs could enjoy a bird's eye view, sandwiches, ping pong, and the occasional show tune performed by Broadway stars. Grete would have liked to join the ranks of young women who volunteered there, playing gin rummy or making small talk to distract the troops. Just last week, she had donned her most professional looking A-line dress in a patriotic shade of blue to come and inquire about a job. Her cheeks flushed at the memory.

"With that accent!" The woman in charge had said while she arched a judicious brow. "We're here to welcome the boys, not frighten them."

Grete had left discouraged, not surprised. After the failed USO interview, she had gone to a typing pool and taken a test with embarrassing results. Her accent ruled out work as a switchboard operator or shop girl. At the Salvage for Victory depot, where she did little more than shred old rubber, the other women were distant. "Oh, another one," a well-coiffed girl, who made it a point to tell the others she had never been to the West Side before, huffed when Grete first arrived. "Sadie and Esther and now her."

"We are all here to help," Grete wanted to say, but she held her tongue. She had already witnessed enough confrontation to last a lifetime.

Now, walking alongside Peter, she pushed those thoughts aside. Peter welcomed her company, and that would have to do for now. All around them, the station was pulsing with energy. The government had threatened to limit vacations and people were eager to depart before they made good on their word.

Peter paused in the center of the hall to admire the ceiling mural, a ribbon of gold stars stretching across a turquoise sky. The mural was tarnished by layers of soot coughed up by thousands of trains and even more smokers. To Grete's eye, the soiling added a natural quality, enhancing, not dulling the brilliance. The mural spoke to her. *Beauty—and nature—would triumph,* she told herself this all the time.

A wiry fellow flicked a cigarette to the ground, where it smoldered at Grete's feet. He took a step closer, grinding the butt under his heel. His suit was jet-black as was his tie, his shirt stark white. Wavy black hair was parted above the corner of his left eye and slicked back, highlighting a silver streak.

"The artist botched the whole thing!" he said as he pointed upwards.

"George." Peter's broad shoulders sagged. "I thought we were meeting downstairs."

Grete took in the nattily dressed man. His tie was too wide and his trousers had cuffs, not at all in keeping with wartime fabric rationing. He had a gaunt face and nervous demeanor that made him seem far older than Peter. She stood back, wondering at the unlikely pair.

"That ceiling has the sun rising in the west and setting in the east," George said, intent on the point he was making.

Grete did a slow pirouette taking in Pisces, Taurus, and the crab whose name she had forgotten. The upside down universe seemed like a message whose meaning she could not interpret. "You're saying it's backwards?"

Peter brushed against her as he looked up. His touch felt like a silent pact. "Do you think the artist did it on purpose?" he asked.

"An intentional blunder twelve stories tall?" George scoffed; his laugh as patronizing as his words.

"This way we can see the stars like the gods do," Peter said.

"Looking down from heaven," Grete mused. She felt a wave of gratitude. Without Peter's reasoning, she would have merely remembered the error every time she looked up at it. Now, this night sky would be unlike any other, which made it even more precious.

George tapped his index finger along the side of his nose as if

indicating the vantage point from which he was looking down at
Grete. "Who's she?" Grete did not appreciate the way he spoke over
her. There was disapproval in his voice and something else: suspicion.

"We met at the . . ." Peter's eyes sought hers. She could not
remember the last time anyone looked at her so intently.

Parade, she mouthed.

"Parade," he said emphatically.

"Huh, how about that." George reached into his pocket to
retrieve a pack of Camels. His fingertips were stained yellow and
he tapped the bottom of the pack as if typing Morse code. "George
Davis here." He lit a fresh cigarette and exhaled, studying her
through a veil of smoke. "I didn't catch your name."

You didn't ask, Grete thought. She had no desire to tell this
strange man her name. The floor vibrated as trains rumbled into
the station and long moments passed while she waited for Peter
to make introductions. Her eyes rested on the opalescent clock
above the information booth.

"Opal," she said, immediately warming to the exotic name.
"My name's Opal." The alias bolstered her sense that this excur-
sion was simply a game without repercussions. She glanced at
Peter to see if he was bothered by her subterfuge. His expression
betrayed nothing.

"Opal. Pretty." George uttered the name with a formality that
suggested he did not believe her but was content to let it go. "My
wife's name is Rose Marie. Isn't that beautiful? But somehow it
didn't suit her. She's too spunky for such a solemn name. I call
her Snooks."

Grete's brow wrinkled as she tried to keep up. George leapt
from topic to topic like an overtired child, excited one moment
and sullen the next.

"George," Peter said, his demeanor seeming to soften, "I didn't
know you were married."

George's face darkened. "Married twelve years, the happi-
est years of my life and now, through no fault of our own, we're
separated."

Since Hitler's rise, Grete had often felt like a blameless victim too. She took a longer, more sympathetic look at George. He had a high forehead, watery eyes, and a distracted air. "Is your wife in Europe?" She could not tell if George was American or German. He didn't have an accent, but his English was peppered with slang as if he were trying too hard to fit in.

"Born and bred in Jefferson County, P.A. You can't get more American than that!" Grete did not understand the abbreviation, but there was no doubt Jefferson County was one hundred percent American. George seemed to be going out of his way to say so. "My poor Snooks was on her way to Spain when the liner she was on was seized."

"Seized?"

"There were Germans onboard," George said, answering her unasked question. "They let the children and old folks go, but the others were diverted to Bermuda. Yep, they got little Snooks locked up in an internment camp like a common criminal, or a Jap."

The explanation only added to Grete's confusion. "But she's American? And you're—" She was going to say "here," when there was a ripple through the crowd. An armed guard crossed the floor. Peter shoved the bag at George, but George was already on the move.

"The luggage office is downstairs," he called over his shoulder, elbowing his way through pedestrians and GIs with an authority Grete found baffling.

Peter started toward the stairs then turned when he noticed Grete was not with him. He returned to her side and took her hand, his fingers curling around hers. They had touched several times, but this was the first time he had reached for her with intention.

"Will you wait for me here?" His eyes met hers, earnest and encouraging. "It won't take long."

Her hand nestled comfortably in his. She could not remember the last time anyone had touched her and had not realized how much she had craved such a simple comfort. Grete would have turned on her heels and left, but Opal was willing to play along. With Peter, she did feel like Opal: a more exotic, more daring version of herself. If not for George, she might even have been happy.

Nodding agreement, she watched Peter descend the stairs. He looked back once and offered a reassuring smile before rounding the landing and disappearing out of sight. Was he aware of the effect he had on her? Grete turned her attention to a young couple locked in an embrace. He was in a private's uniform; she in a lavender dress. The woman's hat fell from her head as the man broke away. He picked it up, brushed it off, and held it out to her. She looked reluctant to accept it as if doing so would give him permission to depart. The little tam hovered between them until, at last, he pushed it forward and she yielded. Duffel bag over his shoulder, the private marched toward the tracks. The woman held an arm up to wave and called after him. His stride faltered, but he did not turn. She replaced her hat, wiped her eyes, and offered Grete a commiserating nod as if they were kindred spirits, both parting with sweethearts.

Grete blinked awake. The entire afternoon felt as if she had been drifting through a dream. The feeling increased as five minutes stretched to ten. She watched the hands of the opal clock advance like daggers with twin hilts in the center and knifepoints marking time. Five more minutes passed before she decided to leave. She was not surprised George was gone, but she would have expected a goodbye from Peter. She was disappointed and a bit embarrassed that she had such strong feelings for someone she had just met.

Boys had been keen on her in Germany. She was flattered, but otherwise unmoved. Only one tall, contemplative boy she knew from the swim club grew to be more than a friend. Otto was an artist as well as an athlete. She found the paint under his fingernails endearing and his musky turpentine scent more appealing than the most expensive cologne. He lived a few blocks away from Grete and their friendship began when they started walking home together after swim practice. Their walks grew to Sunday strolls, ice-skating, and museum outings and their conversation graduated from swim strokes and race times to art and, inevitably, politics.

"Why ban a painting?" she wondered out loud after a failed visit to the Kunsthalle Museum. They had set out that day to view a Max Beckmann piece only to learn that it, and hundreds of other works considered "degenerate" had been confiscated by the Nazis.

"Hitler says Beckmann's a Bolshevik."

"It's art, not politics."

"Nazism is about control." Otto sounded inordinately sad. "Their power comes from dictating what people see and think."

Days later, Otto surprised her with a painting he had made of a sailboat navigating rough seas. The gray hues matched the gravity in his eyes as he told her his family was moving to Holland. They kissed goodbye. It was Grete's first—and only—kiss; somber and sad, not passionate.

She had left Otto's painting and all thoughts of romance behind in Germany. Peter had brought those memories to mind. Now he was gone too. She detested the speed in which people swooped in and out of her life. She looked one last time around the concourse. She was on her way to the door when she heard a low growl that grew into a deafening roar. She put her hands over her ears. All at once she was back in Mannheim, calling for Mama and scrambling for cover. The station vibrated and storefront windows shook. Children cried. Some commuters scattered in disarray, while others seemed nailed to the floor. The guard raced toward the tracks. The siren rose and fell, its roar consuming.

"Grete!" Peter emerged out of nowhere, his chest heaving, face flushed. He took her hand and tugged her toward an exit. They raced up a ramp and had just reached the street when a final shrill note sounded. The bone-chilling wail stopping as suddenly as it had begun.

"False alarm," a guard called out. There was a collective sigh of relief. A woman dropped to her knees engulfing her son in her arms. The boy looked too old for such an all-encompassing embrace yet he willingly submitted, tucking his head in his mother's neck like a gosling. Strangers hugged one another. A few laughed. Most people seemed more bewildered than alarmed.

"Do you think those airplanes triggered it?" someone wondered aloud.

"Airplanes?" Everyone stared warily at the clear June sky as if anticipating a military formation.

"From the parade," the first person clarified.

"Grete." Peter reached out to touch her shoulder. Her heart was hammering; his touch made it pound harder. A moment earlier, she had thought he had gone without saying goodbye. But when the siren rang, he had actually sought her out to make sure she was safe.

"I thought you left," she said, her breath shaky.

His fingers closed softly on her shoulder. "Of course not. I wouldn't just leave." There was a dark smudge high on his left cheek, near his ear.

She did not know which was worse, the embarrassment she felt when she thought he had abandoned her or the relief she felt upon seeing him again. She could not explain what drew her to Peter, but it was impossible to deny her attraction.

"Where were you?" she asked.

"Pete!" George stormed toward them. His demeanor had transformed yet again. He sounded like an excited boy. "What a ruckus!" He tugged at his sleeve as if to check the time, though he seemed more intent on showing off his wristwatch. He waited a beat. "I'm hungry like the dickens."

The clamor had died down quickly. The uproar forgotten amid the cacophony of city noise. Dusk was falling and the blistering day had cooled to a pleasant evening. Grete's affection for Peter was bolstered by the soft twilight. Seized by an overwhelming urge, she removed her handkerchief from her purse. "Come here, Peter." Peter sidled closer and she stood on tiptoe to wipe the smudge off his cheek.

He touched his face, her small gesture seeming to have startled him. His eyes locked on hers. "Have dinner with me."

Had he invited her to accompany *them*, she would have refused, but there was something about the way he said *me* that touched her. She had the same intense sensation as earlier. As if he were reaching out, and without her, he would fall.

CHAPTER 3

PIPING HOT COFFEE, MAC N' CHEESE, APPLE BROWN BETTY. If Grete had known they were going to Horn & Hardart, she would have led the way. She had been to the Eighth Avenue Automat twice before, once for a slice of lemon meringue pie, a second time for a solitary dinner when Uncle Jacques was working late. She was happy to come again with Peter, even if it meant having to put up with George. To her, the Automat epitomized America: sleek and wholesome. Walls of chrome machines showcased a mouth-watering array, what you saw was what you got, and everything was within reach to those who helped themselves.

George immediately warmed to the blend of innovation and choice, too. He held the door open for Grete and Peter, brightening from the odd encounter they had had after leaving Grand Central.

"Holy smokes, George!" A man in a white waiter's jacket had hollered as they walked by a coffee house. Its neon sign, MAYER'S—COFFEE SHOP—BREAKFAST, was dark in the daylight or because of the war. Grete was reassured that someone seemed to know, and like, George well enough to greet him. His sudden appearance at Grand Central had made her feel as if he had materialized out of thin air. The waiter, who had been sitting on his haunches, enjoying a smoke, flicked the cigarette into the gutter and stood stick straight. "That really you, George?"

George lengthened his stride. A yellow cab was honking in the middle of the street, trying to overtake a garbage truck. Men in drab uniforms hung from the rear, dumping trash into the overflowing bed. George eyed the ruckus. He looked as if the possibility of being splattered with yesterday's refuse was the only thing preventing him from darting across the street.

"Who's that?" Peter asked under his breath. They had been walking three astride with Grete between the men and Peter switched places so that Grete was farthest from the waiter.

"Just some fella I used to wait tables with," George said.

"How's Snookums?" the waiter called.

"He seems to know you pretty well," Peter said, uneasily.

"He worked the station next to mine, and I used to clean his clock at pinochle."

Grete could easily picture George as a waiter at some swanky eatery, napkin over his sleeve, slicing roast beef. It explained his blend of superciliousness and servitude.

"Hey, George!" a second man chimed in. He was leaning against the side of the building, holding his cigarette between thumb and forefinger like a European. "Back from Russia so soon? We thought you were a pinko."

Any reassurance Grete had felt at their familiarity morphed into confusion.

"We knew you'd be back," the first waiter said. "America's best after all."

"How's Stalin going to get along without you?" the other man quipped.

The ribbing seemed to chafe. "Laugh all you want, boys," George spat, "You'll be surprised at what I'm going to do."

Peter shot him a sidelong glance, which George steadfastly ignored, striding ahead, muttering to himself. Grete dragged her feet, trying to buy a few seconds. Peter had had ample opportunities to walk away from George.

"I thought we'd be alone." Her words sounded forward, but she was not embarrassed. The afternoon's drama had made her bold.

Peter did not answer immediately and Grete resolved to find a subway station if he did not respond by the time they reached Sixth Avenue. She refused to blindly tag along. She knew the dangers of blind obedience, and thought Peter should too.

Peter ran his hand through his hair. "I didn't think George would come with us."

"Is he really a communist?"

"Nah. He's too selfish to be a communist."

"How do you know him?"

"George is my . . ." Peter hesitated, searching for words or an explanation. It was impossible to know which. "*Kollege*," he said, pronouncing the word with German inflection.

She had trouble imagining Peter and George working together. She had warmed to Peter almost immediately; instantly disliking George. "What kind of work do you do?"

"War."

Oh. It made sense, of course. She had guessed Peter was in his twenties, exactly the right age to be drafted. She made deductions. George was at least a decade older. If they were in military service, it was more than likely George was his superior. That would explain Peter's deference.

"Why aren't you in uniform?" she asked.

"We're part of a . . ." Peter's voice dropped and Grete found herself straining to hear, "It's a special operation. Fighting the enemy. Here."

Her head shot toward him. Peter looked even more handsome now that she knew he was fighting Nazis. She stood a bit straighter. The thought of Nazis on American soil made her skin crawl. If Jews were being persecuted in Germany, a place where her family had prospered for generations, it could happen anywhere. The warning signs were already present. The German-American Bund had recently held a massive rally at Madison Square Garden where they flew the Nazi flag side-by-side with an American one and mocked Roosevelt's New Deal as the "Jew Deal."

"Unfortunately." Peter sighed in frustration. "Our assignment is not going as planned."

A shiver ran up her spine. From the moment she met Peter, she sensed he was in a bind. "What's the matter?" Grete suspected she was delving too deeply, but it would be nice to be needed. She had spent many sleepless nights regretting the way she had allowed her parents to pack her up and send her away as if she were a porcelain doll. Peter seemed to be providing an opportunity for her to right that wrong.

"I'm frightened there's nothing anyone can do," he said. She almost corrected him—*afraid*, not *frightened*—but thought perhaps it was a slip of the tongue, which was far more telling. "Actually," Peter dug his hands into his pockets. "There is one small thing. Could you hold on to this for me?" He held out a rectangular ticket marked *Grand Central Terminal Baggage Claim*.

Grete stared warily at the ticket. It was stamped with a number: thirteen, the red ink coalescing like a bruise. She had a superstitious nature which had become worse since she and her parents were separated. She avoided cracks and knocked on wood as if those small gestures would allow her to ensure their safety. She began to shake her head, but refusing such a small favor seemed petty. The polite young woman, who had been raised to be accommodating, held out her hand. Secretly, she hoped Peter was manufacturing an excuse to see her again. He pressed the ticket into her palm. Thinner than cardboard, thicker than paper, the ticket felt more valuable than its diminutive size implied.

They crossed Sixth Avenue, Grete aware that the subway station had come and gone. It was only at Horn & Hardart that the mood lightened.

"Ah, this is what I dreamed of," George said, fishing in his pocket he removed a fat fold of cash, peeled off a crisp bill, and went to the cashier booth. When he returned, his pockets jingled with coins. "Chow down, Pete. We deserve it."

Peter seemed content to let George foot the bill. He accepted the coins George offered, dumping them onto a single tray.

"After you," he said, brandishing the tray in front of Grete with an exaggerated flourish.

It was Grete's turn to hesitate. Sharing a tray felt more intimate than holding hands—her desires exposed; their tastes mingling. She slid the tray along the stainless steel counter while Peter dropped coins into the slots. The glass doors sprang open with a satisfying click: macaroni with white cheese and tomato and a slice of lemon meringue pie for her; lettuce salad with Russian dressing, meatloaf, green beans, and a baked potato for him.

GEORGE CHOSE A TABLE FOR FOUR along the back wall away from the windows. He wagged his fork toward the empty seats as Peter and Grete approached. His tray was weighed down with Salisbury steak, potatoes au gratin, and tomato salad. A slice of coconut pie and a glass of milk were set to the side. A cigarette rested in an ashtray close at hand. There was something territorial in the way he took up most of the table.

"Here's mud in your eye," he toasted before digging in.

Grete sipped her coffee, watching the other diners over the rim of her cup. A table away, an elderly couple shoveled forkfuls of chopped sirloin into their wrinkled mouths. In the center of the room, secretarial types in stylish hats shared doughnuts, coffee, and gossip. One of them had a shrill laugh that reminded Grete of the parrot who used to live in her building. From a corner table, a man with thin blond hair and a cross-shaped scar slashed across his forehead watched the gaggle with childlike amusement.

George ate ravenously while Grete and Peter talked. This was the first time they had sat down together and Grete found herself aware of his eyes, which were chestnut brown and warm. She explained how she had arrived in this country three years ago and how she lived with her bachelor uncle.

"I graduated high school last week," she said with forced enthusiasm. With school done, her future stretched ahead with less certainty than ever. "Now I'm job hunting." The phrase, lifted from a drugstore romance, was meant to sound sophisticated. She had spent much of the last week in her room, holed up with potboilers. Her favorites featured young women who suffered a minor crisis, like a career setback or romantic mishap, and prevailed. There was no mention of war; no one's parents were missing.

Peter leaned over the table. "What would you like to do?"

Something more than shredding gummy rubber, she thought to herself. "Something useful," she said out loud. Back in Mannheim, she had often left for school at the same time that a young woman lugged a large fold-out table and medicine ball up her neighbor's stairs. The medicine ball caught Grete's interest and she asked the woman about it. *Physiotherapy,* the woman said, explaining her work with the polio-stricken boy. A profession in which she was helping someone appealed to Grete and she had planned to inquire about the woman's training and the clinic where she worked. But war came and she set those goals aside. Peter's question had jogged loose a forgotten interest. "I just need to work on my English." Color rose to her cheeks.

"Your vocabulary's terrific," Peter said. "Just . . . it's *some* . . ." He lifted his chin and curled the tip of his tongue around his front teeth, accentuating the next word, "*Thing.*"

Grete tried raising her chin and curling her tongue exactly as he had, but the word came out as usual, "Some-sing." She didn't think her cheeks could grow any redder, but they did. "And you?" she asked, eager to change the subject. "Do you live in New York?"

"George and I have rooms at the Hotel Governor Clinton."

"You're staying in a hotel?" The snazzy suits, wad of cash, and hotel, she reasoned, all had some-*thing* to do with their work. She wanted to ask Peter more about it, but instinct told her not to pose questions in front of George.

George took a long swig of milk and pulled his salad closer. "My weakness," he said, stabbing a ripe tomato. "Especially in the summertime."

"I'm in room 1421," Peter said proudly. "It has a view of the Chrysler Building."

Laughter rang through the restaurant as the table of chattering secretaries huddled over a photo.

"In the Pacific," a woman in bright lipstick said.

"What's more handsome than a man in uniform?" her friend cooed.

Grete bristled. War was neither distant nor romantic.

She and Peter were only halfway through their meal when George swapped his empty plate for the ashtray. "Boy that hit the spot." He patted his stomach, fumbled in his pocket for matches, lit a cigarette, and took a deep drag. "I first fell in love with this country nearly thirty-nine years ago when a baseball came sailing out of a field where American troops were playing and knocked me cold."

Grete scrambled to do the math. She wasn't sure if there were American troops in Germany in 1903, but only a foreigner would say *American troops*. "You're . . ." She lowered her voice, "German?"

"In Germany, I'm American. In America, I'm German."

Of all George's nonsensical statements, this one was the most confusing. Yet Grete thought she understood. The official term was *Stattenlos*, stateless. A person without a legal nationality. The feeling was that of an intruder.

Peter shifted in his seat as if he were only half listening. His eyes scanned the room and his expression hardened as it took in the man with the blond hair and cross-shaped scar who had been joined by another fellow wearing a plaid sport coat. The coat was double-breasted with a garish blue stripe like something out of a gangster movie. The man tapped his foot impatiently.

George waved an arm, clearing smoke and settling into his story. "When that baseball came flying, I didn't duck in time, and the next thing I knew I was on a bed in the American military hospital. When I came to, a pretty nurse stuffed me with food. *If America's like this, then it's America for me.*"

Grete smiled. George was a windbag. She did not have to look at Peter to know he was thinking the same thing. Still, she nodded encouragingly. She was curious to know more about Peter and if that meant listening to George, she would, for a while at least.

George sat back, crossing his legs and warming to the idea of an audience. "The moment I turned seventeen, I took a job with a shipping company in Hamburg. One day I noticed a ship flying the American flag that was about to set sail for Philadelphia. I managed to sneak into the cargo hold, and was finally on my way." Now that he had started talking, George showed no sign of slowing down. He had taken up most of the space at the table and was now filling the air. "On the sixteenth day out, there were all kinds of noises on deck as the crew opened the holds. Sixteen days without sunshine or exercise are not exactly . . . healthful. My stomach felt like a ball of fire and I was thirsty all the time. The deck was full of longshoremen, but no one seemed to notice me. All those days without washing must have made me inconspicuous; maybe a freshly scrubbed face would have attracted more attention."

"Did you speak any English?" Peter asked. "How did you get by?"

George blinked, jarred by the interruption. "This country isn't like Germany. Americans have a *give-a-kid-a-break* attitude." He gestured around the Automat as if it were proof of his opinion. Grete nodded, surprised to find herself agreeing with George. "If only that were the end of the story," he said. "My life was no Horatio Alger success. Though even during the worst of it, I never thought it'd come to this."

Grete caught a glint out of the corner of her eye as the fellow with the scar pulled a silver flask from his pocket and poured a generous helping of amber-colored liquid into his coffee while the man in plaid scowled. Peter was watching them too. He studied the man with the scar and his companion in the flashy jacket for a long moment before turning back to the table. He set his hand on her wrist, making her heart race. "Opal . . ."

It took a moment for Grete to recognize the fake name she'd assigned herself. Her belly was full and the day's adventure was starting to wear thin. George drummed his fingers on the table. Since he had first interrupted them, Grete assumed he was bad news. She thought she could put up with him for the sake of getting to know Peter, but Peter's reticence was beginning to bother her. She cut him off before he could say anything else.

"Gosh," she said, "I didn't realize it was so late." She pulled her arm out from under his and avoided his eyes. If she looked into his eyes, she might not leave. "Thank you for dinner, but I really must get going." She turned to George, dredging deep for some kind words. "I hope you're reunited with your wife soon." Her feelings toward George had softened slightly since learning his story.

Peter was on his feet before she had pushed back her chair. "Will you be alright getting home?" His eyes roamed the room, settling on the two men dining alone.

Grete nodded. "I'm used to finding my way alone." The remark sounded gloomier than she had intended.

Peter's voice was a mixture of sadness and relief. "Thank you for brightening my day."

A GREEN GLOBE LIGHT ON A CAST-IRON LAMPPOST marked an uptown subway on the corner of 33rd Street. Grete was rounding the corner toward it when she noticed a cloud of smoke hovering low over Fifth Avenue. She was surprised to see the parade was still in progress. The final marchers carried shielded torches, dangling from long wooden poles. The flickering light made the mood more somber than celebratory, the melancholy enhanced by a group of women in Eastern European folk garb singing "The Star Spangled Banner." Their voices rising in unison out of the semidarkness.

With half an eye on the haunting sight, Grete tripped and nearly toppled down the subway steps. Catching her breath, she saw a splintered sign at her feet. She could make out a capital S and a P spray painted on one piece of flimsy wood, LER on another: STOP HITLER. The sign had been popular along the parade route. The debris made her shiver. She should not be out at this lonely hour, when things lay broken and abandoned. She was reaching into her purse for fare when her fingers touched something thicker than paper, thinner than cardboard. The baggage claim ticket throbbed in her hand.

CHAPTER 4

THE APARTMENT SMELLED LIKE SUNDAY MORNING: the scent of leather saddlery and Murphy's oil soap from Uncle Jacques's early morning horseback ride in Central Park mingled with Grete's warm bed linens. Grete nestled into the duvet. Made of Egyptian cotton, puffy with eiderdown, it was one of the few luxuries she had brought from home, a comfort to curl up with at night and a gentle reminder that life had not always been so topsy-turvy. That Sunday, as usual, she rolled onto her side to greet the photograph of her parents, which sat on the nightstand in a slightly tarnished silver frame. In it, Mama, a stout woman with immaculate posture and a regal expression, cradled baby Grete in a bundle of white lace. Papa stood behind Mama, his hand resting on her shoulder. He wasn't old, but there was not a hair on his head (a consequence, he said, of the helmet worn on the Russian front during the Great War and, thus, a sign of bravery). The pair stared somberly ahead. No doubt they were preparing for the camera flash. To Grete, it looked as if they were bracing for the future.

Three crisp knocks interrupted her reverie.

"Gretel?" Her uncle was the only one she allowed to call her Gretel. Since she was a child, he had pronounced her name like that of the girl in the fairytale, sometimes asking about Hansel's whereabouts, other times humming bars from the opera. He still spoke her name in the same affectionate way, but at her request had stopped referring to gingerbread houses.

Grete stretched one leg, then the other, dipping her toes out from under the covers as if testing water. If not for the yellow dress draped across the trunk, she might have believed that yesterday, the war parade, and meeting Peter was a dream.

"Gretel!" Jacques called, more insistently.

Uncle Jacques had left Germany a decade earlier when Nazi trouble first began to brew and the English greeting card company where he worked relocated him to New York City. It was 1932. Grete was nine years old. She did not understand economics or politics, but she saw the beggars in the streets and the Nazi flags blanketing the city. The red flag and gray swastika brought to mind a venomous spider. As time passed, the poison spread. The year Grete turned eleven, the gentile mother of her closest friend came to speak with Mama to explain, with some guilt, that the girls could no longer play together. It was Grete's first brush with anti-Semitism. She felt as if she were being punished, though she wasn't sure what she had done to deserve it. When she questioned Mama, Mama could not, or would not, talk about it. Grete became more and more isolated, and increasingly sad. The widow downstairs with the boisterous parrot began crossing the street to avoid her. At school, her physical education teacher told her that she would no longer be given top grades because "Jews did not deserve top grades."

When Grete entered secondary school, there was a portrait of Hitler hanging in every classroom. Curriculum included "Racial Awareness." The following year, she and all Jewish students were forced to leave school. Grete wanted to hate her former schoolmates, but suspected they were more cowardly than cruel. And in a way, she understood their fear. She had gone to buy Papa's favorite crumb cake one morning and witnessed the baker being kicked to the gutter after refusing to hang a *Juden Unerwünscht*, Jews Not Wanted, sign in his window. The sign was there the next day. The baker and his family were gone. Grete liked to believe she would be as brave as the baker, but, in truth, she was not sure. Tears welled in her eyes as she recalled the all-encompassing dread that overtook her each day as she stood by her front door waiting for Papa to return home from work.

Hatred filled the streets. Still, her parents insisted that Germany was going through a "phase" that would blow over. Then came Kristallnacht, crystal night; a poetic name for the night her life shattered. Grete can still hear the sound of smashing glass. She was fifteen, cowering like an infant beside Papa. The gentile husband of a cousin had warned Papa that something was about to happen and their apartment door was locked, the curtains drawn, lights off. Their family was unscathed materially; the emotional toll was immeasurable. Grete can still see Mama's white face shining through the dark room as an explosion shook the walls. She could not have seen flames, yet she can vividly recall the Haupt Synagogue, which her family attended on the High Holidays, burning to ash. And she can still see hordes of faceless people wielding sledgehammers, smashing windows of Jewish owned stores and destroying Jewish cemeteries, obliterating the living and desecrating the dead.

Smoke still lingered in the air and shards of glass littered the streets, the evening Grete's parents announced they were sending her to live with Mama's brother Jacques in New York City. Mama had cooked Grete's favorite Wiener schnitzel to soften the blow, but neither could swallow a morsel. Grete was fond of her dapper uncle, who visited every year during his vacation, lugging armloads of gifts. Those intended for Grete were thoughtful, but never quite right—a frilly dress two sizes too small, a fat Faulkner novel in English that she couldn't make heads or tails of. Awkwardness ensued as Jacques realized, too late, that the gifts didn't suit her. Grete could not imagine living with him alone in a strange city.

"Uncle Jacques will serve as your guarantor." Mama sounded resigned. "With his help, you'll be able to get a visa." A truck rolled by and Grete strained to hear. The noise grew faint as it passed and she exhaled. "See how lucky you are," Mama announced too brightly. "Jacques has even arranged for you to attend George Washington High School. You'll be a real American!"

Papa looked down at his plate. Grete had never seen him so ashamed. Every part of her shivered as if she had a fever. *No.* She would not leave her friends, her family, and the life she knew. From what she had seen in the copies of *Life* or *Time* Uncle Jacques brought from the States, Americans were clean-cut and whole-some. The ones in Hollywood looked glamorous. But she had no desire to be one of them. Her pleas fell on deaf ears. Mama pushed her chair away from the table and left the room. Papa turned to his meal, slicing the schnitzel without meeting Grete's eye.

Days later, Mama took her to Stuttgart to the nearest American embassy. Grete can recall the mustard-colored room and the metallic smell of fear as they sat, among countless others, waiting for their number to be called. Two medics came and carried a man out on a stretcher. A murmur went through the crowd. His wife and children had passed their medical exams, but he had failed and become so upset he had suffered a heart attack. *76.* Grete recoiled as her number was called. Mama pushed her toward a cubical. The curtain was closed and Grete was told to strip down. Her teeth chattered as a male doctor probed her naked body with icy hands. "You are very attractive," he said. Grete's ears burned with humiliation. Ten minutes later, she was told she had passed the physical. Papers were shuffled and stamped. Uncle Jacques had posted a security bond in an American bank to prove that she would never be a burden to the American government. Grete was *lucky*. It was a word she would come to question then hate. She was lucky, but most of the time she was also very sad.

She passed her sixteenth birthday alone aboard ship with no one to celebrate with and nothing to cheer. Complaining seemed futile; worse, it was selfish. *She was lucky.* Rumor had it that during the crossing a man had jumped into the water, committing suicide. His absence had not been discovered until the next day when it was too late to turn back and search for him.

Uncle Jacques met her at the pier. Jacques was a kind man who took obvious pleasure in showing her the life he had built in New York. He was particularly proud of his office and the candy-colored cards the company produced which featured blue-eyed kittens, rainbows, and puppies. A Valentine greeting showed a girl in pigtails scalding herself with a hot pan. The caption read: *You're too hot to handle*. The cards, even the slightly risqué Valentine one, reminded Grete of children's picture books—American ones. The folktales she had been raised on were far more bleak: a boy who refused to eat his soup, wasted away, and died; a girl who played with matches and burned to death; even the nursery rhyme, *Hoppe hoppe Reiter*, Mama used to sing, while clapping and bouncing Grete on her knees, told of a rider falling into a ditch and being eaten by ravens. As a child, Grete had never questioned the gruesome themes; now they seemed prophetic.

"Gretel, Dépêche-*toi!*" Jacques, who was born in Belgium, only resorted to French when frustrated.

Uncle Jacques had never quite figured out what to make of her. Early on, he caught her in tears over her dog, a smart German shepherd named *Stromer*, Tramp in English. What she never told him was that the Gestapo had ordered her family to turn Stromer over to them. It was a test of loyalty for a young soldier to adopt a dog, earn its trust, and kill it. Instead, Papa had taken Stromer to the backyard next to the lilac bushes, and put a bullet in his head. To this day, the scent of lilacs made Grete sick. She imagined Stromer gazing at Papa with his eager expression as the shot entered his skull behind his velvety ear in the place she most loved to kiss. Grete knew, of course, that so many others had lost husbands and children, but she still ached for Stromer. The day after her outburst, Uncle Jacques brought home a calico kitten, whom he named Vagabond. Grete took one look at the scrawny kitten with ridiculously large ears, whose name she could not pronounce, and again burst into tears.

Grete pulled her covers to her chin, painfully aware of how her presence must have upended her uncle's life. His apartment on Riverside Drive was swathed in masculine shades of brown. A worn club chair sat next to a walnut end table. The table held a reading lamp, brandy decanter, and single lowball glass. The apartment had two bedrooms. Jacques slept in the master at the end of the hall and there was a well-appointed guest room next door. Grete demurred when Jacques offered her the guest room, superstitiously preferring to save the double bed for her parents. She chose to sleep in the small maid's room, tucked behind the kitchen. Her few possessions—schoolbooks, novels, an antique shaving kit that doubled as a jewelry box—filled the tight space. She was careful not to let her things spill into her uncle's bachelor domain. Uncle Jacques would not have objected, but it would have implied a permanence she was unwilling to admit.

She scrunched her eyes shut, allowing herself one more moment of repose. With her eyes closed, she could pretend her parents were breakfasting in the next room and imagine what life would have been like if she had stayed in Mannheim under normal circumstances. If she tried hard enough she could smell burned toast and feel Stromer, asleep at her feet, dog dreaming with twitching legs. Vagabond, whom she insisted on calling Jacques's cat despite her blossoming affection for him, lay curled on the pillow beside her. His fur tickled her nose and she sneezed. Guilt niggled at her. Her uncle was doing his best. Part of her admired the charade, part of her resented it. She could not decide if putting on a brave face was courageous or deceptive. Like Jacques, she went through the motions of her day: high school, volunteering at the salvage depot, shopping and cooking basic meals, which Jacques, unconvincingly, oohed and aahed over. It was not enough to keep her mind off the turmoil in Europe, but she pretended it was. Now, with school over, her days stretched endlessly ahead. Planning her future felt disingenuous while her parents' fate remained unknown.

Grete rubbed the knot in her neck, which seemed to ache with new tension each morning. The day hadn't even begun, but she was exhausted. With a sigh, she tore her covers away and swung her legs out of bed.

SUNDAY, WHILE MANY NEW YORKERS ATTENDED CHURCH, Jacques and Grete participated in their own sacred ritual. Their house of worship was Central Park, their liturgy the *New York Times*. In Germany, her family had attended High Holiday services and lit Shabbat candles out of respect for tradition, but they had never kept kosher and were not really observant. Her bachelor uncle seemed to have foregone religion altogether. Grete did not miss it. Her prayers were in her heart, and she needed neither a synagogue nor bible to access them. For her, nature seemed like a more direct line to God. Grete and Jacques's practice had its own methodology. Following a brisk mile-and-a-half walk around the reservoir, they would settle on their favorite bench under a ginkgo tree. On warm summer days, the foliage provided rich shade. Grete could look east over the water toward the Fifth Avenue penthouses, the bulging Sunday paper between them on the bench, an excess of information that filled a conversational void.

Before departing for New York, Grete was brimming with existential questions about war, human nature, accountability, and guilt. None of which could be answered. Late one evening, when she asked why Jacques had never married, Mama seemed relieved to have a response to a straightforward question. Jacques fell in love with a woman who married another man and broke his heart. The woman was the love of his life and, after that, he could never love again.

Grete had difficulty squaring the romantic story with what she knew of her conservative, balding uncle. "Who was she?"

After much prodding, Mama confessed that Jacques's love was the wife of his employer, the owner of the greeting card company. "That's why Jacques moved to New York," she said, "And now you have a safe place to visit until this madness dies down. See, everything has a way of working out for the best."

Even at the time, Grete was not sure she agreed. She had been led to believe that Jacques left Germany because of the Nazis. The actual story was more complicated, as was her departure from home. Her possessions were crammed into a trunk and she was being uprooted from everything she had ever known. Three years later, her visit had turned into an indefinite stay. Uncle Jacques offered comfort and consistency, but Grete had a hole in her heart, and she suspected Jacques had one as well.

That Sunday, as usual, Jacques had her read out loud from the newspaper. He insisted she read to him so he could correct her pronunciation and she could expand her vocabulary. The front page featured a photo of the parade and the viewing stand along with the headline, "Millions Hail Marchers."

"Two million spectators," Jacques read over her shoulder, punctuating the number with a low whistle.

Grete smiled at her warmhearted uncle. When she arrived home the night before, he had been awake reading in his chair. He looked over his book as if he were on the verge of questioning her, then thought better of it and wished her good night. It was past his usual bedtime. Grete appreciated both that he had waited up for her, and that he had not asked where she had been. She would have told him the truth, but she would not have been able to explain why she had allowed two complete strangers—men— lead her around the city.

Still more confusing was her behavior after finding the baggage claim ticket in her purse. Rather than going straight home, she had returned to Grand Central. The woman on duty slid her glasses down her nose and looked up from her magazine as Grete entered the windowless office. Bare bulbs cast a sickly glow. There were rows of cubbies filled with human flotsam, a torn Saks bag, briefcases in every color and size, a broken umbrella, a pair of men's galoshes, a dented hat. The attendant's nametag caught Grete's eye.

"Your name's Opal?" she asked. Superstition kicked in. A wooden hanger seemed to sway in an invisible breeze.

The attendant pulled her collar up, displaying the badge. "Ophelia." *Just a coincidence*, Grete told herself, reaching into her purse and retrieving the claim ticket with trembling hands. Ophelia peered at it. NOT RESPONSIBLE FOR LOST VALUABLES, read a sign above the counter. NO LIVE ANIMALS, read another. Long moments passed while the ticket lay between them in a way that made Grete even more uneasy. She was relatively sure there were no live animals in the bag; as for valuables, she couldn't say.

Ophelia pulled her glasses further down her nose, scrutinizing Grete more closely before going to retrieve the bag. Grete's eyes locked on a poster which featured a swastika on an arrow pointing toward what looked like Grand Central's underground tunnels. TARGET NO. 1, read the copy, NEW YORK CITY. She looked down the row of cubbies, half expecting a guard to spring from one, but Ophelia passed her the bag, collected a dime, and turned back to her magazine. She had flipped past war news in favor of a Bette Davis look-alike modeling fur: blended sable capes, silver fox jackets, Russian ermine coats. The headline, "Furs Shown as City Swelters" caused a trickle of sweat to run down Grete's chest.

Bag in hand, Grete raced to the ladies room, peering under the stalls to ensure she was alone. She locked herself in one farthest from the door. The room was dead quiet, without as much as the drip of a leaky faucet. The bag was heavier than she remembered. The musty odor even more offensive. She propped her heel on the rim of the toilet, balanced the bag on her thigh, and she opened it. The contents spilled onto the floor, into the toilet bowl, even in her shoes.

Sand.

Fishy, coarse, sand.

A FAINT BREEZE RUSTLED THE NEWSPAPER, pulling Grete back to the park. She set the first section aside and turned to the editorials, "'Alien Restriction Tightens on Coast.'"

"Alien?" she asked.

"Foreign," Jacques clarified.

Foreign was a word she knew. She was a foreigner. Grete read on, "'Over-all Exclusion of Japanese along Pacific Poses Question of Germans and Italians.' Oh," she said, as meaning began to dawn. She had already read that Italian-born garment workers were being barred from plants manufacturing American Army uniforms.

Jacques's chauffer's cap, weekend attire as opposed to the homburg he donned Monday through Friday, bobbed as he urged her on. Grete steadied her voice, "An over-all proclamation this week finally excluding all Japanese from their homes anywhere in the far-west military area No. 1 focused attention on the 'speed tempered with humanity' with which the Army has handled the Japanese evacuation on this coast and almost involuntarily raised the question 'What of the German and Italian aliens?'"

Speed tempered with humanity. She recognized unalloyed propaganda when she saw it. She also knew that exclusion from one's home was inhumane at best. Next to the article was a photograph of a slender, dark haired man with a mustache. The caption read, "Attorney General Francis Biddle set up 'prohibited' zones near vital West Coast defense plants." Her eyes lowered down the page. Biddle's rigid expression left her cold. "Several thousand Germans and Italians were required to move out of prohibited zones." Her voice gave way. Germans had forced her out of Germany. Americans did not trust her in America. She wasn't German or American. She was a Jew—and Jews weren't welcome anywhere.

At last, Jacques took note of her distress. He reached for the section and buried it on the bottom of the pile before finding a replacement.

"Let's read something lighter," he said, handing her the "Society" section.

Grete passed over an article about preserving vegetables for winter and turned to a more enticing piece entitled "East Hampton Arranges Fete."

"The Devon Yacht Club's opening dinner dance on June 27 will be a benefit to aid the United Service Organization's campaign." She scrunched her nose and flipped to another page. "The Maidstone Club," Grete read, attempting a haughty finishing school accent, "opens for the season next Saturday with a luncheon at the beach restaurant and swimming events in the pool," she paused longingly over the words, remembering a time when she too had competed in swimming events, a time when she thought winning or losing a swim race was all that mattered.

Jacques rubbed his chin and spoke with a faux-British elocution. "I am afraid our invitation may have been lost." He tsked while Grete giggled.

Opposite the society column were advertisements for Father's Day gifts and she vowed to get her uncle an umbrella (short, medium, or tall to match his height), or maybe a shaving set. What's more, she resolved to renew her faith in Jacques's ability to rescue her parents. Each week, he went from government office to government office seeking leads, or sat for hours in dreary waiting rooms, refusing to be deterred. She knew her father to be even more persistent. She had heard of refugees smuggled across borders, escaping to the Dominican Republic or Jamaica. Papa would find a way out. She would not allow herself to think otherwise.

A blue jay squawked. Ginkgo leaves performed a fan dance. Grete rested her head on the back of the bench, gazing upward through a canopy of green to the sunlit sky. *Nature will triumph*, she told herself. Steadying her breath, she turned back to the paper. Eager to find something uplifting to read, she flipped past the engagement announcements and book reviews until one headline caught her eye, "Laughs at 'Hitler,' Kicked."

"A woman who expressed her contempt for Hitler by laughing at a caricature of the German dictator in the parade yesterday and carrying a sign that read 'Stop Hitler' was hit and kicked by an unknown assailant." Grete slowed down. From the headline, she had assumed it was Hitler who had been laughed at and kicked; now the meaning was clear. More bad news. She fought an urge to throw the entire newspaper into the reservoir. Like a maestro conducting an orchestra, Jacques waved his hand. Grete sighed.

"The incident occurred about 6:30 o'clock last night in the IRT subway station at Broadway and Thirty-third Street. The victim said she was watching the parade at Fifth Avenue and Thirty-third Street and laughed at a satirical figure of Hitler. She said that her assailant, whom she did not know, appeared annoyed. When she left the parade and went to the West Side IRT subway station at Thirty-third Street she noticed the man was following her. She said that when she reached the top of the subway stairs, carrying her anti-Hitler sign, her assailant turned her around, struck her with his fist and kicked her in the abdomen. A witness who was too rattled to give her name described the man as strong and tall, in his mid-to-late thirties with wide-set eyes and a glen plaid sport coat."

Yesterday pushed forcefully back into Grete's thoughts. She had been at the Thirty-third Street subway stop sometime after half past six. She stared down at the newspaper. STOP HITLER splintered into the capital S and P spray painted on flimsy wood of the sign she had stumbled over. As her eyes scanned the article the black-and-white newsprint blurred into bolts of garish plaid. The same distinctive glen plaid sport coat with a light-blue stripe worn by the man at Horn & Hardart. He was not the only man in the city to wear a glen plaid jacket. But the Thirty-third Street subway was a block away from the Eighth Avenue Automat. The timing was right. She was certain Peter had been watching him and his companion with the cross-shaped scar. A damp breeze blew over the reservoir and her thoughts drifted to the bag of sand. She had little doubt that something was dangerously amiss and the answer lay with Peter. Less clear was what she should, or could, do about it. The first step, she told herself, was to speak with Peter. Grete sprang to her feet, happy to leap into a cause and think about something other than herself.

IN LIEU OF LUNCH, GRETE FOUND HERSELF OUTSIDE the Hotel Governor Clinton. She had invented a hasty excuse to part with her uncle: *The Count of Monte Cristo* overdue at the library. The instant the fib left her mouth she remembered it was Sunday and libraries were closed. Maybe Uncle Jacques assumed she was dropping the book in a return box, more likely he was content to enjoy the "Business" section in peace. Either way, he didn't question her. Assured he would not miss her, she found her way to the Eighty-sixth Street subway. A train pulled into the station before she had time to second-guess her behavior. Keeping busy, she discovered, was the best way to stop worrying about her parents. The train lurched downtown and her thoughts reeled. Was the man in the plaid jacket a Nazi sympathizer? Why had Peter been watching him? Did it have to do with his work fighting the enemy? Why had he asked her to hold a claim ticket—for a bag filled with nothing but sand?

The hotel lobby had paneled ceilings and heavy furniture. Upholstery and carpet alike were plush. Grete approached the front desk, feeling conspicuous in her green poplin and cartwheel hat. Nora Charles would not have been caught dead in shoes soiled with Central Park dust.

"May I help you?" The clerk's manner was efficient, not cordial, his eyes heavily lidded as if it were not worth the effort to open them completely. He wore an excessively groomed mustache that hid, what she was sure, was a smirk.

Grete corrected her posture, shifting her shoulders back like Mama had always instructed. "I'd like to speak with a guest registered here," she said.

"Name?"

"I—umm, Opal."

"The guest's name," he said haughtily.

She sensed the futility of her mission. She did not even know Peter's last name.

"Davis," she said. "George Davis." Was it her imagination or did the clerk cringe?

"The gentleman from San Francisco?" The clerk appeared to accept her befuddled smile as an affirmative because he picked up the house phone and dialed. "No answer," he said, returning the phone to its cradle though it had only rung twice.

"The man traveling with him," Grete tried again. "He's average height with . . ." She held her hands a few inches beyond her shoulders.

The clerk shook his head, clearly eager to be rid of her. "Perhaps the Coral Room," he said, waving dismissively.

She crossed the lobby, her steps quickening at the thought of

Peter then slowing at the idea of running into George. Despite signs of recent activity, stained tablecloths and stray silverware, the cafe was empty. Just as well, she reasoned. What was she hoping to accomplish? To find the man who had assaulted a woman? And then what? Grete knew that she had a more selfish motive as well, which was to see Peter again. She watched the hotel's revolving door spin then eyed the elevator. Peter had told her both the name of his hotel and his room number. It occurred to her that he had divulged that information on purpose. She watched the floor indicator descend, certain that when the elevator doors parted, Peter would emerge. What would he say? Three, two one . . . The doors opened. Like the booth in a magician's show, the elevator was empty. She stepped inside and pressed fourteen.

UPSTAIRS, THE SENSATION THAT SHE HAD STEPPED into a magic show or circus funhouse intensified as the elevator doors parted and she found herself face-to-face with her own wide-eyed reflection. Grete approached the mirror, smoothing down her hair and steadying her nerves. Opal stared boldly back. Off the elevator alcove, the hallway stretched long and narrow. Soiled breakfast trays littered the floor and freshly polished shoes sat outside several doors. As a child on family vacations in Schwartzwald, Grete would make a game of switching the shoes in the hallway, pairing a hiking boot with a peep-toe heel or exchanging boat-sized leather oxfords with tiny Mary Jane's. Longing for the days when she had enjoyed such impish fun, she started down the corridor. The empty hallway fed her anxiety. Room 1421 was on the right side at the end. She was on the verge of turning back when she heard a loud bang.

"There are two windows in this room, Pete," she heard George say, "and if we can't come to an agreement, only one of us will leave here alive." Grete exhaled a breath she hadn't realized she was holding. She primed her ears, anticipating Peter's response. But George kept talking. "I had only the best in America, but didn't realize it at the time. It was Mother who asked me to come home. She was disappointed to learn I was a waiter and said there were better opportunities in the New Germany for a man of my caliber. Mother went on and on about how Hitler was doing great things for Germany like building the Autobahn, but when I got there I learned pretty quick what the Nazis were about. Then I'm asked to return to America and be a part of this thing. Why, that's like a man who, being down and out, is taken in by a good family, given a home and the best of food to eat, and then repays this kindness by sneaking back to the house one night, killing the baby and setting the house afire."

She struggled to make sense of George's admission. Her fortuitous timing in hearing it only added to her sense that she was right to have come. Whatever "this thing" was might be terribly wrong; maybe dangerous. The revelation should have made her turn and run. Instead, she pressed her ear to the door, surprised both by her audacity and the soothing effect Peter's voice had on her.

"Settle down, George. There's no reason for anyone to go out a window." She heard the sound of a window closing. "I share your opinion."

"You mean intention?" George snapped. "There's a difference between opinion and intention."

Grete leaned in as much as she dared. There was a slight creak as the door shifted and she leapt backwards, but Peter's next words made her sidle up again. "The Gestapo threw me in prison. Now those thugs are watching my family."

Grete knew she should feel anger or grief on Peter's behalf, but could only muster a deep sense of relief that he hated the Gestapo as much as she did. The door to a nearby room opened and a couple exited, offering Grete a curious nod as she fumbled in her pocketbook pretending to search for a key. The elevator chimed and a chambermaid appeared. She pushed a squeaky cart full of cleaning supplies down the corridor and disappeared into a supply closet midway down the hall.

When Grete leaned back in, Peter sounded apprehensive. "All night I've been thinking what would be best for me to do. I could walk away, but my family would suffer because of me."

George did not sound nearly as tentative, "By Christ, Pete, you suffered enough at their hands. Six months ago, who could guess we'd be in this together, but we are and now it's our turn. This is our chance to shorten this lousy war and save a lot of lives. The only way to lick those bastards is by beating them at their own game. My plan will keep us out of difficulty here and avoid trouble for our families back in Germany." He launched into a rambling discourse that included words like propaganda and names like Edward R. Murrow. Grete found his logic inscrutable. More confusing than his so-called plan was the fact that he was only now revealing it to Peter. Peter had said they were colleagues, yet they did not seem to know one another well nor did they seem to have much of an agenda.

Wheels squeaked as the maid reappeared with her cart. "Lost your key?" she asked in an Irish brogue. Grete patted her pockets, shrugged, then opened her purse as if to search through it. She was concocting an excuse—wrong floor, sister downstairs with the key—when she realized that the voices inside room 1421 had gone quiet. Grete stepped back. She had come to see Peter and had no desire to hear anymore of George's convoluted stories. Not wanting to be seen, she hurried down the hall and was halfway to the elevator when the door to room 1421 opened. Grete slid past the maid and ducked inside the supply closet, holding her fingers to her lips, imploring silence. Cool as a cucumber, the maid greeted the men.

"Good morning," George said. There was a whiff of stale cigarette smoke as he breezed past the closet.

Grete could not see as much as sense Peter. She strained to listen but the carpet stifled his footsteps. Hidden in the crammed closet, she could not begin to fathom how she had wound up in such a precarious position. She peered out from behind a bundle of rags and saw Peter striding down the hall away from her. She watched the men get into the elevator, the doors closing with a *ding*. A feeling that she was walking into her destiny drove her forward.

OUT ON THE STREET, GRETE CAUGHT SIGHT of Peter's gray snap-brim disappearing down the subway stairs. It took long moments to find her wallet amid her messy pocketbook and she groped in vain for a nickel. A train pulled into the station. People shuffled on and off. Bells rang and the doors threatened to shut. After glancing over her shoulder, she ducked under the turnstile and leapt inside. A secret smile sprang to her lips. She felt like her old mischievous self.

The car was not crowded. A man in a seersucker suit stared vacantly out the window at his own reflection. A group of GIs studied a map. A woman leaned over a pram and cooed to her baby. Grete thought the woman might have seen her slip under the turnstile because her eyes flicked toward her with obvious curiosity as she jiggled the baby carriage in a perfunctory way. Since arriving in New York, Grete had become as docile as a lamb. Any satisfaction she had gleaned from small acts of rebellion—skipping school, quoting Trotsky—had lost all appeal as the situation in Germany grew dire. For the first time in a long while, she embraced her agility and nerve.

Her satisfaction was short-lived. Peter and George had vanished. As the train flew past Forty-second, Fifty-first, and came to a screeching halt at Columbus Circle, she began to wonder if she had gotten on the wrong one. The conductor poked his head out and hollered, "This train will be running express until One-hundred-and-sixteenth Street." It sounded like an ultimatum. Grete stood on wobbly legs. The doors opened and a man entered, playing Bach on the violin, which was enough to make her stay put.

Grete looked forward then back. She was in one of the last cars. If Peter was on the train, chances were he was up ahead. She had never switched between cars before. Signs all over the subway, not to mention common sense, warned against it. But she had also never skipped a fare. A line from *The Thin Man* came to mind, "She's being stupid and she's sure she's being very clever . . ." Clutching the overhead bar, she teetered to the end of the car and pulled the latch. The door was heavier than she expected, and she exhaled sharply as she stepped out onto what looked like shifting puzzle pieces. The door to the next car rolled open as the train hurtled through a station. She switched again as they slowed at Eighty-first, again at Ninety-sixth.

She was nearly convinced she had let her imagination run wild when she finally caught sight of Peter through the scratched window between cars. He was on his feet, swaying with the lurching train, his back to her. George was sitting close by, his hands soaring and diving as he spoke. Both men were wearing the same suits from the day before, now more rumpled than dapper.

The train came to an abrupt stop and Grete was thrown forward. She stumbled into a woman and was scrambling to apologize when she noticed that Peter and George were gone. She flew out of the train as the doors closed and dashed up the steps. Heart pounding, she stood at the top of the subway stairs, assessing the unfamiliar surroundings. The sun was beating down. In the twenty minutes that she had been underground, the temperature must have risen ten degrees. East toward the city, a thick haze lingered low. West, beyond Riverside Park, a rank breeze blew off the Hudson, compounding the heat. One-hundred-and-sixteenth Street was a pretty block lined with trees. On the corner, a gently curving edifice took advantage of Hudson River views.

There was no sign of Peter or George.

A group of boys carrying baseball gloves and bats were walking toward the park, tossing balls and laughing.

"Look, I'm DiMaggio!" one said, uncoiling like a slow-moving spring as he swung his bat.

Another put his hand on his brow, squinting into the sunlight. "And . . . it's . . . outta here!"

At the park entrance, a vendor was shaving flakes off a block of ice and drenching them with cherry-colored syrup as a child held his mother's hand and licked his lips in anticipation. One of the boys dropped a ball, which rolled between Grete's feet. When she stooped to pick it up, she was bumped from behind. She turned, expecting to see a boy. Instead, she found herself staring into the rheumy eyes of a grown man. He looked as overheated as she felt. Beads of sweat ran down from his temples.

"Ach," he said, clearly flustered. The man removed his hat and scratched his head. The cross-shaped scar on his forehead growing whiter and more pronounced as his face flushed in the heat.

When she was twelve, Grete had fallen off a bicycle and cut open her chin. The wound healed into a ragged inch-long scar that made her self-conscious. It was Papa who said that scars tell a story and add character. Grete wondered at the story behind this man's scar. The dual slashes seemed to hide volumes.

CHAPTER 5

THE MAN WITH THE CROSS-SHAPED SCAR was blond and clean-shaven with a boyish face "Do you know the way to the mausoleum?" he asked. His voice was low and trembly as if he were not quite sure of the question—or himself.

Grete debated whether to answer or walk away. To her relief, the man did not seem to recognize her. He pulled a slip of paper from his pocket, squinting at the print. Grete looked sideways at the spiky scrawl, so different from her own round, girlish penmanship. She could make out the name Grant along with a series of numbers, a seven, possibly a four.

"Grant's Tomb?" she asked. It was a sight Uncle Jacques had been meaning to show her ever since a photo had appeared in the newspaper on the anniversary of General Grant's birthday.

The man shifted from foot to foot like a skittish horse. His pants were too short in the leg. His shoes scuffed with chalky watermarks. Grete stared at his shoes in wonder. The leather was dry and grains of what looked like sand were embedded in the cracks: fishy, coarse, sand. Mounds of which she had spilled last night onto the ladies room floor.

"That's where I'm going," she said before she could question the wisdom of walking alone with another stranger. The sun was overhead. People filled the street. She heard the carefree shouts of children drifting from the park. What's more, she knew this man would lead her to Peter. If what she had overheard was correct, the Gestapo had locked Peter in prison and were now watching his family. Her desire to understand his full story, and possibly help him, had increased tenfold. "It's this way," she called, striding ahead.

The newspaper photo of Grant's tomb showed it on the banks above the Hudson. Uncle Jacques's apartment was on Ninety-eighth Street and she was reasonably certain Grant's Tomb was north. Walking with authority she did not feel, Grete turned uptown along Riverside Drive. The fellow with the scar lagged behind. His hands stuffed in his pockets as if he were searching for an excuse to part ways. "It's not far," she said with false confidence. He dropped his shoulders and tagged along. Grete reevaluated her opinion. This man wasn't a bit like a skittish horse. He was more like an obstinate mule being dragged by a lead. She slowed to match his pace. They trudged up the wide sidewalk, his feet slapping the pavement and scattering a flock of pigeons. Their progress was marked by streetlamps that could not have been more than a few dozen yards apart yet felt like milestones.

"Are you sightseeing?" she asked. He gave her an apprehensive look. Slow-witted as well as slow moving, the question seemed to stump him. "Visiting New York?" she clarified. A vapid smile hung on his lips and she forged on. "Where are you from?"

"Wilkes-Barre?"

"Where?"

"Vilkes?" He rubbed his head. "Vilkes-Bar? P.A."

"Really?" It was impossible not to notice that the abbreviation was the same one used by George. (She had since looked it up and understood that it stood for Pennsylvania). "Pennsylvania isn't too far, right?"

He did not bother responding. It struck her that he may not have known the answer. They walked a few more blocks in silence. The sky was eggshell blue, the Hudson wide and majestic. Twice, she turned, having the niggling sense they were being followed. Her vague sense of anxiety gave way to nervous chatter.

"What brings you here?" She was referring to Grant's Tomb and his answer came as another surprise.

"War."

It was the same curt response Peter had offered when she had asked about his work. And this man, like Peter, was not in uniform.

"When does your work begin?" she pressed, feeling a bit cruel. This fellow seemed almost helpless.

"We're waiting to hear." His response was singsong, like a child repeating what he had been told.

"We?" She had little doubt he was referring to the sinister man in the plaid jacket he had been dining with at the Automat. That man had kicked a woman. He was violent. This dim-witted fellow seemed harmless enough, but Grete was still happy to part ways. She looked ahead, relieved to see the monument appear high atop a bluff, its gray dome austere against the summer sky. The epitaph carved above the entrance, LET US HAVE PEACE, struck her as exceedingly appropriate now that the entire world was at war. General Grant had fought to keep his country whole. She wished there was a way to do the same for Germany.

"Here we are," she said, gesturing toward the tourists who were milling about.

"*Ja* . . . Yes." He offered a brisk nod and dashed ahead with swiftness she hadn't realized he was capable of.

Grete watched him mount the stairs and vanish beyond the enormous bronze doors. She planned to wait a few moments then follow, confident he would lead her to Peter. While she waited, she admired the granite structure that rose above Morningside Heights like a wedding cake. Her eyes fell on the pair of large, stone eagles with outstretched beaks and spread wings that guarded the stairs. She followed their fierce glare, and there was Peter, hovering half out-of- sight in an outcropping of trees. He looked utterly alone, lost in thought. He turned his hat in his hands before offering a slight shrug. It was difficult to say if the gesture was meant for her. Grete flushed as she wondered how to explain her presence. She had just taken a step toward him when the man in the glen plaid jacket sidled up behind him, whispered something, and stormed up the stairs. He looked rough and seemed more threatening than she recalled. Peter replaced his hat on his head and followed him inside.

A group of students climbed the stairs and entered the mausoleum and, without thinking, Grete blended into the crowd. With stained-glass windows reflecting onto white marble floors, the interior of the mausoleum was solemn. The tourists spoke in deferential tones, which bounced off the walls like otherworldly whispers. A staleness in the air made Grete think of roaming spirits. This was a tomb, she reminded herself, death hovered nearby. Dusty rays of sunlight filtered down from the dome. In the center of the rotunda, a marble balustrade surrounded an open crypt. She peered over the rail. Like something unearthed from a pyramid, two red marble sarcophagi lay side by side. She could see four men huddled in a tight circle: the slow man with the scar, the gangster in plaid, George—and Peter. She leaned so far forward her heels left the ground. The man in plaid was florid and visibly angry. His words bounced off the marble.

"We waited over an hour," he hissed. "Where were you?"

"Calm down, Dick," George said. "Pete and I started talking and lost track of the time."

The man named Dick jabbed his finger into George's face "You, *Herr Strich*, are a danger to us all."

George slapped his hand away. Tittering schoolgirls muffled his words. Peter raised his eyes and Grete held her breath. Abruptly, the men stepped apart, marching up the stairs toward her. She slipped into a room to the side of the rotunda and hid behind a display of battlefield flags, counting faded stars and bullet-ridden stripes as she waited for her heartbeat to slow. She looked up in time to see the man named Dick and his friend with the scar storming away in one direction; George in the other. She was on the verge of admitting defeat when someone tapped her shoulder.

"*Nicht hier,*" Peter said, cuffing his hand around her wrist and leading her outside.

THE DAY HAD TURNED CLOUDY and there was a threat of storms in the air. Peter kept a tight hold as they entered the park. His grip was more protective than menacing. Still, Grete shrugged free, making it clear she was there on her own accord. Children played nearby, their laughter soothing but altogether distant from the cloak-and-dagger intrigue she found herself in. Peter gestured toward a bench on a rise overlooking the Hudson and sat with a frustrated sigh.

"*Was machst du hier?*" he asked. His German sounded accusatory.

Grete's back stiffened. All at once, she felt exhausted, and defensive. Peter was the one who owed her answers, not the other way around. "What are you doing here?" she parroted in English. "Who were those men you were talking to?" she asked without bothering to say she had seen them at the Automat.

Peter gestured over his shoulder toward Grant's Tomb. "This is George's idea of a rendezvous." The word rendezvous was straight out of a film, *Foreign Correspondent* or *Night Train to Munich*. He let out a disparaging laugh. "Go home. It's better for you to forget all this."

She knew she should leave, but she was also aware that forgetting Peter might not be easy. He had stirred feelings she thought she had lost. "Tell me what's going on and then I'll decide what to do."

Peter patted the bench by his side. When she did not sit, he leaned forward, his body folding into itself. "I am a German, like you."

"I'm not German!" She bristled. Along with everything else, the Nazis had stolen her heritage. "I'm American." *Or at least I will be*, she thought to herself. Two years would pass before she was eligible to become a citizen. It was impossible to say how long it would take to expunge the stories, foods, songs, and games that she had been raised on. The Nazis had made her hate all she had loved. Worst of all, the United States would never truly be home until she was reunited with her parents. "I'm American," she said again as if repeating it would make it so, "and a Jew." As little as five years ago, she would have described herself as a talented athlete and a mediocre student, a bit of a mischief with an insatiable sweet tooth. Now, being Jewish was her sole defining trait. She winced recalling how a teacher in Mannheim had stopped calling her "Grete" and referred to her, and the three other Jewish girls in her class, as "Sarah."

Peter's barely audible response lacked conviction. "This has nothing to do with religion."

Her ears burned. No Jew would say such a thing. "You said you were—" She stopped short. Peter had never said he was Jewish. She had simply assumed. "You said you were American." She was confident he had said that.

"A *naturalized* citizen. *Deutschland liegt mi rim Blut.*"

"Well, it's not in my blood! The Nazis made that clear enough!" A couple walking arm in arm gave them a wide berth. Grete took a deep breath. If she wanted answers, she would have to soften her approach. She sat down, careful to keep a safe distance between herself and Peter. "At the parade you said it would be nice to talk. Well, talk. I'm listening. And," she added, "speak English."

A smile flittered across Peter's lips. "Anyone ever tell you you're *stur . . .*," he started to say the word in German and switched mid-syllable, ". . . bborn."

"Yes," she said bluntly. Papa often called her stubborn. To her ears, it sounded more like a compliment than criticism. Even as a young child, Grete had a stick-to-her-guns nature. She recalled a rainy day outing with Papa when she was four or five. She could not remember where they were going, but she recalled his bewilderment as they approached a puddle and she dropped his hand and charged straight through. "*Kindela?*" he had said, "You're making your shoes all wet." Grete smiled and splashed. As far as she was concerned, going through the puddle got her where she wanted to go faster, and splashing was fun. As a swimmer, she was known for her dive and the way she propelled her body forward. Teachers called her obstinate. She preferred to think of herself as determined. So what if she was willful? Strong-mindedness was a good thing. A pigeon cooed at her feet, and reality dawned. Papa was gone and she had become a meek person she did not recognize, or like. She sat up, preferring her former self. The tenacious person who would not take no as an answer. "Peter, tell me what's going on."

"Telling you would be selfish. I'd be burdening you just to clear my own conscience."

"Were you in prison?"

Peter looked up as if to question her, then thought better of it and remained silent.

"I went to your hotel," she confessed. She was about to bring up the claim ticket, the sack of sand, the broken sign and the man in the plaid jacket, but the truth was more straightforward. "I wanted to see you again. Please tell me what this is about."

He slid closer and his leg settled against hers. "It's a long story. A complicated one." Grete remained quiet. Moments passed as Peter seemed to collect his thoughts. He began slowly. She had the sense he was trying not to distress her, which only made her more alarmed. "It's true my family lived in this country for six years. My father worked as a chauffeur, my mother was a maid, and life here was difficult. The year I became a citizen, we moved back to Germany. My parents believed the National Socialists would restore German pride." Grete inhaled. Now that Peter was talking she was suddenly unsure. He put his hand gently, but insistently, over hers. "Of course, the situation in Germany only got worse." He turned, his eyes pleading. "You were there. Children were in rags and old people were begging in the streets. The Nazis promised to do away with all that, so I went along with them."

She wrenched her hand out from under his. "What?"

He looked up at her, confused.

"How did you go along with them?" she demanded.

"I became a soldier."

"A *Nazi* soldier?" It was remarkable, she thought. She had traveled halfway around the world to escape the Nazis and was now sitting on a park bench beside one. Had been holding his hand, in fact, moments earlier. She scrambled to her feet so quickly she became lightheaded. Her knees buckled and she sank breathlessly back onto the bench. She was not sure what she had been expecting, but it wasn't this.

"Grete—" He reached out as if to comfort her then, seeming to think better of it, placed his hand back down in his lap. "I'm not one of them." She waved him away, which he took as an invitation to say more. "I was drafted as a storm trooper under Röhm. We were fighting communists."

Grete squinted as if it would help her remember what she knew of Ernst Röhm. He was one of Hitler's closest allies before the friendship soured and Hitler had him killed. At the time, she was more interested in friends and sports. Entirely ignorant that her life was on the brink of disaster.

"Röhm wanted to return Germany to its former glory," Peter insisted. Grete wasn't at all sure that was the case, but she did not interrupt. "It was Hitler who corrupted the Party. Those hoodlums were offensive to me from the start. I hated the songfests and speeches, grown men strutting around in costume, heel-clicking."

"But you went along with them?"

"Once you're in the Party, you can't get out."

Her disappointment surged. "You turned a blind eye like everyone else."

"That's not true. When I realized what was really happening, I did what I could. Some of the people being harassed were my friends. One girl, Eva, lived in our boardinghouse. Her father was dead, so it was just Eva and her mother. She was English, born in Singapore, half Jewish. Eva was secretary to the Chief of the Associated Press in Berlin. There was a little café in the Tiergarten we used to go to . . ." His voice trailed.

Irrational as it was, Grete felt the tug of jealousy.

"Before Poland was invaded, when circumstances were bad but not lost, I told Eva and her mother to get out of Germany. I also told her the truth about the Party so she could pass it along to the Associated Press. They fled to London."

Grete found herself softening. Perhaps her instinct about Peter hadn't been totally off.

"When the war started, I was assigned to a division that

wrote propaganda. They had me take journalism courses at the University of Berlin. One of my professors took a fatherly interest in me. His name was Haushofer and he was an associate of Hess—"

"Rudolph Hess?" The air seemed to swirl. She caught her breath, expecting Peter to correct her, but he remained quiet. "Hess is Deputy Führer!"

"Grete." Peter held his hand up to curtail her protests. "You asked to hear *my* story. I can't defend Hess, Haushofer, or anyone else."

Grete pinched her palm, willing herself to listen.

"After I graduated university, I was sent to Poland to report on conditions there." His voice grew melancholy and his knee trembled against hers. "I saw people who were left on trains for days starving and freezing to death. I couldn't save them, so I convinced myself that the best thing I could do was return to Berlin and write an honest report, which I did." Peter sat back as if that were the end of the story.

A bumblebee hovered nearby. Grete listened to it hum, waiting for it to settle on a pansy before speaking. "You still haven't said what you're doing here or why you're mixed up with those other men."

"No." He smiled. His smile was disarming. For an instant, she could almost believe they were friends, enjoying a warm June afternoon in the park. "It's enough for you to know that I'm trying to do the right thing." His expression grew somber. "Knowing more won't help. It might actually harm you."

She considered what Peter had shared. His confession had only raised more questions. "Why were you in prison?" she asked.

Peter sighed. It was clear he had given the matter lots of thought and not reached a conclusion. "I handed the report over to Haushofer like I'd been asked. Who knows maybe he expected me to toe the party line? Or maybe he had enemies within the Gestapo? All I know is the Gestapo got hold of it. They accused me of falsifying documents and injuring the reputation of the Schutzstaffel and threw me in the basement of a Berlin prison.

After a few months, I was moved to a camp along with Jews, and Catholic priests, and anyone else who opposed them."

Pain seared through her. Grete wondered if the camp was anything like the ones her parents were in. *If they were still there.* She shook those dark thoughts away. It was easier to focus on Peter than her parents. "But you got out," she said softly. "How?"

He shrugged, his eyes wide, as if he too were confused by the strange series of events. "I spent seventeen months in that pit and then one day in April—"

She could not help but interrupt. "Two months ago?"

"They called me into an office and had me sign a concentration camp—" Peter lapsed into German, *"Erklärung."*

"A declaration," she supplied without insisting on English. The story he was imparting was difficult enough. "Saying what?"

"Promising to keep everything I had seen secret. I returned home for Easter and less than a week later received a typed letter." He sat up, barking the letter's content, "'Soldier Peter Burger, I ask you if you would like to go on special assignment to a country where you have been before.' The letter was unsigned and was not on letterhead. I ignored it, but the Gestapo showed up every day." His voice wobbled and he blotted his eyes with a knuckle. His distress was so sincere, Grete found herself resisting the urge to console him. "I thought I would be sent back to Poland. Instead, I was sent to a training camp where I met George and the others."

"The men I saw you with?"

"Dick and Henry. We were all recruited because of our . . . It might be hard to believe, but I was recruited because of my English. All of us have lived in America. I was a citizen. That made me an excellent candidate."

"Candidate for what?" She braced herself for his answer.

"Abwehr."

The Nazi intelligence service. She clamped her hand over her mouth.

"Grete, try to understand, I was told this was my last chance at rehabilitation and if I didn't go along with it I'd be sent back to a detention center."

Her head was spinning as she stood on trembling legs. The pathway leading out of the park sloped upward and she moved at such a furious pace that her breathing grew ragged. She understood why Peter had not wanted to share his story and she regretted having heard it. Her heart pounded. She had thought she could hear his explanation and be satisfied. She had not foreseen the magnitude of his trouble nor how strongly she would feel about his plight. She had just reached the street when he caught up.

"You must understand." Peter no longer sounded reluctant to share his story. He sounded determined for her to accept it. "My life was already ruined, but I couldn't harm the people I loved most. I had to do what they said."

Grete stopped midstride. She looked beyond the sidewalk into the woods running down to the river, then across the street, afraid to see the horrible man named Dick. *"Du bist ein—"* Peter's disclosure had shocked her into speaking German. She should have realized then that her principles were evaporating. Instead, she swallowed, quickly correcting herself. "You're a . . ." Sweat trickled down her brow. She thought she might faint, "Spy?"

"No," he said, shaking his head too adamantly. "I was trained in sabotage."

"That's spying."

"We were never asked to collect information or pass anything to anyone."

"George Davis and the others are spies too," she said, more statement then question. The loquacious George seemed anything but discreet. It was even harder picturing the childlike man who had accompanied her to Grant's Tomb as a threat. Grete felt herself go pale at the thought of Dick. She was now certain that he had kicked the woman at the subway station. It was easy to imagine him doing far worse.

"George has a plan to get us out of this," Peter said.

Grete recalled the conversation she had overheard at the hotel. George had said something about *licking those bastards at their own game.* "George is a loose cannon," she said. That much was obvious.

"I don't have much choice but to go along with him. The Gestapo is watching my family. I can't back out or run." Peter took her face between his hands and looked into her eyes. "Hitler and his butchers are digging Germany's grave. They need to be stopped. I know it's crazy to think I can do anything about it, but even if I do one small thing, it would be something."

She found herself nodding in support. Doing anything was better than feeling helpless. Peter said he had been in prison alongside Jews and other Nazi opponents. As a Party member, he could have kept silent like countless others. Instead, he was risking everything. For the first time since they entered the park, she was able to meet his eye. "What will you do?" she asked.

"We were told to lay low for now. I'm waiting and watching and, when the time is right, I'll act."

"And until then?"

Peter's expression grew markedly lighter. He sighed, and she sensed his relief. She thought she understood why he had been so quick to confess. Telling his story to her—a young woman who was no threat—eased his burden. "Until then, I thought I'd visit my sister in Astoria."

"You have a sister who lives in Queens?" Given everything Peter had shared, this was perfectly ordinary information, yet it surprised her as much as the rest.

"I haven't seen her in years." Peter smiled inwardly. He removed a thick manila envelope from his pocket. "And I have a gift for her from the Führer."

CHAPTER 6

GRETE TIPTOED PAST UNCLE JACQUES, napping in his chair. She scribbled a note on the pad by the phone. *Back after dinner.* Vagabond watched with an accusatory glare. With a twinge of guilt Grete added, *Visiting friend from Germany.*

"You look prettier each time I see you," Peter said when she came back downstairs in a fresh dress, her favorite. He touched her hair where it curled below her chin. The compliment caught her off guard, and felt wonderful. Heat rose to her cheeks. She could not put her finger on why Peter needed her, but she was sure he did. Even if, as he said, he was only doing one small thing to stop the Nazis, he was trying to fight back. And she was helping. It was why she had agreed to come along to visit his sister. Standing outside Riverside Park, she had been taken aback by his invitation.

"Why don't you come with me?" he had said, slapping the manila envelope against his thigh as if the idea had just occurred to him.

"To your sister's?" Her head was swimming with everything he had told her, her body charged with the knowledge of his secret mission.

"You don't want to come," he said sheepishly. "You shouldn't have anything more to do with me."

"It's not that," she bluffed. Of course, she should have nothing more to do with Peter. "It's just . . . I wouldn't want to intrude."

"It would be nice to have company." Peter broke into a wide grin. "And I'd like to spend more time with you."

Grete found herself flattered, then relieved. Being with Peter gave her a sense of purpose and kept her darkest thoughts at bay. She wasn't prepared to say goodbye just yet. Later, she would mull over his invitation, each time drawing a different conclusion.

THEY RODE THE TRAIN TO QUEENS in companionable silence. Grete was grateful for the quiet. Her head was a muddle and she needed time to collect her thoughts. Peter's story was incredible and there was still so much she did not know. *What was he doing here?* He had spoken for close to an hour without revealing that crucial fact. At the Lexington Avenue stop, he stood to offer an elderly woman his seat. He held the bar over Grete's head, occasionally holding her eye contact and then breaking into his wide grin as if he were both surprised and pleased by her company.

From the Astoria subway stop, they walked long blocks past Irish bars, German cabinetmakers, and Italian bakeries. It was late afternoon, and the sight of the bakeries' bare shelves made her empty stomach ache. Twice, she opened her mouth to question Peter, and closed it again. He had endured so much, he deserved a single afternoon to set his worries aside. She did too. As they passed a movie theater, Peter confessed a weakness for Cary Grant, who could play either screwball or scoundrel. At the time, the remark sounded completely innocent.

They turned onto a tree-lined street comprised of tidy row houses with small yards boxed in with chain-link fences or low hedges. Many had victory gardens beginning to bud. Several displayed small banners in the windows, a white field with a red border and a star: blue stars for family members serving in the armed forces, silver for someone who was wounded, and a gold star for a boy who had been killed. Her mood grew somber again. The sky had turned completely gray. Thunder rumbled in the distance.

"We'd better hurry," Peter said.

The wind picked up and a smattering of raindrops hit the pavement. Peter stopped in front of an attached two-story home. Except for open windows and curtains fluttering in the breeze, it looked identical to the others. He held the gate for her. They climbed the stoop. Peter ran his hand through his hair and straightened his jacket. She was moved to see his fist tremble as he knocked. Some time passed before Peter knocked again. He shifted his weight and smiled anxiously at her.

"Are they expecting you?" she asked.

Peter shook his head. "Hannelore doesn't know about any of this."

A scarecrow of a man came to the door. His pants were crinkled and he wore a cardigan and slippers. He removed his bifocals and rubbed his eyes. "Ernest, is that you?" He did not offer a handshake let alone a hug. "How on earth?"

Grete turned to Peter. Who was Ernest, she wondered, and why was he receiving such a lukewarm welcome?

Peter ignored the slight and made introductions. "My brother-in-law, Robert. Robert, this is my friend Grete."

Robert looked even more confused. "Friend?" he asked, as if such a thing were unlikely.

The rain fell harder. "Can we come in?" Peter asked.

"Of course," Robert apologized, "Excuse me. I was . . . surprised." When he turned to lead them inside, Grete saw that his hair was matted in back as if they had woken him from a nap. Peter raised his eyebrows apologetically, but gave no explanation for the name or anything else.

The smell of something warm and nourishing wafted down the narrow hallway as Robert led them into a cozy living room. Books, mostly histories and biographies, from what Grete could see, were haphazardly stacked on a coffee table along with pewter candlesticks and a plate of almonds. Oil paintings and a few sketches crowded the walls. As in Jacques's apartment, a radio with amber-colored wood and black dials occupied a prominent position and the Sunday *Times* was folded and discarded in sections across the floor. The front page and its large photo of the war parade lay in stark juxtaposition to the intricately patterned Persian rug. Grete stared at the date-line above the photo. It seemed impossible that she had met Peter only yesterday.

On the couch, a pillow yawned. Or rather, what Grete had taken to be a pillow was actually a small black dog, who stretched, revealing a spotted white paw.

"Spotty!" Peter's brother-in-law turned to the dog. "You know you shouldn't be up there!" Spotty cocked an ear, looking less than impressed.

"Spotty!" Peter beamed. He went to the sofa and lowered his head to meet the dog's nose. "I didn't expect to see you!"

"He'll be fourteen this month," Robert said with pride and a touch of sadness. Spotty offered a few tail wags before setting his head back down and resuming his nap.

Grete fought an urge to nestle in with him. She flashed back to Sunday afternoons in her own living room in Mannheim, reading on the sofa with Stromer by her side.

Peter approached a Queen Anne desk, with its warren of cubbyholes and drawers, and picked up a framed photo of three boys. Grete recognized him instantly. He was in short pants and looked to be about eight, his smile brighter than that of the man he had grown into.

"My brothers," he said, wistfully. "Walter is somewhere in Austria. No one has heard from Fred since last fall."

An enamel clock struck six. Robert had still not invited them to sit. "How did you get here?" he asked. Fully awake, he still seemed genuinely confused.

Peter set the photo down. "Is Hannelore home?"

"She's at a neighbor's," Robert said, nodding as if he were finally coming to his senses. "Sit, please." He looked apologetically at Grete and gestured to a chair. "Forgive my manners. It's just . . ." He turned to Peter. "I'll telephone your sister."

Robert excused himself. "Come home right away," Grete could hear him whisper from the hallway. "Everything's fine, but it would be better if you came right away."

He reappeared with a curt nod. Rain was pouring down and he closed the windows, making the comfy space at once confining. Grete dug her fingers into the chair cushion. The enamel clock ticked, drawing attention to the silence. Her belly growled and she shifted in her seat to disguise the noise. Ten excruciating minutes later, the front door opened. There was a gust of damp air and the sound of someone stomping rain off their shoes. A small, angular woman entered the room, saw Peter, and stopped dead.

"Hannelore," Peter said, rushing to his sister and engulfing her in a warm embrace.

Hannelore's entire body seemed to crumple as Peter led her to the sofa. She did not sit so much as collapse, gaping at him, at a loss for words. The dog stood, circled three times, and resettled himself with his head on Hannelore's lap. Peter sat on her other side. Robert brought a glass of water, which Hannelore drank with trembling hands. The rain slowed to a steady patter and the thunder began to disperse.

Grete studied Peter. He looked younger beside his sister, and more vulnerable. His chest was hollow and his shoulders did not seem nearly as broad. The siblings shared the same olive complexion, straight nose, and worry lines.

When Hannelore finally spoke, her words were faint. "Mother wrote you were in prison." Robert had addressed Peter in English and Grete noticed that his sister did too.

Peter clasped his hands on his lap. "I'm sorry to have caused so much worry."

Hannelore took his hands in hers. "How on earth?" It was the same phrase her husband had used.

"I got out," was all Peter would say.

"Ernest!" Hannelore sounded stern, an older sister reprimanding her naughty brother. "How did you get out? When?"

Grete tried to catch Peter's eye, but he was consoling his sister. "Calm down. I'll tell you everything, but you have to calm down first."

"Hannelore," Robert interrupted. "This is Grete. Ernest's friend."

Hannelore's attention shifted to Grete and she looked as confused as her husband had when Peter first introduced Grete. Grete raised a hand weakly in greeting. Peter cleared his throat. It seemed he was deliberately not looking Grete's way.

"Grete and I just met. She has been tremendously kind."

The explanation was as vague as the message Grete had left for her uncle. Rain slapped the window and the room grew quiet again. Hannelore and Robert exchanged an impenetrable look. It felt to Grete as if everyone was engaged in a game in which something significant was at stake but no one knew the players, or the rules.

Robert made the first move. "Sundays we usually have an early supper," he said. "Everything's almost ready. Maybe it would be best for us to catch up on a full stomach. Grete, will you help me set the meal out?"

"Yes, of course," Grete said, leaping to her feet. She was relieved to be excused from the reunion, and her stomach rumbled enthusiastically.

She followed Robert into the kitchen, where a large iron pot simmered on the stove. There was a sturdy round table in a small alcove surrounded by windows filled with blooming African violets. A glimpse of the life she dreamed of having with her own family. The table was set for two with white dinner plates and cloth napkins rolled into monogramed silver rings. Robert passed her two more place settings. Rain lashed the windows as Grete set the plates in place. The purple flowers contrasting starkly against the stormy sky.

Robert uncorked a bottle of wine. "I think the occasion calls for it," he said. But it felt like anything but a celebration.

SUPPER WAS CHICKEN STEW, brimming with mushrooms, celery, and peas. Hannelore ladled the dish over rice, serving Grete first, then Peter and Robert. Robert sneaked pieces of chicken to Spotty, who had abandoned the sofa and was now perched hopefully at Robert's feet. Hannelore had recovered from her shock enough to play the diligent hostess, offering seconds and thirds and refilling everyone's glass until a lull settled over the table.

"This was delicious," Grete said, the color was back in her cheeks and she was settling into a satisfied drowsiness.

"Robert's the cook," Hannelore said, gazing affectionately at her husband. Grete recognized that the couple shared an indefinable quality. Maybe it was happiness.

"Only once a week," Robert said. "My mother thought it was important for a man to know how to cook at least one dish, preferably his favorite. She taught me her recipe for chicken fricassee and on Sundays I like to honor her memory. The chopping and stirring, and the smell, it's like spending the afternoon with her." He smiled to himself before turning to Grete. "Would you like to know the secret?"

Grete wasn't sure how many more secrets she could handle, but she forced herself to nod politely.

"Nutmeg!" he exclaimed. "And cream, of course. It's not kosher, but Mother liked to say that kosher was what comes out of your mouth, not what goes in."

Grete jolted upright, scanning the dinette until her eyes found a pair of candlesticks tucked on the windowsill next to an African violet. *Shabbos candles.* Robert was Jewish. There was a reason the creased newspaper, Sunday nap, and warm but slightly guarded demeanor reminded her of Uncle Jacques. Hannelore was married to a Jew. Grete thought there must be a very romantic, if fraught, story behind their courtship.

"I'd love the recipe," she said.

"Grete lives with her uncle," Peter explained. "Her parents are in Europe." The calm respite became a tense silence. Hannelore furrowed her brow and Robert nodded gravely. Peter shifted uncomfortably in his seat. "I know I owe you an explanation," he said.

Robert folded his arms across his chest. "I'd say."

"Robert, please," Hannelore softly chided. "We're family."

Grete's heart sank as the tension mounted. She and Peter had arrived in a happy home and filled it with discord. She stood and began clearing plates. Peter touched her forearm. "Stay, you've been by my side this entire time. I want you to hear this." He tipped his wineglass back and Hannelore poured him another which he swallowed in three gulps. With his eyes lowered, he began painstakingly recounting what he had told Grete about Poland and his imprisonment and release. His English became peppered with German as he became more animated before switching over entirely. Grete had the same sense that she had had earlier: Peter seemed eager to defend himself.

"I'd been out of prison for a week when I got a letter, instructing me to go to a home outside of Berlin called Quenz Farm. I didn't want to go but the Gestapo showed up at my door . . ." Peter reached for his wine glass, saw it was empty, and took a gulp of water instead. "Please understand, I had no choice but to go and I didn't know why I was there until our training began."

"Our?" Grete interrupted. "You mean George and the other men I saw you with?"

Hannelore looked even more distressed. "Who's George? What other men?"

Peter held up his hand, asking for patience. "Our day began at seven with calisthenics. We were told to only speak English and they had us practice by reading the *New York Times*, *Colliers*, *Life*, and the *Saturday Evening Post*." Grete thought of Sundays in the park with Uncle Jacques and the tender way in which he corrected her English. She was coddled with kid gloves while Peter was forced to fall in line. "The copies were as recent as January," he said. "All of them were stamped 'Property of the *Oberkommando der Wehrmacht*.'" German High Command. Hannelore crimped her lips. "They had us share stories about ourselves." Peter spoke quickly as if his confession would absolve him. "On Friday and Saturday, we would all gather early in the classroom and discuss the story each man should tell once we arrived here. Something close enough to the truth so it would not raise suspicion. Because of my coloring, I was told to pose as a Czech refugee who had stowed away on a Spanish ship. Another man planned to say he was born in San Francisco before the earthquake, which would make his identity difficult to verify. Another fellow was to say he was from Pennsylvania."

"Wilkes-Barre," Grete mumbled to herself.

"Quenz Farm is run by a Lieutenant named Kappe. He's a formidable man." Peter stared out the rain soaked window as if Lieutenant Kappe were hovering just outside. "It was a school of sorts. They took us on fieldtrips to railway stations and factories and we learned about fuses and timing devices and how to write in secret ink on cloth handkerchiefs. The name of a contact in Lisbon through which the group leader could communicate with the High Command was stored that way."

A strained look settled over Hannelore's face as she drew back in her seat. "I don't understand."

"It's easy. All one needs is a bit of alcohol mixed with a laxative, of all things. It's best to write with something thin like a toothpick or matchstick. When the writing dries it's invisible, but it turns red when exposed to ammonia fumes."

"Enough!" The cutlery clattered as Robert pounded his fist into the table. His tone was worlds away from the soft-spoken man who had talked so warmly about his mother. "You've got a lot of nerve sitting under my roof, at my table, and confessing this treachery."

"I'm not asking you to forgive me." Peter looked beseechingly around the table. "Just understand. I am no more in favor of the Reich than any of you. I'm no Nazi. We had three weeks of training before they sent us off with a fistful of cash and forged identity papers." He shook his head. "As if a false name could save us."

Grete fidgeted in her seat. Beneath the table, Peter reached for her hand. "Peter's my name," he said, finally realizing her confusion. "Ernest Peter Burger. Only family calls me Ernest."

Obfuscation was the English word that came to Grete's mind. A tricky word that she had gotten wrong more than once on vocabulary tests. She had thought it was a ridiculous word with no practical purpose, and yet here it was, perfectly applicable.

"And the others?" she asked. The wine had gone to her head, making her dizzy. Or maybe it was the intricacies of Peter's subterfuge that were making her light-headed.

"Richard Quirin goes by his real name, but we call him Dick. Henry is Heinrich. George's surname is Dasch, not Davis."

"*Herr Strich,*" Grete said, recalling how Dick had called him that at Grant's Tomb. *Strich* in English meant line or dash. The pun might have been clever if the information were not so damning.

Hannelore seemed to agree. "Why do you need a false name?"

"I don't," Peter said. "I didn't change my name because I have nothing to hide."

Robert's chair scraped against the floor as he shifted backward. "We've heard more than enough about invisible ink and code names. Why are you here?"

"I won't go through with it," Peter insisted, "but it's a simple enough plan. They gave us dynamite painted to look like coal. Just a few lumps put in the furnace of a train will crack and ruin the boiler. If that happens, trains can't run and the Army won't be able to move troops or equipment." The chicken curdled in Grete's stomach as she thought about their visit to Grand Central. "I won't go through with it," Peter said again, "and I'm fairly certain George won't either, but we have to pretend to go along with the plan until the time is right to stop it. We can't raise suspicions."

"Fairly certain?" Hannelore said, doubt creeping into her voice.

"Hannelore," Robert said. "These men are spies. They're motivated by hatred and money. They can't be trusted." It was not clear if he was referring to Peter as well. Robert turned to Grete. "You seem like a nice girl. How did you get mixed up in this?"

Grete's cheeks burned. She had been asking herself that all day and still did not have an answer. At least not one she could articulate.

"Peter," Grete said. "What were you doing in Grand Central? Where did you go?"

"Looking around," Peter said.

"Reconnaissance," Robert spat.

"We were told there is a secret basement in the station. Ten stories underground, where the government stores power converters. The power from there runs trains along the northeast. If it were to stop, 80 percent of all troops and equipment would stop with it."

"Your instructions are only to stop troop transports?" Hannelore said. She sounded relieved.

"Isn't that enough?" Robert said, looking sharply at his wife. "Do you understand what will happen to our boys on the front line if they don't receive fresh troops or supplies?"

"Stopping power would do more harm than that," Peter said, glumly. "The power from Grand Central also runs aluminum plants. Right now, aluminum for airplanes and engines is more precious than gold. If power is cut for as little as eight hours, the electrolyte baths used to mix the aluminum would harden and be destroyed. They would have to be dismantled and rebuilt, which would take more than a year. Airplane production would be crippled."

"Germany would win the war," Robert supplied.

Hannelore turned to Peter. "Why do they need you to dynamite them? Germany's wiped out half of London. Why can't they bomb the factories here?"

"The U.S. is too far away for that kind of operation," Robert said.

"Besides," Peter said, "we weren't ordered to dynamite Grand Central. It doesn't take dynamite to destroy power converters. All it takes is a bucket, or bag, of sand."

Grete bolted upright. She saw herself dumping two sandcastles worth of sand in a pile on the ladies room floor. Her toes curled as they touched tiny grains still left in her shoes. She had unknowingly thwarted a disaster, and was secretly pleased.

"I think we've heard more than enough," Robert said. "You say you're worried about your loved ones. How could you show up here and expose your sister to this."

"You're right, I shouldn't have come. I just wanted to see Hannelore. If anything should happen to me, I need *Mutti* to know the truth. Promise me, you'll tell her. I'm innocent of this—" He raked fingers through his hair. "They gave us money." He reached into his pocket for the manila envelope he had shown Grete earlier and set it on the table. "I know that just by being here, I'm putting you in danger. You should have this." He pushed the envelope forward.

Robert shoved it away. "It's blood money. We don't want it."

Hannelore nodded and looked away. The envelope sat in the center of the table until Peter stuffed it back in his pocket, defeated. Grete's heart went out to him. There was little he could do that would not jeopardize his family.

"This is a big country," Hannelore said. "Take the money and disappear."

"You have to look out for yourself," Grete agreed. "The others aren't trustworthy." Hannelore looked at her as if surprised she was still sitting there.

Peter refilled his wine glass and drank it down. "Each man took an oath to do away with any man who did not fulfill the mission."

"An oath?" Hannelore seethed. "What's a promise to a bunch of monsters?"

"I'm not worried about going back on my word. I'm worried about what might happen to . . ." Peter's head dropped. *"Mutti und . . ."* Hannelore clasped her hand over her mouth. "Hannelore," Peter said. "This was my only chance to escape Germany without causing further harm. I never intended to go through with any of it. I won't."

"It doesn't matter what you do if the others are moving ahead," Robert pointed out.

"Two might," Peter said. "One's not very bright. The other is too mean for his own good. I'm working with the group leader, George. He has a plan to stop the operation before it begins."

"You crossed enemy lines," Robert said. "It's already begun!"

Hannelore swiveled toward Peter. "How did you get here?" she asked.

"They put us on a train to Paris. We spent a few days there before they took us to Lorient where we boarded a U-202."

"A U-boat!" Robert exploded. "You landed on an American beach!"

Grete blinked, startled. She had not given any thought to how Peter had arrived here. The realization that he had crossed the Atlantic on a German U-boat as part of a deadly wolf pack made her shudder.

Robert sat forward, clutching the side of the table as if he were about to say more, but Hannelore cut him off. "What do you plan to do? How will you stop this?"

"George and I are going to the FBI."

"Like Sebold!" Hannelore said. She sounded as if she had struck upon the solution to a riddle, and Grete understood why. Last fall, she and most Americans had been riveted by coverage of a foiled spy ring. William Sebold, a U.S. citizen living in Germany, had been coerced into spying for the Reich. His grandfather was a Jew and the Nazis threatened his family if he didn't cooperate. Sebold became a double agent and helped to reveal Nazi plans to bomb a General Electric factory and Roosevelt's Hyde Park Chapel. In a matter of weeks, the German agents and spies were rounded up, tried, and sentenced. Sebold was a hero.

"You say you're afraid of what will happen to family back home if you don't cooperate," Robert fumed. "What do you think will happen when you go to the FBI? Your name will be all over the papers and the Gestapo will track down everyone you love."

"No," Peter said, definitively. "George says the FBI will keep it under wraps."

Grete flashed to weaselly George. It sounded exactly like something he would say. She did not know what George was playing at, and she didn't trust him.

"When are you going to the FBI?" Hannelore asked, wringing her hands.

"We're calling tonight."

Robert swept his arm toward the door. "Go."

THE DOWNPOUR HAD LEFT BEHIND A SLICK STREET and dark puddles. Over Hannelore's shoulder as they hugged goodbye, Grete saw Robert take Peter by the arm. He spoke softly, but she had no trouble reading his lips, "Don't come back here again."

Peter joined Grete on the sidewalk. "There's just enough time for me to get you home before I meet George," he said. Grete nodded agreement, not consent. She was part of something bigger than herself—and she had no intention of being swept aside.

CHAPTER 7

FOR THE SECOND TIME IN AS MANY DAYS Grete found herself in Grand Central at a reckless hour. A janitor, too old and infirm for war, pushed a mop across the pink marble floor, making a soapy tide drift to and fro under the trompe l'oeil sky. Echoes replaced the usual daytime din. All but two ticket windows were shuttered. A handful of people watched the board displaying arrival and departure times. Grete's heart thumped, anxious and excited. It had taken some convincing to persuade Peter she should come along.

"No," he had said as their subway barreled toward the city. "It was good of you to come to Hannelore's, but that wasn't dangerous."

His insistence that she leave only made her more determined to stay. "That's ridiculous," her voice rose and she took several deep breaths to calm down. "Put yourself in my shoes." They were sitting side by side in the rattling subway car. Hearing Peter's story had filled her with a keener sense of purpose. If she walked away only to discover that the other men had completed their so-called mission or, worse, some innocent had been hurt, she would never forgive herself. "Peter this isn't just about you and George. It concerns me." *It concerns my parents.* "Knowing what I know, do you think I can just go home? Could you?"

Sullen after the cool reception he had received at Hannelore's home, Peter did not bother answering. "Did you hear the way Robert spoke to me?" he asked, kneading his hands in one another. "You'd think I was a . . ." He looked around the subway car. "One of them."

"Well, you're not," Grete said. Peter had spent seventeen months in a Gestapo prison and was still suffering. "Time will prove him wrong," she said. "You will."

Peter turned to Grete, taking her hand, caressing her fingers. "That means a lot."

Happiness surged through her. "Where are we meeting George?"

He dropped her hand. "We're not. I am. I told you, it's not safe."

"So why was it safe for me to hold that baggage claim ticket?"

"That was only a piece of paper." A crease formed on his forehead. It was clear he was just now remembering the ticket. "What did you do with it?"

"I turned it in, got the bag, and dumped the sand." Pride stirred within her as she recalled the lopsided bag and its unwieldy weight. "Why lug a bag full of sand around on the hottest day of the year?"

Peter flashed her a wary look. "We brought it from the beach where we landed. There's nowhere to get that much sand in the city and George wanted to show the others he was thinking ahead. You should have seen him at the Automat after you left. He made a big show of telling Dick and Henry how the bag was in the luggage office and the plan was 'in motion.'"

"And now it's not." She expected Peter to praise her or, at least, agree, but he continued to brood. "See," she said, "I can help."

"What'd you do with the bag?"

"I told you, I dumped it."

"Not the sand. The bag."

Grete shifted on the bench. After spilling the sand, she had dropped the canvas bag on top of the heap and had been halfway out the ladies room door when she reconsidered. She went back to throw the bag into the trash, then decided it was better to discard it on the street—several blocks away. "I covered my tracks," she said, trying to make light of her paranoid behavior.

"This isn't a game."

Embarrassment swept over her. She had trailed Peter to Grant's Tomb as if it were an elaborate game of hide-and-seek. "I know."

"Listen carefully, Grete, before we left Germany Lieutenant Kappe introduced us to a man but didn't use his name. Everyone was told to take a good look because we might come in contact with him when we arrived here. I think he's SS, assigned to watch over our activities, undoubtedly with orders to destroy anyone who lies down on the job."

"Why would the Lieutenant introduce you to someone who's meant to be watching you?"

"To scare us. Kappe liked to say there was no escaping the protective eye of the Reich. He warned we'd be watched until our death beds."

She felt a twinge of apprehension as she sorted through all the people she had seen and spoken to at the parade, in Central Park, on the subway. "What's he look like?"

"He's tall, close to fifty, speaks English fluently. His hair is black with a little gray around the temples and he weighs maybe two hundred pounds." Grete frowned at the generic description. Of course, someone whose job was to follow others would hardly stand out in a crowd. "George and I haven't seen any sign of him."

"That's good." She hesitated. "Right?"

Peter held his hand out and rocked it like a teetering kite, maybe yes, maybe no. "If no one is watching us, nothing is preventing George from taking the money and running. He could live out his life on what we were given."

Grete remembered the fat envelope Peter had offered to Hannelore. "How much is there?"

"Each of the men received $4,000 and George got $80,000—in cash."

"$8,000 dollars?" A new car cost about a thousand dollars. A house, five. With that amount of cash, George could do exactly what Hannelore had urged Peter to do: Disappear.

"Eighty," Peter corrected her. "He's got it all stashed in some old Gladstone bag. He tried to put it in a safety deposit box, but the bag was too big for the box."

Grete blinked. The exorbitant amount highlighted the gravity of the situation. "He could also turn you in." She couldn't pretend confidence in George.

"That's why I needed Hannelore to know the truth, and you too."

"Me? People don't listen to me. They hear my accent and think I'm the enemy. Even those who should know better think I'm German and a Nazi or Jewish and depraved."

Peter did not disagree. "Still," he said. "Hannelore's my sister. It goes without saying she'd defend me. Your trust means a lot to me."

The subway rolled into Grand Central. "Where are we meeting George?" she asked again.

"Here. In the Great Hall." He offered a weak smile. "By the clock."

"The *opal* clock," she said as if that alone were justification for her to stay. Deep down her confidence faltered. She had envisioned another theatrical rendezvous, a foggy west side pier or dank meatpacking warehouse, and the immediacy of the meeting caught her by surprise. All at once she was uneasy. She remembered the guards she had seen patrolling the station. Given what Peter had said about the secret basement, Grand Central seemed rife with danger. The subway doors opened and Grete peered out at the platform.

She could not decide if leaving or staying would be more agonizing. From the instant they first spoke, she had wanted to help Peter, though she could never have guessed the enormity of his dilemma. Her determination had only increased now that she understood what was at stake. The doors began to close. Peter jumped between them, straddling train and platform. Grete sprang to her feet. He held out his hand. The bell rang, the doors started to close, and she leapt out.

TEN MINUTES LATER, GEORGE STILL HAD NOT SHOWN.

Grete's eyes darted from the ramps leading into the main concourse to the dagger-like hands on the opal clock. She worried George would not come, and feared he would. Standing in the open hall under the indigo night sky, she felt utterly exposed. She looked up at the constellations and down the shadowy tunnels and held her breath as a man in a plaid sport coat hurried toward them. The man was short and fat, not a bit like Dick, yet she could not draw air.

"I'm going to look downstairs," Peter said.

Grete twined her fingers through his, making it clear she would not be left behind. Peter had said that he and George were calling the FBI, and she had come along to ensure they did. While she did not doubt Peter, it was impossible to guess what George would or would not do. They walked down the stairs, their footsteps growing unnaturally loud as they strayed deeper underground. The ceilings were lower downstairs but the space was just as vast. A long wall on the left had a dozen or so doors; all closed. The luggage office was bolted shut. Unseen beyond the locked doors, convertors turned.

Peter led her toward a far corner that housed a bank of phone booths and walked down the row until they reached the final booth. The accordion door opened with a squeak. "Wait inside. Don't let George see you."

Grete's nose twitched. The booth smelled of stale cigarettes and something else, possibly urine. There were scratches on the wood paneled walls, cigarette butts on the floor, and wads of chewing-gum under the phone shelf. The glass door was cloudy with oily handprints and grime as if someone had struggled to get out.

Grete eyed the tiny seat. She had no desire to sit. "Where will you be?" she asked.

"Right out here."

Like a daredevil at the Barnum & Bailey show, Peter was tread-ing a razor-thin tightrope. What's more, she was balancing pre-cariously by his side. She had never feared heights or small places, but cold panic trickled through her veins as she stepped into the suffocating booth. Peter had confessed everything. Did he regret his indiscretion? He moved closer, and she pulled back. So much of Peter's appeal hinged on the unknown. His behavior confused her. Her feelings were even more perplexing. She felt a shiver and drew him toward her, suddenly grateful for the confined space. It made her bold.

"Why wait?" She picked up the phone and forced it into his hands. "You don't need George to call the FBI. You know as much as he does." Peter was shaking his head, but she refused to be deterred. "Sebold went to the consulate on his own. Believe me, I understand what it's like to worry about loved ones. If I allowed myself to think about my parents, it would tear me apart." Her thoughts pivoted to Mama. "Trust yourself and you'll know how to live," she said, paraphrasing Goethe.

"Trust myself? I don't even know who I am anymore. I'm not a Nazi. I'm not American." Peter grasped the receiver, but she refused to let go. The phone trembled between them before Grete gave in, allowing Peter to place it back on the hook. It was one thing to march up Fifth Avenue in starched uniforms while bands blared and crowds cheered; another to stand far from home in an empty train station on a rainy night. His was a lonely war without battle lines or comrades and, no matter what he did, he was on the losing side.

"You're afraid?"

He did not deny it. "There isn't a stone big enough for Sebold to hide under. If the Gestapo don't kill him, his—" Peter tapped his temple, "will. No one can escape their own thoughts. Sebold's no hero. He's a snitch who turned a lot of men in. It's a dirty thing to do."

"Dozens of Nazi spies were arrested because of him."

"Spies like me?"

"No," she protested. "Men like Dick who could cause serious harm."

"How can you tell the difference? Who's evil and who's just unlucky? If I had stayed in the United States, I'd be an American soldier. A hero instead of a traitor."

Grete considered their countrymen locked inside Germany. Circumstances determined their fate. Was the corner shoemaker, whose business flourished after his Jewish competitor vanished, evil? She closed her eyes envisioning her family home; the wide windows, the *secret* cupboard that doubled as a liquor cabinet (for her parents) and play space (for her). Who was living there now? Did a boy or girl sleep in her bed? Did they ever consider who had lived there before? Did they know they were benefiting at someone else's expense? Were they evil?

"Doing nothing is dangerous," she said. "You won't be able to live with yourself."

Peter was as calm as she was agitated. "You may think I'm being cowardly, but patience takes courage. 'A leaf that's supposed to grow is full of wrinkles,'" he said, reciting Goethe back to her with far more skill.

"You're doing the same thing you did when you were in Poland. You're abiding by their rules when there are no rules."

He flinched as if slapped. "It's better to let George make the first move."

"It doesn't matter if he's the group leader," she said. "Rank doesn't apply anymore."

"It's got nothing to do with rank. When George calls the FBI, I need to look as if I was eager for him to do it."

"Aren't you?" The air was stifling. A trickle ran down her chest.

"Of course, and if he gets through to the right people and all goes according to plan then we might be able to shorten this war and save lives. But I have to prepare for every possibility."

She put her hands on his face. "Peter." Her throat tightened, making it hard to speak. "You can stop this now with a single phone call."

Peter leaned close enough so that she could see the scruff of his whiskers. "George is calling. That's what we agreed."

She was about to protest when he curled his arm around her and drew her near. He bent down and pressed his forehead into hers until she felt the full weight of his grief. A gesture more intimate than a kiss.

AFTER PETER LEFT TO FIND GEORGE, Grete pulled the phone booth door closed and picked up the receiver. She had come to Grand

Central to ensure that Peter called the FBI and if he was not going to call, she would.

"Operator." She gulped. "This is an emergency."

"What is your emergency?" the woman droned.

The operator's tone was mechanical, cold, and efficient like a German. Grete slammed the phone into its cradle. She could report George, but could not bring herself to turn Peter in. Maybe patience was best for now. She would see if George showed up, gather more information, and then decide what to do.

Peter returned with George who was ranting in a cloud of cigarette smoke. "Christ, Pete," he said, waving his gangly arms, "It's nearly ten!"

"I told you," Peter offered a half-hearted apology. "I was at the clock at nine, exactly like we said. I waited ten minutes and left because I didn't want to stand around looking suspicious."

George took a drag of his cigarette and his features relaxed. "The newsreel ran late. You should have seen it. What a show! The Arizona was gone in one . . . Kaboom!" He swept both arms into an all-encompassing smoke-filled circle that ended in a point like a heart. "Those Japs sure are dirty bastards!"

Hidden behind the scratched window in the corner booth, Grete caught her own reflection in the glass. It was impossible to see her entire face, only dark hair fading into woodwork and the oversized pupils of some frightened creature. As Peter steered George toward the booth beside hers, Grete pulled at the neckline of her dress, eager for George to pick up the phone and dial.

All at once, the door to the phone booth was flung open and she was yanked out by the arm.

"For crying out loud!" George snapped, dropping her arm and whirling toward Peter. He shoved Peter against the booth with a bang.

Peter regained his footing and pulled Grete aside. He was not much taller than George, but he was broader. His fists were clenched into tight balls and he was clearly struggling to restrain himself.

"You alright?" he asked, glancing at her sideways. She nodded, more shaken then hurt. Peter turned back toward George. "Calm down," he said, holding his arms out, palms forward as if to settle a rabid dog.

Grete looked down at her heels. They were sling-back shoes, her most flattering pair. The slings were loose from too much wear and tended to slip. There would be no way to outrun George, or for anyone to hear her shout.

"You trying to make me blow my stack?" George fumbled for a fresh cigarette, furiously striking a match until it ignited. His eyes traveled from Peter to Grete and back as he inhaled. The nicotine had its intended effect, and slowly his breathing returned to normal. "You two lovebirds been together this whole time?" A warm blush threatened to consume Grete. Her moods, she noted with dismay, were as mercurial as George's. "Dammit, Pete," George swore. "If we're not on the same team, I got to assume we're on opposite ones."

Peter took George by the elbow, ushering him along the length of the booths. "Don't you see, two fellas alone will stand out." He seemed to be implying that she was a mere diversion and, while Grete wanted to believe he was protecting her, she didn't like the sound of it. She leaned forward to hear more, but Peter's voice faded as they receded down the line.

George was not nearly as discreet. She heard the phrase "honey trap" and blushed to her roots before indignation took hold. Let George say what he would. Peter too. She knew why she was here.

"Are you going to call or not?" she asked.

George spun around, storming toward her. "Don't think I don't know what's going on here." His eyes bounded from Grete back to Peter.

"George," Peter said, his voice slow and steady. "We all want the same thing."

"Yeah, what's that?"

"We want this over with as soon as possible."

George's shoulders softened. "You can say that again," he said, still doubtful but resigned. "This thing has me tied up in knots. I'll tell you one thing. Those boys can't ever know that I'm a stool pigeon—for the sake of my life, and not only my life but also for the sake and security of Snookums and Mother."

"I swear on my life," Peter said.

"I'll tell you something else," George went on. "Dick better not find out about Toots here. Me, I'm a nice guy and Henry's a namby-pamby, but Dick means business."

Grete steadied herself by resting her hand on the phone booth. She thought about how Dick had assaulted a woman and peered helplessly around the deserted hall before her eyes settled on Peter. She had known him for two days, but war had intensified their unlikely bond. Though it was impossible to explain why, she trusted him. More than that, she sensed that what they were doing was essential.

"Let's get this over with," George said, brushing against her as he stepped into the booth. He dug his hand into his pocket, rummaging through scraps of paper before seeming to find the one he was looking for.

Peter stood in the doorway, preventing him from closing it. Grete positioned herself at his side, listening to the scratch and release of the dial. The number seemed inordinately long. There was a lengthy delay as the call went through. The line rang several times before someone picked up.

"Who's this?" George demanded. "Can you take a statement? Yeah, okay. Transfer me to your top man." He fumbled for a cigarette. "Who is this?" he barked again. "I got a message of great importance and I need to know who I'm speaking to." George looked at Peter, shook his head, and frowned. Whoever was on the other end of the line had declined to give his name. "If you won't give me your name, why do you expect me to tell you mine?"

Grete's hopes sank. George could not manage a basic introduction; he was incapable of handling such a sensitive matter. For the hundredth time, she wondered why Peter was aligning himself with George.

"It is essential you make a detailed record of this call," George said. "The statement I will be giving is of the utmost importance to national security." Grete inhaled. Peter looked somber. Both braced themselves for a serious disclosure, which did not come. "I can't reveal my name," George repeated like a child engaged in a schoolyard prank. "For now, you can call me Franz Daniel Pastorius." There was a significant pause before he spoke again. "Very funny, not Napoleon. I said Franz Daniel Pastorius and I'm warning you right now this is no laughing matter."

"Another crackpot for the nutter desk!" The agent on the line scoffed loud enough for Grete to hear.

Peter met her eye. He looked as crestfallen as she felt. "They must get a lot of crank calls."

"Wouldn't a simple Frank or Dan have done?" she whispered.

"Franz Daniel Pastorius is the name of the mission," Peter said, while George explained the same to the agent.

"Pastorius is the name of a sabotage mission which landed early yesterday morning from a German submarine on the shore of Long Island. In this landing were four men under my leadership. What?" George shook his head, swore under his breath, and spelled, "P-A-S-T-O-R-I-U-S," adding with a disturbing amount of pride, "We're the first group to receive instruction to come here and commit acts of military sabotage."

"Lieutenant Kappe has a sense of humor," Peter told Grete. "He named the mission Franz Daniel Pastorius after the leader of the first group of German Mennonites who settled in Philadelphia in colonial times. It's a catchword. If any of us need assistance and are forced to approach a contact we are to say 'Greetings from Franz Daniel' and the contact is to reply 'Pastorius.' If everything is fine and we need to communicate in writing, we are to simply write, 'My dear friend so-and-so.'"

In the phone booth, George puffed anxiously on his cigarette, clouding the glass. "Nope. I don't want agents meeting me. No . . . Washington D.C., not New York . . . Because New York could be compromised!" Long moments passed while he remained silent, seeming to take in what the party on the line was saying. "Gestapo?" he finally said. "Sure, I'm afraid." George did sound sincerely frightened, but an instant later, his ego reappeared. "This case is too big! I got to spring it in Washington. Listen, the only thing you need to do is let your top men know that Franz Daniel Pastorius will be at FBI headquarters to deliver a full report of military importance this Thursday, or Friday."

Grete grabbed Peter's arm. "Thursday or Friday?" The assignation sounded disturbingly noncommittal.

The color drained from Peter's face. "George?" he mouthed. "I thought we were doing this now, here in New York."

George cupped his hand over the phone. "Trust me. The Gestapo are less likely to have infiltrated the ranks in D.C."

"But why wait until Friday? Let's get this over with."

"Check and recheck. I know exactly what I'm doing. If that sand pounder had reported us, the FBI would have known by now. I bet they'd play ball and put me in touch with someone other than this numbskull."

"Sand pounder?" Grete asked. She imagined someone pounding the sand with a mallet, or fist. "What's a sand pounder?"

Peter waved her off. "George, I didn't come this far to play games."

The phone cord twisted as George turned his back and spoke into the receiver. "I'll be in Washington later this week, and I refuse to speak with anyone but J. Edgar Hoover himself." He slammed the receiver down and stormed away.

Grete was happy to see him go. Peter was better off without George. "What's he talking about? What's a sand pounder?" she asked again.

"The night we landed," Peter said. "There was a guard on the beach."

"Guard? You mean the Coast Guard?"

"He was just a boy. Alone and scared."

"The Coast Guard is part of the U.S. Military. How can you be so dismissive?"

"It was foggy and Dick and Henry were already in the dunes with the crates."

Grete's ears pricked. "Crates? What crates?"

"The dynamite they gave us was packed in crates. We buried it in the dunes."

CHAPTER 8

AZY SKY BLENDED INTO OCEAN WATER as Grete looked out on the horizon. Crossing the Atlantic, the vast ocean and distant shores had seemed foreboding. Sitting on the beach where Nazi saboteurs had landed, her perspective was entirely changed, and dangers she never could have imagined were real.

That morning, for the first time since leaving Germany, she woke feeling eager about the day ahead. She could not recall the last time she had worn lipstick, and she applied a blushing shade of red. After Uncle Jacques left for work, she packed lunch for two and took the subway to Penn Station. Peter was exactly where he said he would be by the ticket counter. From a distance, he looked like any other dark-haired man with full lips, a straight nose, and strong physique. Looking closer, she could see the cleft in his chin, his heavy brow, the worry in his eyes and slight tremble in his hands. He had not wanted to come and it was clear he would rather be anywhere else. Convincing him to return to Amagansett had not been easy. She understood his reluctance, but did not believe he had a choice. She had been asking herself since she first met Peter how or why she had gone along with him so readily, and it seemed to her that she now had an answer. Peter had said there was dynamite buried on the beach and she was sure it needed to be destroyed before a lunatic like Dick could get his hands on it. Grete watched Peter for another moment before the enormity of their shared secret drew her toward him. She crossed the floor, vaguely aware that she was now fully vested in his plight.

Instead of greeting her, Peter picked up their conversation exactly where they had left off the night before. "I promised myself I'd never go back there." She realized that he must have been awake all night, mulling it over.

She answered in-kind, exactly as she had the previous night. "We'll dump the crates in the ocean where they belong and no one will be harmed."

"What happens if they wash up? Maybe it's better to leave them."

"If they wash up the Coast Guard will know about the danger, but not about you. That's the best possible outcome." She slipped her arm through his and led him toward the tracks.

They rode the railroad to the east end of Long Island. Grete watched through the window as residential buildings became storefronts and warehouses. The stations grew further apart. Now that they were seated on the train, Peter seemed more at ease.

"I've missed this," he said. Grete smiled, encouraging him to say more. Peter had shared top secret details, but he was usually tightlipped about home. He rested his head on the back of the seat and closed his eyes. "It feels almost normal, sitting here with the sun shining through the window, and it's nice to be with you." Grete nestled closer. For the first time since they had met, Peter seemed almost content. Their relationship was complicated, yet he summed it up simply: It was nice. The train rounded a bend and his weight shifted toward her. "There are so many things I miss about my former life. All the little things I took for granted." She sighed in agreement and he opened his eyes. "What do you miss?"

Mama and Papa were the first to spring to mind. "My home isn't there anymore," she said, more to herself than him. "You can't be homesick for a place that doesn't exist."

"You can still have memories. They can't rob you of those." Peter looked out the window. "I miss my brothers." Grete recalled the photo she had seen at Hannelore's house of the three smiling boys, their knobby knees sprouting out of short pants. "Walter's five years older than me and Fred is only a year younger than him. They were a team and didn't include me much, but once when it snowed, I must have been about five, we went sledding on a steep hill the local children called *Selbstmorehügel.*" Grete translated to herself, *suicide hill.* "I felt very proud being with them." Peter smiled. "We had a long toboggan and they sat me between them so I wouldn't slip off, but we hit a bump and crashed, and I lost a tooth." Peter tapped his lower jaw. "It was only a baby tooth. Still, *Mutti* was angry. Then Walter, who had a good sense of humor, explained how we had saved her the trouble of having to pull it. *Mutti* made us hot cocoa. She always made cocoa just the right temperature so it warmed your insides without scalding your tongue."

"Sounds perfect."

"Too idyllic, really. I think I remember it that way to block out everything that followed."

Grete closed her eyes, allowing herself to imagine there was no war. "I miss Mannemer Dreck," she conceded. Her mouth watered at the thought of macaroon pastry smothered in rich chocolate.

"That was delicious," Peter agreed. "Chocolate here is too sweet."

Grete settled back in her seat, happy to be so well understood. Peter's shoulder rested against hers, growing warmer as the train rattled along the tracks, jostling them together in drowsy comfort. His eyelashes fluttered closed and his breath grew steady. Grete watched him doze, her breath slowing to match his.

They passed through towns with funny sounding names—Speonk, Quogue—and the scenery changed again from pinelands to open fields. For a man who had suffered so much, a spy on a top secret mission, Peter was remarkably relaxed with her. He slept so soundly she had the sense that it was the first time he had truly closed his eyes in days, maybe weeks.

Three hours later, they arrived in the small resort village of Amagansett. It was another scorching day, relieved only a little by the salty ocean breeze. They strolled past farmhouses where dogs slept on porches, and stopped to pick ripe strawberries.

"Taste this," Peter said, his mouth full. He brushed a berry on his sleeve before holding it out by the stem. Grete stooped beside him, lips parted. The scent filled her nose and the berry tickled her tongue. She bit down. It was sweet and juicy with a trace of summer rain and soil. She closed her eyes and let the sun caress her shoulders.

They walked a mile or so into the sea breeze, all urgency lost. The road was straight and the ocean was visible as they descended a bluff. The dunes were spotted with small bungalows. A truck drove by towing a small fishing boat with the name Beach Plum painted on its side.

When Peter's feet touched sand, he dropped the picnic basket and took off, shedding clothing as he raced across the wide beach and dove under a wave. Moments passed until he surfaced, waving toward her and calling for her to join him.

Grete's shoes were already in hand and the bottoms of her bare feet broiled in the hot sand. She hated nylons and never wore them. With the war in high gear, nylons were used as powder bags for guns and she could pretend she was just being patriotic. She went to the shoreline and let the waves wash her toes.

"Come in!" Peter splashed water toward her.

"I don't have a swimsuit," she protested.

He half-heartedly covered his eyes. "I'm not looking."

She pulled her skirt to her thighs and waded in. The surf was gentle with rolling waves. One brushed her hem and she felt her former self, the champion swimmer, emerge.

"Turn around," she shouted as she stepped out of her skirt. She was grateful to be wearing a relatively new pearl-colored silk slip. Peter was spurting saltwater in the air. She unbuttoned her blouse, pulled it off, and plunged in. The water that had felt refreshing on her toes was icy cold, the shock invigorating. She swam parallel to shore, stroking steadily with cupped hands and fluttering her feet, kicking until she found her rhythm. It was the first time she had swum since the Nazi threw her into the Rhine and she embraced the broad stretch and gentle release, letting the water wash away sadness.

"You swim like a fish," Peter called when she came up for air.

His praise spread through her, easing the chill. "I haven't been in the water since . . ." She swam closer and her breath became shallow. It was impossible to say whether from the cold water, exertion, or the story that tumbled from her lips; one she had never shared with anyone.

Peter treaded water beside her, listening as she described the day her beloved swim club had been overrun by strangers. How grown men and women had run in fear, and how the Nazi thug had lifted her off her feet and hurled her into the raging river. His mouth pinched closed as she told how she had struggled against the strong current and how she had been too frightened to return to the changing room and had walked home barefoot in her wet swimsuit, while people jeered and children threw stones.

"I've never been much of a student," she confessed, "but swimming came naturally. I always felt confident in the water, always felt most like myself. Then this stranger came along and stole that away. He didn't know me, but he hated me." She waited, expecting Peter to be outraged on her behalf. Instead, he dove under a wave. When he surfaced his features were calm.

"Dive as deep as you can," he said. "Let the ocean wash the bad memory away."

Grete turned toward the horizon. Peter was voicing her thoughts: *Nature will triumph. Look to nature and find yourself again.* She took a deep breath and dove into a swell. The water temperature dropped as she descended. She swam a few strokes and, when she could go no further, she rose for air. Cleansing and cathartic, the saltwater made her entire body tingle. Feeling buoyant, she tilted backwards to float, closed her eyes, and let her hair fan out behind her. Peter swam up beside her. His leg brushed against hers and she shivered, aware of his near-naked body.

Peter got out first. Water glistened on his olive skin. She watched as he shook himself off and slipped into his shirt, the fabric sticking to his wet chest and shoulders. She could not help but admire his muscular calves and trim hips as he stepped into his trousers. Peter went to collect the picnic basket and Grete used the opportunity to dry off as best she could and dress, combing her fingers through her hair, untangling salty knots. Her blouse clung. She brushed sand from her skirt, not the least bit self-conscious. Peter crossed the beach, basket in hand, and she stood on tiptoe to smooth down his spiky hair.

"I'm starved," he said.

"I'm afraid it's not much." She had thrown together what she could: half a baguette, a wedge of brie that had ripened nicely in the warm weather, a couple of peaches, some almonds, and two bottles of Donald Duck Lime Cola.

Peter held the bottle out, studying the label with its long-billed duck in his Navy cap. "A fine vintage."

"It's what we had," she said. "And it happens to be my favorite."

He clinked his bottle with hers. "To blue skies." He took a long swig and a broad smile spread across his lips. "It's delicious."

Later, after every scrap was gone, Peter lay back on his elbows. Suddenly somber, he began to share a fantastical scene. Seagulls wheeled overhead and the sand bubbled as crabs burrowed underfoot. The surf was hypnotic. Grete pulled her knees to her chest entranced by the scene Peter was describing.

THE LANDING WAS TIMED TO COINCIDE with the new moon. Periscope jutting inches above water, the sub slithered toward shore, using electric motors rather than noisy diesel engines. When the hull scraped sandy sea bottom, the captain ordered all motors cut. After seventeen days at sea, the U-boat surfaced at midnight. George handed each man a canvas money belt with $4,000 cash and reminded them to search their belongings and destroy any incriminating papers, cigarettes, or wrappers. The captain gave strict orders to overpower anyone they encountered and "feed them to the fish."

The hatch was opened and salty mist flooded inside. A sailor, selected because he was husky enough to row back to the sub with only one mate, climbed through, inflated a rubber raft, and dropped it into the sea, where it bobbed like a helpless whale calf next to its predatory mother. A second brawny sailor lowered a

rope ladder to the dinghy. The men quickly passed four wooden
crates filled with explosives, a canvas sea bag of civilian clothes,
two shovels, and George's old Gladstone bag with $80,000 dollars
sewn into the lining down the shaky rope ladder. Once the raft
was fully loaded, they clambered aboard. The sub was parallel to
shore and the captain advised them to pull the raft at a 90-degree
angle and head straight for the beach. A towline was attached to
the sub to allow the sailors to find their way back after depositing
their cache.

"Christ, this is perfect," George said.

The sky was pitch-black, made to order for landing. The sea
was smothered in fog. The overcrowded raft rocked perilously. The
sailor in the bow leaned far over the dark surf and shined a blue
torch into the mist. George sat in the stern, clutching the Gladstone
on his lap. He had traded his ship cap for a brown fedora, which he
held to his head against the wind. The hat and bag made him look
more like a door-to-door salesman than an enemy combatant infiltrating American shores. The other men paddled. Salty sea spray
coated Peter's face as the dinghy was swallowed by fog.

The pounding swells seemed to come from every direction as
the men struggled to find their way. Peter watched the towrope
stretch, grow taut, and slacken again as the line let out. Waves
crashed into the side of the raft, spilling over and filling it with
water. The men had practiced this landing in a collapsible rubber
raft on a lake at Quenz Farm. Part of the lake was still frozen in
April and the water was icy cold, but it had not prepared them for
the vast ocean. The raft plunged and rocked for ten minutes before
the breakers came into view.

"Come on boys, let's get to it!" George shouted over the roar-
ing surf.

The boxes of explosives had been sealed against water, but the
men were drenched. Dick and Henry lost their paddles, still the
dinghy managed to crest the waves toward shore. George leaned
over the side and used an oar to feel for the ocean floor. "We made
it, boys," he said when he hit sand. Peter watched as Dick and

Henry exchanged a dubious glance. Their ordeal had only begun.

The six men tumbled out of the boat into waist-deep surf, their uniforms growing increasingly waterlogged as they unloaded the heavy crates and passed them in a line toward shore. When the stash was safely ashore, Peter, Dick, and Henry began carrying them up a steep sandbar and over the sloping beach while George went to look around. The tide was out, the beach wide. Their feet sank as they made their way over the hard-packed sand at the water's edge and further inland. The dunes were covered with tall seagrass and low-lying scrub. Bushes and spindly evergreens snagged their clothing and scratched faces and hands.

The final box and the canvas sea bag were still by the shoreline when George returned, panting, and waving his arms. A yellow beam of light was swinging steadily down the beach toward them. Ankle deep in surf, the sailors struggled to turn the dinghy over and rid it of water for their journey back to the sub.

"Get back where you came from," George hissed in English.

Peter could not tell if the sailors understood, but George's urgency was clear. The sailors had been told to take all uniforms back to the submarine, but there was no time for that. They leapt into the righted boat and rowed furiously over crashing whitecaps toward open water.

"Get to the dunes, take off your caps and dungarees, put on civilian clothes, and lay low," George told the others.

The men had been instructed to wear German army fatigues: khaki dungarees, a slipover khaki jacket, and a ship cap boasting a golden eagle and swastika. It was the same uniform worn by the crew. Once on shore, they had been told to put on American-made clothing to disguise their identity.

As the light drew closer, Dick snatched his cap with its swastika insignia off his head, and Peter did the same, shoving it deep into his pocket.

"George," he whispered. "Take this." He reached into the duffel bag and passed him a red sweater to cover his uniform.

Peter squinted into the darkness but was unable to see who was wielding the light or how many men there were. Their leisurely pace seemed to indicate the crew had not been spotted. Without pausing to remove his soaked dungarees, which were now coated with sand, George pulled on the sweater and raced up the beach. Peter, who had always considered George a blowhard, marveled at his courage. He removed his German uniform down to his swim trunks and crammed it into the sea bag. Trembling more from adrenaline than the night air, he trailed George down the beach.

"What are you doing down here?" the stranger yelled, lifting a flashlight and shining it into George's gaunt face and down the length of his body.

Along with wet fatigues and the red sweater, George wore white tennis shoes that seemed to glow in the mist and the brown fedora he had managed to keep on over the choppy waves. The quivering light also illuminated the stranger's young, round face and dark blue pullover.

Peter's relief that there was only one man was quickly surpassed by the realization that the man was in uniform.

"Coast Guard?" George asked. He spoke loudly, but Peter could hear a tremor in his voice.

"Yes, sir." The Coast Guardsman sounded hesitant, more boy than man. "What's going on here?" He directed his light into the surf and stared out to sea, where it was just possible to make out the sailors in the small boat, silhouetted in mist. His fingers tightened around his flashlight, giving the impression he had no actual weapon.

"We're a couple of fishermen from Southampton who ran ashore," George offered.

"Do you know where you are?" the man asked.

"You're Coast Guard. You tell me," George said. Peter grimaced. The man's youth had emboldened him. "Where's your station?" he asked.

The boy pointed over his shoulder. "Amagansett."

Peter weighed the information. The sub had planned to land a few miles west, in the town of East Hampton, where George had once worked as a caretaker.

"What do you intend to do?" the boy asked.

"We'll stay here until sunrise," George said, "then we'll be alright."

"That's four hours. Why don't you come up to the station and wait there," the fellow suggested. His tone softened, "There was grilled bologna for dinner and may be some left over."

George hesitated. Peter's stomach clenched as he thought back to the captain's orders to overpower anyone they encountered.

"Sure," George agreed. The pair walked a few feet into the soupy fog before George stopped. In the flickering light, the Coast Guard's shadow dwarfed his. "Actually, I'm not going with you," George said.

"Why not?" The boy's surprise made him seem even younger than Peter first thought.

Peter crouched in the darkness, dressed in nothing but swim trunks, the canvas duffel by his feet. He was not carrying a weapon, but a shovel could knock the boy out.

The breeze shifted and a waft of diesel oil blew off the water.

"Hey," the boy said, squinting out toward the ocean. The sub was a low-lying shadow parallel to shore. "What's going on?"

Peter left the bag and approached. *"Bist du in Schwierigkeiten?"* He felt the blood drain from his face. He had inadvertently spoken German.

The boy whirled toward Peter. "What'd you say?"

"Shut up, you damn fool." George spoke over his shoulder to Peter. "Everything's alright. Go back with the boys and stay with them," he said, making the Coast Guardsman aware that there were more men to reckon with up the beach.

Trembling, Peter took the duffel by its strap and began dragging it toward the tall beach grass. The Coast Guard's flashlight leapt along the sand, then lit on the bag.

"What's that?" he asked.

"Clams," George said.

"Clams?"

George seemed to realize he had made a gaffe. Either clams

were not to be found in this strip of ocean or it was the wrong season. "Problem is," he said, "we don't have any identification papers or a fishing permit."

Peter tugged the duffel up the beach back to the others.

"*Dummkopf,*" Dick swore. "You're leaving a track."

Dick and Henry were shivering in their wet swim trunks, too. Their discarded uniforms and the crates of explosives lay unburied at their feet while they passed a bottle of Schnapps between themselves.

"Keep your heads down," Peter said. With one eye out for the Coast Guard, Peter changed into a dress suit. A week before departure, Lieutenant Kappe had brought him to a heavily guarded two-story warehouse. They were directed to rows and rows of men's suits, overcoats, and raincoats in every size, all used. In another row were hats, luggage, even underwear. Shoes were in the cellar. All the clothing had different labels from Sweden, Germany, Czechoslovakia, and America. Kappe led Peter to the American items. Under Kappe's watchful eye, Peter chose a midnight blue suit that fit like a glove. He had little doubt he was stepping into the clothing of some unfortunate soul who had been slaughtered by Nazi hands. Dressing in the foggy darkness, his nose twitched at a lingering hint of cologne and he had the sickening sense he was inhabiting someone else's skin. He turned back to the duffel and laid out Henry's gray suit and Dick's brown gabardine.

"Put the wet uniforms in here," he told them, passing the duffel. Neither man budged.

"There's only one of him," Dick reasoned. "We can tackle him, use the blinker to signal the sailors, and let the crew take care of him." He started toward the stranger.

"The sailors are gone," Peter said, though he had no real idea of how far they had gone. "If we use a blinker, we'll give ourselves away."

Dick looked out at the water.

"George is in charge now," Peter pressed. "He's the leader and it's up to him to issue orders."

"*Herr Strich?*" Dick muttered, making it clear what he thought of George.

"Kappe said to do away with any man who didn't abide by the orders," Henry added in his singsong way. Both men seemed eager to dispose of the Coast Guardsman—and George—if necessary.

Peter didn't argue. Instead, he took a step forward, straining to hear and indicating the others should do the same.

"Come along now," the boy was saying. "We'll work it out at the station."

There was the sound of a skirmish. Peter peeked over the dune in time to see George grab the fellow's arm and twist it behind his back.

"Now wait a minute," the boy said, yanking his arm back. He may have been young, but he was broad and muscular. He could easily best George.

Peter could feel Dick tense beside him.

"You're a young fellow," George said, suddenly cordial. "How old are you anyway?"

The Coast Guardsman seemed thrown. "Twenty-one," he said, shifting his weight and looking over his shoulder as if eager to escape.

"Do you have a father and a mother? How about a sweetheart?" George did not wait for his response. "I'm sure they wouldn't want any harm to come to you." Though it was impossible to tell if he saw them, George seemed to sense the other men's presence.

The boy took several steps backwards, swinging his light toward the dunes where Peter, Dick, and Henry stood waiting. "What's your name?" he asked, trying to sound authoritative, as his voice wobbled and broke.

"George. What's yours?"

Waves crashed and long moments passed before the fellow answered. "Frank . . . um . . . Collins."

"Well, Frank." George's tone shifted yet again, now confidential. "Why don't we forget about this and I'll give you a little something for your trouble." He reached into his money belt and pulled out four bills.

Frank Collins recoiled. "I don't want your money."

George peeled more from the roll. "Take $300."

"No." Collins shook his head. "It's alright."

"Take it," George insisted. "Count it." He lowered his voice, making it impossible to hear his next words.

Collins' shoulders tensed as he accepted the cash. He ran the flashlight over the wad and shoved it haphazardly into his pocket.

"What will you do with it?" George asked, clearly relieved. "Going to spend it on your sweetheart?"

"Some of it, I'll give to my parents. Some of it, I'll put in the bank." Collins sounded dazed.

"And you'll remember to have a good time."

Collins offered a stiff nod. "Yes, sir."

"Good." George removed his hat and spoke up. "Take a good look at me. Look into my eyes." He set the hat back on his head. "I'll be meeting you in East Hampton sometime. Do you know me?"

"No, sir," Collins said. "I never saw you before in my life." Still facing George, he stepped backward again until he was out of arm's reach, then turned and sprinted into the haze.

ONCE COLLINS WAS OUT OF SIGHT, George made his way to the dunes. Peter, Dick, and Henry had donned their rumpled civilian clothing. All sat on a large piece of driftwood. Peter at one end, several feet away from the others.

George rifled through the duffel bag. "Where are my Scotch tweeds and my jacket?"

Peter froze. The clothing must have toppled out when he was searching for the sweater to cover George's uniform. George started to retrace his steps.

"You going back?" Dick said incredulously.

"They can't be far."

"I'll go with you," Peter said.

When they were out of earshot, George turned to Peter. "Christ, that fella was just a kid. I couldn't kill him."

Peter was about to agree when he stumbled over something soft. "Here they are," he said. He stooped to retrieve George's trousers.

"When he took the money, I told him he'd be hearing from me again. I saved his life," George boasted. "He'll make a good ally."

Peter tensed. He and George had not had an opportunity to talk openly at Quenz Farm, but they had come to a tenuous understanding. They shared a hatred of the Gestapo. Now, moments after landing, George was ignoring explicit orders and calling an American Coast Guardsman his ally.

George picked up his shirt and jacket. "The boy said his name was Frank Collins. Remember that. It could be important one day." He was searching his jacket pocket then his pants. "Did something fall out?" He dropped to hands and knees, searching the sand. "Dammit. There was a little book I had."

There was a loud swish as the sub blew water from its tanks. The electric motor chugged, then the diesel engine thrummed full throttle. A cloud of oil wafted toward shore.

"Sounds like it's stuck," Peter said. His relief at the thought of sixty comrades still nearby was quickly tempered by the certainty they would be caught. George seemed to have a contingency plan, but his mood changed with the breeze and Peter did not fully trust him.

"Come on, Pete. Let's scram."

When they returned to the others, Henry was swigging Schnapps and Dick looked as if he might take a swing at Peter. A searchlight began scanning the beach. Henry dropped the bottle. "The jig's up."

Dick turned his fury on George. "They're looking for us and it's all your fault."

"Don't worry about that young fella," George said. "I had him buffaloed."

"You should have killed him," Dick said. "Or let me."

"Now boys," George said, "Be quiet, hold your nerves, and do exactly what I say. Each of you get some crates and follow me. Pete, take the duffel."

Peter waited for the others to move before kicking sand over Henry's forgotten Schnapps bottle. He strung the duffel by its strap across his shoulder and picked up a crate. They made slow progress. Peter allowed himself to fall behind before pulling off his ship cap and burying it in the sand. A high-pitched bell chimed nearby. The bell rang again and he recognized it as a telephone. Yards away, a light switched on and off, shining through the mist and illuminating a small home with a porch.

"It's a signal!" Henry said.

A dog barked and a screen door creaked open.

George directed the men farther inland. At a shallow gulley between the dunes, Dick and Henry dug a trench for the crates. The breeze picked up, carrying the smell of burnt oil and the sound of an engine.

"It's either a patrol boat moving along the shore or the U-202 going full speed ahead," George said.

Neither was reassuring. All four men stood at attention as the noise died away and realization hit. They were on their own.

"Get back to work," George said. He changed into civilian clothing while Dick and Henry resumed digging. George tossed his wet uniform into the hole then shook the other uniforms out of the duffel and into the pit. He took Henry's shovel and began filling the empty duffel with sand.

"What the hell you doing that for?" Dick asked.

"We'll need sand for the power convertors."

Glaring, Dick covered the rest of the hole. George threw clumps of seaweed on top.

"It'll dry by morning," he said, admiring his work.

Dick, who had buried his shovel, frowned at the one in George's hand. "You forgot that," he said.

"I want to leave it out," George said, stabbing the shovel into the sand. "It will help us find the spot when we come back." When Dick looked like he would object, George passed him the sea bag. "Take this and let's go."

Too exhausted and hungry to argue, the men followed George's lead. After several miles on a dirt road, they came upon a row of sea-weathered bungalows. George looked right and left. They walked a hundred yards before he changed course and turned.

"I thought you knew the area," Dick grumbled.

"Are we lost?" Henry asked.

"Just getting my bearings," George said.

A car approached and they scrambled into the bushes. Two more cars followed. With every passing headlight, Henry fell flat on his stomach. A truck carrying sailors headed toward the Coast Guard Station. Henry shivered like a dog and said, "Boys, we're surrounded."

As the sky grew lighter, the fog lifted and beacons from the Coast Guard Station flooded over them. They had no choice but to move on. They came upon a main roadway and walked single file until it met a railroad track. Not far down the track, the rail split.

"We're going the wrong way," Peter said.

Dick stopped walking. "How do you know?" he asked.

"The double track has more traffic so it must lead to the city. The other way goes out to the end of the island."

Even George seemed to accept this logic. They reluctantly turned back.

"More time wasted," Dick said, glowering at George.

A mile past where they had originally set out on the tracks, they came to a small, shingled railway station with a peaked roof and single chimney. An overhang outside the door had a long sign that read AMAGANSETT.

The doors were locked. There was no timetable posted.

George, who was still wearing wet swim trunks under his trousers, ducked into the bushes to change. The others brushed mud and grass off themselves and settled in.

An hour passed.

Henry paced the platform. Peter looked down the road. The sailors had been headed for the beach but it was only a matter of time before they showed up at the railway station.

"I haven't heard so much as a whistle," Dick said.

George stuck his neck out over the tracks. "I wonder if there is weekend service out to Montauk."

Dick glared at George as if he'd like to shove him under an approaching train.

Peter noticed smoke coming from the station chimney. "It's open," he said, running his hand through his hair, relieved.

The rickety ticket window inched open. The stationmaster looked out in surprise. "Good . . ." His words drifted off mid-sentence.

"Lousy weather for fishing," George said loudly.

The stationmaster gave him a suspicious look. "You're not from around here, are you?"

"That today's paper?" George asked, pointing past the stationmaster and inside the window where a stack of newspapers lay tied with twine. He purchased four papers and four tickets on a direct train to Jamaica Station. From there, it was one stop to Penn Station and all the anonymity that New York City had to offer.

CHAPTER 9

THE SUN WAS STREAKING THE SKY with crimson hues by the time Peter finished speaking. Grete looked down the broad expanse of sand. The beach extended in both directions as far as the eye could see. Unlike the rocky Mediterranean where she had vacationed as a child, the sand was soft and fine. Rich amber and buttery yellow shells dotted the shore. Jones Beach, Rockaway, and Coney Island were subject to wartime regulations and curfews. Grete did not know the laws governing this tranquil strip, but she was sure they were breaking them.

"We paired off when we reached Jamaica Station," Peter explained. "I went with George. Henry stayed with Dick. We agreed to meet again that evening at Horn & Hardart. There were some shops outside the station and George and I bought shoes and cheap suits. We changed in the men's room, dumped our old, sandy stuff in the trash, and took the subway into Manhattan. The Governor Clinton is a busy hotel and we thought we would be inconspicuous there. After we checked in, George stopped to buy a wristwatch at Macy's. We went to the parade—and I met you."

Grete scrunched her toes in the warm sand and looked out across the ocean in disbelief. Peter had endured cruelty in prison and isolation on a U-boat filled with comrades who could not be trusted. It was difficult to reconcile so much brutality with the gentle man sitting beside her and she began to understand why he had sought her out at the parade. Peter was alone. A bird drifted on the rolling swells, dove, and disappeared. She sat forward, hugging her knees, waiting and watching until it bobbed to the surface. The bird's long, black neck and narrow head twisted and turned, scanning the water like a periscope.

"This happened . . ."

"Two days ago."

She shook her head. It seemed inconceivable that it had happened at all.

Peter wrapped his arm around her shoulder. She had the sense that he would have been happy to remain sitting there indefinitely. But there was too much at stake. She stood, brushed herself off, and offered her hand, pulling Peter to his feet with exaggerated effort that made them both smile. They walked east. The sun was behind them and their figures cast long shadows. They passed fishermen in waders pulling in nets with flopping fish. A boy ran along the shore tossing a kite into the air, only to have it nose-dive back down again. The tide was coming in, the waves crashing harder. A row of gulls stood sentry by the waterline.

Peter stopped and pointed toward a large piece of gray driftwood. "Up there."

She stepped toward the dunes, but he held her back, opening his palm. Cupped inside was a small volute shell: impossibly delicate, beautifully spiraled with an ivory exterior and glossy pink core.

The shell was both intricate and simple, like her feelings for Peter.

"I don't have the words to express my gratitude in English or German." His cheeks bloomed with color. "This is a small token. Who knows how long it was home to some tiny creature. It kept him safe. See the inside? It's opal."

Grete stretched her hand out and he pressed the shell into her palm, closing his fingers around hers.

"Keep it safe," Peter said. "Always remember—we tried to do the right thing."

"That's all we can do," she said, cherishing their camaraderie. She was not alone in thinking that they were working together. She looked into his eyes with a deepening sense that they were right to have returned to this beach and that together they might thwart disaster.

Peter brought her hand to his lips and held it there. She had the impression he was praying and she rendered her own private prayer for her parents, for Peter, and for the countless others who were suffering. Tears filled her eyes. She and Peter had known each other for such a short time, but the gravity of his dilemma intensified every emotion.

She looked out past the breakers. It was impossible to imagine a U-boat prowling less than a mile offshore, landing enemy spies, delivering Peter. Yesterday's rain had obliterated any footprints in the sand. She walked up toward the driftwood and skimmed the base, but did not see a bottle of Schnapps or anything else. Peter forged ahead. His shirt snagged as he slipped through a jagged opening in a partially buried fence and into the spiky seagrass. They trekked over another dune and down a gully. Peter stepped between two raggedy bushes and came to an abrupt halt. The trench stretched in front of them, long, narrow—and empty.

"They beat us to it." He sounded resigned. The seagrass had been tramped down; the area thoroughly searched.

"Who?"

"Dick and Henry?" he speculated. "We had orders to move the explosives as soon as possible. After the run-in with the Coast Guard, George told us to hold off until things quieted down, but Dick doesn't listen to George, and Henry only does what Dick says."

"I thought you didn't know your orders. You said you were waiting."

"We were told to wait to carry out the operation, but we had instructions to move the explosives quickly. Part of the reason Dick and Henry were recruited was because they had worked at Volkswagenwerk. They were told to open an automobile shop here, somewhere out of the way where the TNT could be easily hidden. Kappe suggested the Blue Ridge Mountains or the Catskills."

"They couldn't have bought a place and moved the crates in

a day. The Catskills are hours away. I don't even know where the Blue Mountains are."

"Blue *Ridge* Mountains. They're in the Carolinas."

"Gas is rationed. They couldn't have driven that far."

Peter turned. "Gasoline is rationed?"

She nodded.

"Another glitch," Peter said with a desperate chuckle.

"What do you mean?"

"How are we supposed to transport the explosives with gas rationing in place?" He looked furious. "Kappe liked to say that a small group of men could do more damage than divisions of fighting men, but he doesn't have any regard for our safety. Back at Quenz Farm, when he handed out U.S. currency, one of the men noticed the bills were a type that had been taken out of circulation years ago. If we had used them, we would have been arrested right away."

"Maybe that would have been best."

"How can you say that?"

"Then this whole thing would have been stopped immediately."

"We're nothing but cannon fodder," Peter swore.

"But you were never going to do it."

"That doesn't matter. The moment Kappe thinks we have no value we'll be cast aside, or worse. It's why I have to keep up this sham. We're completely expendable." Peter peered down at the grave-like pit, sand-colored for an arm's length then loamy and dark. "Dick and Henry couldn't have moved that quickly. The Coast Guard must have found the explosives."

"The Coast Guard!" Grete fought an urge to run as three men in blue pullovers and sailor caps marched down the beach toward them.

"Pretend we're sweethearts." Peter grabbed her with trembling arms, his lips desperately seeking hers. He sank to his knees, laying her back in the sand, and smothering her body with his. His chest was firm, his body so unlike her own. Peter tasted salty, exactly as she imagined he would. She returned his kisses without any need to pretend.

IT WAS IMPOSSIBLE TO SAY HOW MUCH TIME PASSED before Peter sat up. "They're gone." He brushed the sandy hair off her face and traced his fingertips along her lips. Relieved, Grete gave in to the full breadth of her desire. She raised her head to his. Her lips to his mouth. She was back in the sea, buoyant. Peter's hand cupped her chin, slid down her neck then to her blouse, his fingers toying with the buttons. She pulled him down toward her and his kisses grew deeper as she pressed into him. She felt the heat of his body on hers and the thrum of her pulse. The warm sand sifted and conformed to her weight as she sank deeper—and a sharp edge jabbed the crook of her back.

Peter sensed her distraction. "What is it?"

She disentangled herself, twisting to reach into the sand behind her. Dizzy with desire, it took her a moment to comprehend. "A notebook?" Thin with a warped black cover, the book looked innocent enough.

"That's George's." Peter sounded equally dazed. Grete's desire fizzled as Peter grew more alert. She turned away to button her blouse. The fact was they could not escape, not for an afternoon or a moment of intimacy.

She brushed sand off the cover. "What's it doing here?"

"It fell from his pocket the night we landed. Remember, I said he was looking for it."

Grete flipped the book open. The pages were damp and crinkly but the handwriting was stylized as if it were a reflection of the man George wanted to be. She held it up, squinting at the blurred ink.

Peter pointed at a row of numbers. "These are figures on U.S. production of tanks and planes. George said it was proof the United States was just getting started and that our work here was essential. He used to read from it on the sub to bolster the men."

"That doesn't sound like a man planning to betray the mission."

"He had to act that way."

Grete turned a page. "There are addresses here too."

Peter leaned over her shoulder. "This one's our contact in New Jersey. And here," he tapped the page as if it were the proof he was searching for. "Attorney General Francis Biddle, Department of Justice, Constitution Avenue."

The name should have been reassuring. Instead, Grete recalled the article she had read about Japanese internment camps and doing the same thing to Italian and German Americans. The attorney general did not strike her as much of an ally.

"I thought you were told to get rid of any papers from Germany. Weren't those George's orders?"

"Those were Kappe's orders, but George doesn't think he's bound by any orders. Besides, it doesn't look German." Peter took the book, smacking it against his thigh. "I knew you were my good luck charm. This proves it."

"Why would you say that?"

"This is important evidence. Proof that George was planning to turn himself in from the start. No wonder he was so shaken when he lost it."

"Even if it says that about George, it doesn't say anything about you."

"George will defend me." Peter did not give her time to disagree. "I've got the book, which proves we're working together."

"He didn't exactly give it to you; you found it."

"No one knows that."

"I do," Grete said, her voice so low it was barely audible above the sound of crashing waves.

Grete looked down the beach. As the sun lowered, fog crept across the sand. Disappointment at their failed attempt to find the crates collided with her feelings for Peter. The pleasure she felt kissing him was tainted with the sinking awareness that any possible future together was doomed. Either the explosives had been confiscated by the Coast Guard, Dick and Henry had them, or George was lying. Each scenario was more troubling then the last.

Peter flipped a soggy page. "Sketches," he said, leaning close to study them. "This is the submarine nose that holds the torpedoes. There were ten onboard and the captain was eager to use all of them. But he had orders not to attack until after we were safely landed."

Grete shuddered at a detailed diagram labeled *Verteilung der Feuerleitgerate auf den U-Botten*, Torpedo Fire Control System. She could make out propellers on the backs of the torpedoes and imagined the blades spinning at impossible speeds as they shot toward their target.

Peter pried apart another damp page. "This is the first deck below the conning tower where we used to sneak a smoke. And this is the control room and periscope." He pointed. "Radio room. We sure as heck weren't allowed in there."

"Why would George have these?"

"He shouldn't." Peter said, sounding uncertain. "But information like this would be invaluable to the U.S. military." He thumbed through a few more pages. There in bleeding ink were descriptions of Henry and Dick.

Name: *Heinrich Heinck, alias Henry Kaynard*
Age: *32-33*
Weight: *160-170 lbs.*
Hair: *very thin, light brown, parted on left side*
Eyes: *gray*
Features: *high forehead; normal eyebrows; nose, straight;*
    medium full lips, round face
Speech: *clipped sentences; low voice; knowledge of English*
    limited
Scars: *peculiarly shaped cross scar on forehead*
Peculiarities: *slow moving, phlegmatic type, gives impression*
    unsure of himself.
Occupation: *mechanic and electrician*
Clothing furnished to wear on arrival: *U.S. green gray dou-*
    bled-breasted suit, gray soiled hat, brown shoes.

Name: *Richard Quirin, alias Richard or Dick Quirin*
Age: *34*
Height: *5'10"*
Build: *slender*
Hair: *gray, curly*
Eyes: *green*
Features: *high forehead, bent protruding fleshy nose, full lips, large protruding ears*
Peculiarities: *habit of keeping lips apart when not talking, walks with forward slouch*
Occupation: *tool and die maker, painter and domestic*
Clothing furnished to wear on arrival: *dark brown gabardine suit and low brown shoes.*

The book trembled in Peter's hands. "George always said we should be most afraid of our comrades because they knew so much about us."

Grete took the book and read on. "Who's Warner Thiel? And Scottie?" Peter ran his hand over his mouth and she grasped his face to force his eyes on hers. "Who are they?"

He peeled her hands off his cheeks. "I don't know Scottie's real name. We called him that because he looked like a Scotchman. No one trusted him. He claimed to have syphilis and went back to Hamburg."

Syphilis, she recoiled, but there were far more pressing issues at hand. "Hermann Neubauer? Ernest Zuber? Edward Kerling?" she asked, skimming descriptions, *Gray Stetson hat . . . usually keeps one hand in pocket or has a newspaper in it . . . good shot.* "I don't understand. If these men dropped out, why couldn't you?"

"Only Scottie left."

A wave crashed hard. Grete felt as if she'd been tossed. "I thought it was only George, Dick, Henry, and you. Who are these others? Where are they?"

"I don't know. Kappe likes to compartmentalize. It's better for the left hand not to know what the right hand is up to."

Surf and sky merged as fog closed in. Grete stood and began

walking down the beach back the way they came. Her hopes sinking with each step. It was impossible to see more than ten feet ahead. She had the sickening sense that an army of men would spring from the mist. Though she couldn't say if they would be Coast Guardsmen or Nazi spies.

Peter kept pace with her. "Grete, listen, there wasn't any need for you to know about the other men because we never saw them again after Lorient."

"How many are there? Where'd they go?"

"Four. As far as I know, they were to come over on a different sub and land somewhere in Florida."

Grete shuddered at the image of more Nazis infiltrating American shores. How many others would follow?

"And their mission?" A knot formed in her chest. The terminology came too easily.

"Same as ours. We were told to meet them on the Fourth of July. Until then, we won't know where they are."

"How will you know where to meet them?"

"That's why George has a contact in New Jersey."

"And if George abandons the plan or something happens to him?"

"If something happens to George, I was to establish myself as a violin teacher and place an ad in the *Herald* on the first and fifteenth of each month, giving my name and address. The others all know to look for it."

"You play the violin," she said faintly. She didn't give Peter a chance to respond. "Why not place the ad now? The others would assemble and the FBI could be there waiting."

"An ambush?"

Grete hesitated. It felt like a trick question. *An ambush.*

"The other men haven't landed yet. Their route is longer. They'll probably arrive tomorrow or Wednesday. That's part of the reason George is waiting to go to the FBI. We won't be able to do anything until then."

"Why didn't George say something when he called the FBI?

The Coast Guard might have been able to stop them."

"The Florida coast is hundreds of miles long. Do you really think the Coast Guard could find a few men dropped off in the middle of the night?"

"They found you."

"That was an unlucky coincidence."

Unlucky? Grete wondered at his choice of words.

"The agent didn't believe George to begin with. Sending them on a wild goose chase up the Florida coast wasn't going to help."

"If they had found them, this whole thing would be over," she said for what felt like the hundredth time. Peter had had ample opportunity to stop the mission. "What are you waiting for?"

"Grete, try to understand. Some of these fellows are just like me. They aren't good or bad. One of the boys, Herbie, is my pal. He was dragged into this just like me. The others didn't trust him because they considered him more American than German and didn't think he'd go through with the plan. I can't just run to the FBI for my own safety. To be decent, I have to wait and give Herbie a chance to come forward on his own."

Grete ran her hand through her hair, which was as tangled as her thoughts. "Why did they consider him American?"

"Herbie was born in Germany, but moved to Chicago with his parents when he was very young so now he's a citizen. He's got no business being in this thing. I can't rat him out."

Grete took the book, searching until she found the description of Herbert Haupt: *Age twenty-two or twenty-three. Hair: black, wavy, on which he uses smelly brilliantine. Wears a prominent heavy rectangular ring on left hand with a large inscription of a Mexican eagle.*

"If he lived in Chicago, how did he get involved in this?"

"He was in trouble."

"What kind of trouble?"

"The kind where it's really the girl who's in trouble."

Grete blushed as she recalled Peter's touch, her lips on his.

"Herbie promised he'd marry her then got, what do you say?"

Peter rubbed his shoulders and pretended to shiver.

"Cold feet," she said drily.

"He ran off to Mexico, but couldn't get work without papers. Some German approached him at a cafe and suggested he go to the consulate. They gave him a passport and passage on a blockade breaker to Bordeaux. He arrived in Berlin in December, the day after Germany declared war on the U.S. Even before he got there he knew he'd made a terrible mistake."

"Another one. Imagine how the mother of his child feels."

"There was a self-appointed trial board on the ship."

"How very German."

"They reprimanded him for some nonsense like a crooked armband and reported him in Berlin. He thought he would be arrested, but the Gestapo had other plans. The German consulate in Mexico had already alerted them. With his American English and citizenship, Herbie was an ideal candidate for this operation. He had no interest in joining Kappe's group, but he couldn't find work without papers and the government was demanding he repay the money for his passage. Herbie still refused. He had been in Germany a few months. His parents live in Chicago and he was being ordered to come here and defend the fatherland. No one in their right mind would do that."

"But he did."

"He didn't have a choice!"

"No one forced him to abandon his girlfriend or leave the United States. He's American. He should be fighting for this country."

"You're right, but this is a high price to pay for being young and selfish. I can't give him up to save my own neck."

"Does Herbie know what you and George are planning?"

"There was nowhere to discuss any of this before we landed. The first opportunity George and I got to speak freely was in the hotel."

Grete walked ahead, creating as much distance as she could. Right or wrong, Peter had a soft spot for his comrades. Quenz Farm, with its calisthenics and field trips, sounded like summer camp. No doubt the Gestapo had the men share their personal stories to create a bond. She stopped short, flipping pages in George's book until she found what she was looking for. Her eyes grew wide as she read what George had recorded about Peter: *swarthy complexion, stocky, to pose as Jewish refugee who had spent time in concentration camp.* Her fingers clenched the slender book. She understood why she had immediately assumed Peter was Jewish; he'd wanted her to believe it. Lonely and gullible, she had happily gone along with him. She narrowed her lips. Of all Peter's half-truths, passing himself off as Jewish was probably the least harmful, and most offensive. She thought of her parents and how they were suffering. The idea that Peter was soliciting sympathy this way made her sick.

"Were you really in prison or is that just something you said?"

"What?" The healthy glow Peter had gained from the day's outing faded. Hard lines returned to his face. "*Mein Gott.*" He laid her hand on his chest and she could feel his heartbeat. "I would never lie about a thing like that."

She pried her hand away. "These are pretty detailed descriptions."

"George must have his reasons."

"Of course he has. He's planning to double-cross you."

Peter snatched the book away and flipped to the end: page after page of addresses. His eyes shot to one in Astoria, Queens. "That bastard!" A vein bulged in his neck and he looked as if he wanted to rip the book, or George, in two.

IT WAS CLOSE TO TEN O'CLOCK by the time Grete arrived home. Her uncle's brandy snifter was empty, his cigar no more than a soggy stub, his patience frayed. For the first time since coming to live with him, she had crossed a line.

"Where were you?" Uncle Jacques sat upright. A book lay closed on his lap. His reading glasses were askew and the radio was tuned to opera, more static than libretto. He had been asleep.

Conscious of the sand in her hair and her sunburned nose, Grete was overwhelmed with guilt. Vagabond rubbed against her legs, drawing attention to her freshly bronzed calves. "I went to the beach." She was prepared to do many things to help Peter, but lying to her uncle was not one of them.

"The beach?" He straightened his glasses and studied her. She may as well have said the moon.

Grete held her breath, praying he would not ask which one. She would never be able to explain her pilgrimage to the nether lands of Long Island. The ivory shell Peter had given her, no larger than her thumbnail, dug through her skirt pocket and into her skin.

"Who did you go to the beach with?"

"A friend." There was that word again. Just yesterday, she had been happy to call Peter her friend. Twenty-four hours later, the description felt inadequate.

"A boy?" Peter was not exactly a boy, but she did not contradict him. "Someone from school?" he persisted.

A simple "yes" would have absolved her. Her uncle would have been satisfied at the notion of a fellow student. He might even have been happy that she had finally made a friend.

"No." She shook her head. "Peter and I met at the parade."

Jacques reached for his cigar before realizing there was nothing left. "You spent the day with a boy you met on Saturday?" He frowned at the cigar nub, though Grete had the impression the unhappy expression was meant for her.

"He's from Germany."

Her uncle looked up abruptly.

"Like me," she added, hoping that might help him understand the connection she and Peter shared. "I had supper with his sister and her husband yesterday," she said. "They're lovely. Today we went to the shore. It was a last minute plan, because of the heat."

Jacques picked up his empty glass, running his finger around the rim. Her uncle, more than anyone, knew how lonely she had been. He seemed to sense her semi-truths but was reluctant to squelch her happiness.

"What did you say his name was?"

"Peter." Though she now knew Peter's last name, she did not think it would help matters to divulge it.

Jacques held the empty glass to the light, turning it as if to test an imaginary bouquet. "If you intend to keep seeing this boy, I expect you to bring him around and introduce him."

"We were here Sunday afternoon, but you were napping and I did not want to disturb you," she said, flabbergasted by the agility of her lies. She was spending too much time with Peter and his easy subterfuge was beginning to rub off on her.

Jacques was too sophisticated to say *hooey*, though he looked as if he might want to. He pulled himself out of the chair and carried his full ashtray and empty glass to the kitchen where she heard him pour another brandy. "Are you volunteering tomorrow?" he asked instead.

"Yes." She nodded, relieved to answer so simply.

CHAPTER 18

GRETE'S HEART WASN'T IN IT.

"Look around and try to find bits of rubber, any kind!" she chanted with waning enthusiasm. Women plodded toward the subway in chunky heels and utility suits of jackets with wide shoulders and nipped waists that could be mixed and matched with skirts for myriad looks on the cheap. Businessmen with newspapers tucked under their arms hurried down the stairs. Most were fatherly types who wore their hats forward to hide receding hairlines. The younger men had more severe impairments: a pronounced limp, thick glasses, or a distracted tic. They fit the classification 4-F, Grete noted sadly. She was sympathetic to the shame of being marked *unacceptable*.

A gust of air blew trash up the stairs as a train screeched into the station.

Earlier that morning, when Grete and her partner Rose, another Salvage for Victory volunteer, set up their donation box on the northwest corner of Seventy-ninth Street in front of a church, the caretaker was hosing down the sidewalk and the awning provided ample shade. Hours later, the pavement had dried, sun was encroaching on their cover, and they had collected precious little. Rose had decorated the cardboard box with a drawing of a garden hose, easily mistaken for a snake, and a doughnut-like tire. She had inscribed the other sides with encouraging slogans: THROW YOUR SCRAP IN THE FIGHT! GET IN THE SCRAP!

Few had taken heed.

"Hurry up and bring them in, if you want to help us win!" Rose bellowed. Rose was short and curvy with a sassy voice that belied her size.

The previous Friday, Roosevelt had announced a two-week drive to collect scrap rubber lurking in discarded footwear, toys, and tires. Fala, his adored terrier, had contributed his favorite ball. Joe DiMaggio donated his baby's rubber pants.

Happy to escape the stifling confines of the salvage depot, Grete had set out believing that any donations collected that day would contribute to dozens of airplanes. An hour later, she had revised her estimate down to a single airplane, then spare parts. Her optimism lasted another hour, after that, duty kicked in, followed by disappointment. The girls retreated to a thin band of shade. Grete peered into the box. She and Rose had managed to collect a clump of rubber bands, half a sink stopper, and a leaky hot water bottle.

"Maybe we'd have better luck outside an apartment building," Rose suggested, pointing across the street at the Apthorp, a fortress-like home to the rich and famous that straddled an entire city block.

Grete admired her perseverance. Rose had explained, while she and Grete set up, that she was from a *shtetl* on the Ukraine plain at the base of the Carpathian Mountains. She was also Jewish. Grete suspected they had been paired together for that reason. They had little else in common. Rose's father had served in the Czech army in a horse artillery regiment. Her mother had been raised in a village without running water or electricity and had never attended school, though since their arrival in America she had taught herself to read and write in English, Rose added with pride.

A boy, who was not much taller than the donation box, approached and peered in. "Got a ball?" he asked.

"We're here for donations," Rose chastised. "Not handouts!"

Grete smiled. Her new friend was as thorny as a rose. And she was beginning to grow on Grete. The boy skulked away and Rose prattled on. Grete listened, happy for the distraction.

"When Chamberlain handed the Sudetenland over to Germany to 'keep peace,'" Rose scoffed, "my father made for America. He worked nights unloading trucks at the Bronx Terminal Market and when he made enough, he sent for my brother Phil. The two of them earned enough for me, Ma, and my little brother, Heshie, to come here."

"He had a lot of foresight," Grete said. It was difficult to understand how her parents could have been so blind. They were unwilling to give up the lives they had built. When she was not sad, Grete was angry.

Rose seemed to sense her pain. "My family was lucky," she said. "Ma's favorite saying is 'don't be smart, be lucky.' Our visas arrived in December of '38 and we left three days later on an overnight freight train to Prague. I was fifteen; Heshie was only three. None of us had ever traveled farther than the next village and we were all scared, especially Ma. A week after we received our green cards from the American Embassy, the Hungarians invaded Czechoslovakia and all American visas were cancelled."

Grete shuddered as she considered all those, including her own parents, trapped under the bloodthirsty regime. Rose had made the cut by days. Peter's friend Herbie had arrived in Germany the day after Germany declared war on the United States. Grete, who had always resented it when people called her lucky, could not deny fate's role.

"Fortunately, my father had booked our tickets on the Cunard Line, thinking a British ship would be safest. The clerk in Prague took pity on two women and a toddler traveling alone. He booked our passage through Germany and arranged for a hotel room in Paris until it was time for us to depart from Cherbourg. His kindness helped us more than he will ever know."

"One small gesture can mean so much." Grete was thinking of herself and Peter. She wasn't convinced her compassion toward Peter could change the course of the war, but helping one person, helping Peter, might make a difference for him, and for her. She was channeling sadness into hope, frustration into action.

Grete turned back to Rose. She had promised herself not to think about Peter for a day. "I can't imagine traveling halfway around the world with children," she said. Rose's parents had taken a leap of faith across war-torn Europe and the Atlantic Ocean to save their family.

"Our train had to cross all of Nazi Germany. It was a long trip and Heshie got restless. A group of soldiers boarded, and he popped his head out of our compartment to say hi—in Yiddish. My mother slapped him so hard his cheek turned red and he burst into tears. Thankfully, the soldiers must not have heard him clearly or they just didn't care. Either way, they left us alone. Ma says she can still feel the sting in her hand from slapping her child."

Grete reconsidered Rose. She had been wrong to think they had nothing in common. Grete was from a cosmopolitan city. Her family owned—had owned—a factory and a car. Rose came from a village of Jews. She had probably never been in a car before arriving in America. Yet here they both were.

Rose turned back to business, placing her hands on her hips and shouting, "Things that stretch and things that bounce. We can use each precious ounce!"

A woman with a passing resemblance to Grete's mother approached. Grete's lip quivered. Each day, she conjured up her parents' voices and idiosyncrasies. Her father sang in a rich baritone, though he often forgot lyrics. Her mother hid chocolate in the breadbox. The sound of their laughter had faded long ago.

The woman reached into a string bag, removing two worn welcome mats, a mildewed raincoat, and a torn bathing cap. Faced with an actual donation, Grete and Rose hesitated. They had been given a butcher scale to weigh goods and donations were supposed to be reimbursed at a cent per pound, but they had yet to conduct a transaction. Nor were they given money for reimbursement, just a small pad and pencil to write IOUs. Grete reached for the scale.

"You can have it for free," the woman said. "I have a son in the Pacific and want to do everything I can."

Grete nodded. She was also trying to do everything she could.

She and Peter had agreed that it would be wiser to spend the day apart. The four men, Dick, Henry, George, and Peter, planned to meet again at the Automat. Who could say how George would react when Peter confronted him about the notebook? Peter was furious, but George had a talent for talking Peter off a ledge. Grete was certain he would have some convoluted excuse as to why he had recorded Hannelore's address in his book. And she was equally sure that Peter would accept it, if only to delay the inevitable. Sooner than later, he would have to break ranks. *Trust yourself and you'll know how to live*, she had told him. She realized now how hollow it sounded.

Grete set the moldy rubber in the donation box and looked up in time to see a group of fashionable women in slacks leaving the Apthorp courtyard. She snatched the box and tugged Rose by the elbow. They ignored a red light and blaring car horn and dodged a crosstown bus to set the box in front of the building's elaborate wrought-iron gate. On the day Pearl Harbor was attacked, Mrs. Roosevelt had said it was essential to rise above the "clutch of fear," even knowing that one of her sons was on an aircraft carrier in the Pacific. The least Grete could do was round up a few girdles.

"Uncle Sam needs rubber for the war effort," she called. "To be melted down for tires, tanks, and medical supplies. Please donate what you can."

Rose placed both hands on the sides of her mouth. "Junk needed for war!" she shouted.

The women strode purposely around the box without a second glance. Grete kicked it in frustration. Yesterday, she and Peter had traveled for hours with nothing to show for it. Today, she could not manage to collect a discarded brassier. She had not even been aware that there was rubber in a bra until she had seen an ad in the newspaper for lingerie using whalebone and piano wire instead. The tagline read: "The Corset and Brassier Creators of America Faced—and Met—a Challenging Situation in the Midst of a Desperate Rubber Shortage." Grete smiled to herself, a sagging bust hardly qualified as a challenging situation. "You would think some of those ladies could spare a corset," she said.

"And give up those hour-glass figures." Rose giggled. "Besides, corsets are important for morale." Grete started to laugh before she saw Rose was serious. "Women need to feel our best to help the war effort," Rose said, playing with the wide patent leather belt that cinched her waist and highlighted her curves. Her mouth twisted as she folded her arms, seeming to take stock of Grete. "You're a skinny minny. After this, I'll treat you to ice cream or, better yet, come to Shabbos dinner at my house."

"That would be nice," Grete agreed. If only Peter were not consuming her every thought.

"Come Friday!" Rose said. "We live in the Bronx a few steps from the Westchester Avenue El. Easy-peasy." Rose used nearly as much American slang as George. "In the summer, we celebrate before sundown because my father keeps such early hours. I hope that's okay?

"I'll try," Grete said. Her heart went out to Rose. Despite her bravado, she was just another refugee trying to find her way.

Satisfied, Rose turned back to the task at hand. "Collect scraps to slap a Jap!" she hollered. Passersby turned to look at the petite girl with the outsized mouth.

Grete suppressed another smile and feigned outrage. In truth, she found Rose's devil-may-care attitude refreshing.

"Ma wouldn't approve," Rose agreed. "She'd rather slap a Kraut, but that doesn't rhyme." She leaned closer to whisper. "Don't look now, but that fellow on the corner is staring."

"Of course he is!" Grete laughed. For an instant, she felt as if she were fourteen again, in the schoolyard, ogling boys and giggling with friends.

"Not at me. He's been watching you since we crossed the street." Her brow wrinkled. "He's a bit old for a crush. Don't you think?"

Grete's head shot up. The man was wearing a black suit and charcoal gray fedora. His polished shoes glimmered in the sunlight. She shielded her eyes, but the sun was behind him and she couldn't see his face. She would have recognized Peter anywhere. It wasn't Peter. The man was too thickset to be George. Descriptions from George's notebook cluttered her thoughts . . . *stocky/slender, gray curly hair/thin-light brown hair, high forehead, steely expression*. She felt a stab of fear. It could be anyone.

"Let's go," she said, picking up the donation box before Rose could object. Rose opened her mouth but must have sensed Grete's alarm because she quickly followed along.

They strode up Broadway. Grete avoided looking over her shoulder and instead caught a glimpse of the man from the side of her eye as they crossed the street. He moved too fast to be Henry. It could be Dick or even the SS man Peter had told her about. Heat radiated off the sidewalk and sweat gathered on her chest. Her throat was desperately parched. She picked up her pace. She had not thought there were SS men on American soil, but she hadn't thought there were Nazi saboteurs either. She made a sharp right down Eighty-first Street, cutting Rose off so that she banged into a trash can, sending the lid to the ground with a loud clatter. Rose stooped to pick it up, but Grete tugged her forward.

"What happened? What's wrong?" Rose asked, clearly concerned.

"Nothing," Grete insisted as they turned on to Amsterdam Avenue.

"Is that man following us?"

If he was following them, he was not trying to hide. Grete did not dare look.

"Grete," Rose said insistently, "What's going on?"

"I'll tell you," Grete said, "Just not now. Please." The fear she had been suppressing since Peter first shared his story bubbled to the surface.

The salvage depot was only a block away. Grete rushed to catch the light, tripped over the curb, stumbled to her knees, and spilled their hard-earned collection into the street. When she looked up, the man was gone.

GRETE DID NOT SLOW DOWN UNTIL she turned into the entrance of Jacques's apartment house. The awning provided protection from the scorching sun and she took a moment to catch her breath. She looked down the street for the man in the dark suit, but there was no one. Despite a bloody knee, she had walked twenty blocks at a furious pace. Shaking off Rose had been more challenging. Grete had to beg her to leave her alone with a promise to explain everything on Friday at Shabbos dinner. By the time Grete reached Jacques's block, her hair was damp and there were angry blisters on her heels.

"Someone left a package for you," the doorman said. He held the door and followed her inside, reaching under his desk and removing a small, rectangular box, wrapped in brown paper and tied with twine. Her name was written across the front in generic block letters.

Grete kept her arms pinned to her side, reluctant to take the package until the befuddled doorman pushed it toward her stomach. Smaller than a drugstore romance, it seemed daunting.

"Who dropped it off?" she asked, looking over her shoulder for the man who had been following her. SS. She was sure of it. The idea made her want to race upstairs and bolt the door.

"Don't know," the doorman said. He removed his cap and scratched his head. "I was helping 9F with her shopping bags and when I came back to the desk it was sitting here."

Grete did not expect any less. She rode the elevator to twelve, gingerly shaking the box beside her ear then stopping cold at the thought of fuses and timing devices. Outside the apartment door, she set the package on the mat and lowered her head to listen for ticks. Satisfied there was no imminent threat, she carried it inside, carefully removing the twine and unwrapping the paper. Inside was a plain white handkerchief. Grete picked it up, searching for a card, and a battered ten-cent book with a black cover fell to the floor.

She leapt back as if it were dynamite. George's flimsy notebook with its detailed descriptions of torpedoes and spies seemed more dangerous than explosives. She stared down at it. Its appearance could mean any number of things. Peter had asked her to hold the baggage claim ticket for safekeeping, was he asking her to hold this too? Was he in danger? Another wave of heat poured through her as she imagined Peter confronting George and George snatching the book away and sending it to her as a warning.

No. If George had the book back, he would not give it up.

Grete double-checked the lock on the front door and tested the chain before picking up the notebook and walking to the living room. Vagabond was curled in a ball on the sofa and she watched his ribcage rise and fall, envying his tranquility. She slipped out of her shoes and sank into a chair, turning the book upside down and over, trying to intuit its meaning. The cover was damaged and several pages were glued together with dry sand. She pried the sheets apart, her hackles rising with every turn of the page. Her eyes watered over the detailed sketches and menacing names: listening room, attack periscope, 20mm guns. Small wonder Peter said the book was important. It held enough incriminating information to hang each of his companions. No doubt, the United States military would find it immensely valuable.

And here it was.

She ran her hand over the cover wondering what to do—and felt a small lump. The weather-beaten notebook was riddled with bulges and buckles. Grete could not explain why she singled out this particular one; she attributed it to fate. On inspection, she could see where the black leather separated from the spine. She held the book closer and noticed a scrap of paper wedged inside. A secret within a secret. She tucked sweaty strands of hair behind her ear. Carefully, so as not to rip the paper, she coaxed the paper out.

Another sketch. This one labeled: TRACK 61. Grete wiped her brow and squinted at the tiny drawing. It was not cigar-shaped like the submarine diagrams. Instead, two parallel rails stretched off the page. Arrows pointed to a series of rectangles that she guessed was a train and a platform beside it. The drawing was unadorned with the exception of what looked like the passenger car on the train. Someone had taken the time to drape small curtains in the windows. A jumbled name was scratched along the body. Grete narrowed her eyes: Ferdinand Magell . . . Letters blurred, not the looping Ls and coiled Es of George's script, but a spiky, angry scrawl. On the lower left corner, bolder than anything else, was a square with the words *freight elevator* gouged inside. An arrow pointed upward from the elevator and the shaft was marked *W-A*. Directly across the rail tracks, a staircase snaked up to what Grete knew to be Grand Central Terminal.

The paper fluttered in her trembling hands. She had not known what to do with the book and she had even less idea about what to do with this new secret. She tried to slide the paper back in its nook, but it refused to go. She had the sickening sense that she had unleashed a monster. She set the diagram and book on the table and went to retrieve a glass of water. She guzzled two full glasses before her head stopped spinning. The cut on her knee throbbed and she went to the bathroom to clean and bandage it. Returning to the living room, she collapsed back into a chair. It was the first time since she had met Peter that she had slowed down long enough to think clearly. Racing around town had allowed her to forget her problems, and she couldn't deny her attraction to Peter, but their relationship had developed into something far more than a distraction. Peter's freedom was at stake and innocent people might be injured, or worse. Innocent people like her. Peter had told her it was not safe for her to accompany him and she had, foolishly, brushed his concerns aside. For the first time since meeting Peter, she began to fear for her safety. She eyed the notebook. Reasonably certain that Peter had left it for her, she had a strong hunch he knew nothing about the scrap of paper hidden inside. The smart thing would be to throw all of it in the trash and forget she had ever seen it. But she had abandoned common sense the moment she left the parade with Peter. The notebook and the information it contained were too serious to ignore. War made people do barbaric things; it also caused ordinary people to do brave things. She did not understand why Peter had left the book for her or what he wanted her to do with it, but she felt an obligation—a patriotic duty—not to toss it aside.

Sinking back in the chair, her eyes fell on the handkerchief:

plain, white, cotton, exactly the type Peter said could be used to convey invisible writing. She held it to the light, trying to recall what he had said. Something about matchsticks or toothpicks and laxatives. Some kind of fumes? Her nose twitched. Ammonia. She leapt to her feet. Jacques kept cleaning supplies under the kitchen sink. A search yielded white vinegar, dish detergent, garbage bags, and sponges. No ammonia. The bathrooms proved equally fruitless. Grete turned to the hallway linen closet where the ironing board was stored. Aroused from his nap, Vagabond watched with interest as she stood on tiptoe and ran her hand along the top shelf. Her fingers hit cold metal and the iron came crashing down, nearly knocking her out. Vagabond scurried under the sofa. "Sorry," she called after him. She reached back up. There was bleach, and another tall bottle adorned with a skull and crossbones.

In the kitchen, she studied the sinister black-and-white label before twisting off the ammonia bottle's cap. The fumes made the hairs in her nose stand on end. No doubt only a miniscule amount was needed. Still, she was reluctant to pour it into a bowl and leave the poisonous remnants for Vagabond or Uncle Jacques to ingest. She opened the refrigerator in search of a container and settled on a half-empty carton of cream, pouring the cream into the cat's bowl. She washed the carton, then cut it into a shallow square. She cracked open the window and removed the ammonia cap again. The smell sent Vagabond, who had been intrigued by the cream, scurrying to the other room. Grete watched him go, marveling at his wisdom. Sighing, she opened the window wider before pouring a few tablespoons of the liquid into the carton bottom. Holding her breath, she stretched the fabric taut over the carton, and waited.

Nothing.

She lifted the handkerchief, then lowered it so that it touched the top of the carton.

Nothing.

Frustrated, she held the handkerchief to the light and noticed a tiny tag in the corner. What she thought was the front was actually the back. She turned the cloth over.

Slowly, like witchcraft, flaming red letters began to emerge. Some were missing. Others faded as quickly as they appeared. Her pulse quickened as she deciphered what she could.

Greetings from Frank Dan . . .

Letters flitted by and vanished but Peter's warning resounded in her head. *If any of us needed assistance, we were to say "Greetings from Franz Daniel."* If she were not on the verge of panicking, she might have smiled. *Frank Dan* was the Americanized version of *Franz Daniel,* intended solely for her.

Grete pulled the fabric taut over the ammonia. Toward the top, there was a capital *G* she assumed referred to George, followed by the word *gone.* Had George gone to Washington? She could only hope. Reading on, she saw the word *come,* absent an *o,* and the number nine. She shook her head in frustration and stretched the thin cotton until it began to tear. Did nine refer to an address or time? Morning or night? Either way, she had told her uncle she would cook his favorite spaghetti Bolognaise for dinner and she intended to keep her promise. Grete began wrapping the book inside the handkerchief. Whatever it was Peter needed would have to wait. She was folding the notebook back into the handkerchief when a final word blazed to life: *Chrysler.*

CHAPTER 11

THE CHRYSLER BUILDING'S POLISHED chrome entranceway was set back from the street and framed in tombstone-gray brick. Grete positioned herself inside the alcove; a place to see without being seen. It was the height of the morning rush. Lexington Avenue was snarled in traffic, gas rationing be damned. Every blaring horn, skidding tire, and slamming door made her stomach lurch. Ten minutes later, she was pacing the block. Peter's message did not specify where to meet, or that part had been lost, or she had misunderstood, or something had happened to Peter. Twenty flights overhead, gargoyles looked ready to pounce. The building's steel spire pierced low-lying haze. Its silhouette was her favorite among the skyline but she had never ventured inside, preferring to admire the architecture from afar. In her mind, the interior could never match the dazzling crown.

Another misperception shattered. Grete saw at once that the lobby was a treasure. A huge yet intricate ceiling mural featured airplanes and factory workers, the motif oddly communistic. But Walter Chrysler was all capitalist. The proof was front and center, where three gleaming automobiles with polished grills and white-walled tires sat atop a revolving platform. Grete imagined herself behind the convertible's wheel on open road with a scarf tied round her head. Peter was by her side, his arm slung around her shoulder. They were on a long stretch of highway that led anywhere they wanted it to. The platform rotated and the convertible was replaced by a tan hardtop with the muscular definition and grace of a ballerina. Another turn and a shiny black vehicle took center stage. In the reflection of its door, Grete caught a glimpse of a man standing several feet behind her. He had the same general carriage as the man who had followed her yesterday. She felt a twinge of fear. The cars pivoted again, obscuring her view. She peered over her shoulder just as the man removed his hat to scratch his forehead. His hair was black and flecked with silver at the temples. Her fear mounted. He fit Peter's description of the SS man. Then again, thousands of men fit the same generic description and her suspicion seemed to know no bounds.

Grete leapt as a young boy brushed up next to her. He and his father wore the same open-mouthed expression of delight. "That's a DeSoto," the father explained. She scanned the lobby. She couldn't see the SS man. Peter was nowhere. Someone tapped her on the shoulder and she spun around.

"Can I help you?" a security guard asked. The innocent question left her stumped. Germany had taught her to fear men in uniform. The air around her felt close, and she tried to concentrate on the guard's face, which was kind.

"Looking for the observation deck?" He spoke loudly and pointed upward. *The observation deck.* Peter's penchant for dramatic rendezvous seemed to match George's. The Chrysler Building observation deck had to be one of the most romantic meeting places in the city. "Take the fourth elevator on the right to the seventy-first floor." The guard gestured toward the elevator bank.

Grete stepped toward the elevators then froze. There was only one other passenger waiting: the man in the black suit who had followed her yesterday. She recognized his charcoal gray hat and the pristine shine of his shoes. His face was obscured by a newspaper. The *Brooklyn Eagle*, a paper she never read. A front page photo of a man and woman gripping each other by the elbows and staring into one another's eyes drew her attention. "Life and Death for Lovers," read the headline. It seemed like a veiled threat, or maybe she was finally grasping the full measure of her involvement. She took another inadvertent step forward. The man in the photo was tall and stooped, but he may as well have been Peter. The woman had a broad face and closely set eyes, but Grete felt like her twin.

The elevator chimed. The doors opened.

The man lowered his newspaper. His expression was indecipherable. He was clean-shaven and impeccably dressed in a crisp white shirt and pressed tie. He held out the paper to indicate that she should enter before him. Wild horses could not have dragged her inside that elevator. Too frightened to turn her back, she stood rooted in place.

"I think you'll want to talk to me," he said. His *talk* sounded like *tawk*. Her ears perked up at the sound of his New York accent. "Grete."

She jumped as her name left his lips. "Who are you?" she asked. "How do you know my name?"

He gestured inside the elevator. When Grete didn't budge, he reached inside his jacket. Her eyes scrunched closed. Just as she suspected, she wasn't truly brave. This stranger was about to shoot her and all she could do was flinch. An eternity passed.

"Grete," his voice was low and confidential. "I'm Special Agent Charles Lanman, Federal Bureau of Investigation." Her eyes sprang open. He had removed his wallet and flipped it open to reveal a badge. The badge was gold, in the shape of a shield, and straight out of a movie. *FBI, not SS.*

"Grete," Agent Lanman said again. She had the sense that he was repeating her name on purpose to unnerve her, and it was working. "I may be able to help you—and your parents."

She was inside the elevator without a second thought. Agent Lanman pressed the button for seventy-one. Grete had never been to the observation deck, but she pictured a narrow ledge in the clouds with a perilously low rail. It was bound to be empty at this early hour. Anything could happen. Still, she was prepared to follow Lanman to the ends of the earth if there were the slightest chance to rescue her parents. Air whistled down the shaft as the elevator rose, thirty then forty floors. Her ears

popped and her heart skipped. Agent Lanman seemed intentionally silent as if he were giving her time to process all that
was at stake. They rose another ten flights before he flipped an
emergency switch. The elevator shuddered and stopped. A bell
rang. Grete stumbled backward, resting her hand on the wall for
balance. Lanman opened a small panel below the buttons and
turned a key to silence the alarm.

"How can you help my parents?" she asked.

"First things first." He held up his hand to command silence.
"I've been tailing you since Amagansett." He sounded like a parody
of an FBI agent, but she did not doubt his authenticity. Lanman
had a wide neck, ears that sprouted from a closely cropped hair-
cut, and an air of righteous American authority.

She took in his words. *Amagansett*. She had been half naked
with Peter in the ocean, kissing him in the sand. Too much blood
had drained from her head to blush. Still, Lanman's admission
made her heart seize with guilt. Peter had been dead-set against
returning to Amagansett. She was the one who had insisted they
go and destroy the explosives. The Coast Guard must have alerted
the FBI who were lying in wait.

"Why me?" she asked. She had meant to ask Lanman why he
was following her, not Peter, but her thoughts were too muddled
to speak clearly.

Agent Lanman intuited her meaning. "Burger can't know we're
on to him."

"Peter called the FBI because he wants help. He needs help.
He's . . ." She struck on Peter's phrase, "trying to do the right thing."

"Peter Burger won't do us much good so long as the other
saboteurs are at large. We need to round them up together,
red-handed."

"How can you help my parents?" Her voice cracked.

"Tell me what you know about Peter's mission."

"I . . ." She felt as if she had just arrived in New York and could
barely speak English. "I . . ." She stammered, shrugged.

"Look, Grete, we can talk here or we can go down to FBI

headquarters and have a chat there. You've been busy the past couple days and we should have a lot to discuss."

Red-handed, mission, headquarters, FBI. Grete's thoughts flashed to Uncle Jacques sitting quietly at home, the telephone ringing, and the voice on the other end of the phone spouting those treasonous words. She was jeopardizing all he had done to help her, his security, and the welfare of her parents. Tears stung her eyes. She reached into her pocketbook for her handkerchief and was reminded of the handkerchief Peter had sent her, the one with the invisible ink. She was hit with another wave of remorse. How could she have gone along with Peter? And how could she betray him now? She tucked her handkerchief deeper into her purse and wiped her arm across her eyes.

"Power convertors," she blurted. "It has something to do with power convertors and Grand Central Station and," she said illogically, "sand."

If this was news to Lanman, his expression did not show it. "Do you know dates and times?"

"No." She wanted to explain that she was not involved, that she would never have known those details, but she realized the opposite was true. Her cooperation began the moment she left the parade with Peter. "I don't believe they have dates yet. Peter said they're waiting."

"For what?" Grete did not know the answer, or she wasn't sure how to phrase it. "Grete," Lanman pressed, "Boats to Germany go both ways."

The elevator floor seemed to drop out and she braced her hand against the wall. "There's another group of men landing," she said, horrified at how quickly she had betrayed Peter.

"When?"

"Any day. I don't think Peter knows exactly. They traveled here separately and Peter doesn't know where they'll come ashore. He says it will be somewhere along the Florida coast. Both groups plan to meet on the Fourth of July."

Lanman shook his head as if the date alone illustrated evil

intent. "Where?"

"I don't know. The group leader is a man named George Dasch." Lanman's face showed no sign of recognition. "He has a contact in New Jersey." Sensing the information she was providing was insufficient, she kept talking. "George and Peter are working together. They've already called the FBI," she stressed. Again, Lanman's expression registered nothing. She forged on, "And now George is going to Washington while Peter keeps an eye on the other men."

Lanman held up his hand. He did not seem interested in Peter or George's defense. "Keep doing what you're doing. Stay with Burger and make sure you know where he is at all times. Encourage him to track down the others and move ahead. The sooner they get caught, the sooner I can help your parents."

"But Peter won't go through with it," she said again. Lanman's eyes flashed with pity. She had incriminated herself and Peter, or Peter had incriminated her. Either way, they were both trapped. "Can you really help my parents?" Doubt crept in. It seemed too good to be true.

"Your parents are at Camp de Gurs in southern France," Lanman said. "We can get them out, get them visas, and get them here. But you need to do your part first. The saboteurs must be brought in, then we'll talk." Lanman pressed another button. The elevator door opened and he was gone.

GRETE ARRIVED ON THE OBSERVATION DECK as breathlessly as if she had climbed each of the seventy-one flights on foot. She had spent three years consumed with worry about her parents and now this man, Special Agent Lanman, was offering to wave a wand, or an American flag, and save them. If what he was saying was true and her parents were alive, she should have been relieved. Instead, she was plagued by doubts. Could Lanman really help? She cursed herself for not asking more questions or insisting on proof. But the truth was, she was in no position to negotiate. Lanman had said her parents were in France, not Germany, which was consistent with the last letter she had received from them. If they were in Germany or in a camp farther east, she would have disbelieved the government's sway. As it was, she could only hope that Lanman would be true to his word. He had said he was approaching her, not Peter, because Peter could not know he was being followed. But she knew the real reason: Peter was a seasoned soldier; she was a malleable target.

At last, the elevator doors parted. Far more than a narrow ledge, the seventy-first floor was a labyrinth of hard angles and long shadows. Inverted triangular pillars fanned out toward a ceiling of stars from which globe lights with Saturn rings hung down. The globes provided the only curves along an avenue of sharp edges. Tall triangular windows, framed in chrome, created sunlit pyramids across the floor. The air was at least ten degrees cooler than it had been on the street. Grete had the impression she had stepped out onto an alien planet.

The feeling intensified when Peter appeared, engulfing her in a wordless embrace. From their first meeting, it was as if he were relying on her for support. Now as they leaned together, Grete wobbled. She reached up and stroked his face. She had every intention of doing exactly what Lanman asked. She would do anything to help her parents. Still, she couldn't suppress her guilt. She buried her face in Peter's chest.

Peter wrapped his arms around her waist. "What's wrong?"

"I've never been up this high," she fibbed, tottering slightly and allowing Peter to steady her. It was easier to play the part of tourists, a young couple in love, or honeymooners visiting the big city. Her knees trembled. She was afraid, but it was not the height that frightened her.

Peter led her into a window bay where the view was clear. It also provided at least a sense of privacy. Grete looked into the adjacent alcoves for signs of Lanman or another agent, but they appeared to be alone. From this height, the East River looked like a moat. Sunlight dappled the water and shimmered along the loops of a large, red Pepsi-Cola sign on the opposite shore.

"The ink works!" Peter's smile was bright. "I never actually tried it. It's good to know you were able to read it."

She withdrew, startled by his sunny demeanor. Was he testing his spying techniques—or her?

"Obviously, I read it." Her voice was far harsher than she intended. "Why did you leave me that book?" George's book. She had been so blindsided by Agent Lanman, she had forgotten to mention it.

Peter's smile faded. "Someone broke into my hotel room." He hugged her to his chest and his lips brushed the top of her head. "I'm sorry I keep pulling you into this. I've nowhere else to turn. That little book is the most important proof I have that we planned to abort the operation even before we landed. I need to keep it safe."

With her ear to his chest, Grete could hear Peter's heart thrumming. Her questions spilled out just as quickly. "Who broke into your room? Was it George? What did he say when you told him you had the book?"

"Nothing."

"How is that possible?" George was many things; silent was not one of them.

"George wasn't there."

"At the hotel?"

"Not Monday night when we got back from Amagansett or all day Tuesday. We had an appointment to meet Dick and Henry yesterday, but when I called his room no one answered. The chambermaid said the room hadn't been slept in. The others were furious. George is always going his own way. It's bad for morale."

"That doesn't matter now."

"It matters more than ever. Dick won't follow orders if he has no faith in George, and Henry only does what Dick says."

The boy Grete had seen downstairs skipped around the corner and his father raced after him, shouting for him to slow down. Grete waited for them to pass and turned back to Peter. She lowered her voice.

"Peter," she treaded carefully, "Did you ever discuss what

would happen if you were caught?"

Peter rubbed his hand over his face. "We all think about it. No one talks about it. Before we left Germany, Kappe said the only thing for us to do if we got into trouble would be to try to get to Chile or Argentina. We're on our own."

"You are," she said, trying not to sound too cruel. "If you're waiting for George to do the right thing, you'll be waiting a long while. He may never go to the FBI. Peter, please turn yourself in without him. I'll go with you."

"What?" Peter snapped. "The FBI can't know anything about you. They'd send you back to Germany without a second thought." Her heart seized. Everyone but her seemed to understand the risk. She wondered now how she could have been so naïve. Peter put his hand on her chin, lifting it to force her eyes on him. "I don't like George either, but he's risking a lot. Any other man might have killed that boy on the beach. Dick wanted to snap his neck. George saved his life. Calling the FBI, especially after that run-in, took a lot of courage. I can't just desert him."

Grete couldn't help but speak up. "He refused to give his name or any details. If he had gone with the Coast Guard to begin with, this whole thing could have been stopped that very first night."

The elevator chimed, unloading four women in nurse's uniforms with dark blue capes and garrison caps. One bent over a Brownie camera while the others lined up, flashing smiles. There was a commotion while they changed positions and another round of photos before they moved around the corner.

Peter lowered his voice and Grete leaned closer to hear. "We had to wait so the FBI knew we came forward voluntarily and we got to give those other boys a chance to come forward on their own. How can I make you understand?" He raked his fingers through his hair. "Say you wanted to kill someone—"

She stepped back. "What?"

"I'm trying to explain." His words gained momentum. "Say you wanted someone dead and you planned to kill him by, I don't know, pushing him in front of a train or buying a gun to shoot him. Is that a crime?"

"I'd never kill anyone."

"Not even if they hurt your family? Or murdered someone you loved?"

She flushed. She was lying to Peter to save her parents. Who could say what else she might do? She shook her head as if it would erase the gruesome images flooding her thoughts. "Why are you asking me this?"

"Just answer."

"Pushing someone in front of a train is a crime. So is shooting him."

"You're not listening. I'm saying you *planned* to push him or shoot him, but didn't actually do it."

"Well, if you didn't actually do it, and no one died, it's not murder. As far as being a crime—" Grete faltered.

"None of us men have pushed anyone in front of a train. We didn't buy guns or explosives. The German High Command gave them to us. We were in no position to refuse. As soon as we could, we buried them in the sand."

"Your orders were to bury them."

"The point is, none of us have done anything. We're not even responsible for the plan. You can't charge a fellow with a crime he didn't commit. And I can't turn the others in just to save my own neck."

Peter's argument made some sense. Grete began to see why Lanman was not arresting him immediately. Peter and the others hadn't done anything; not yet.

"You don't even know where George is," she said. "How do you know what he is or isn't doing?"

"George will go to Washington and I'll watch Dick and Henry. That's what we decided and that's what I intend to do."

"Why can't it be the other way around?"

"Dick hates George."

"George rubs everyone the wrong way. You're much better spoken."

Peter shook his head. "My English."

"Your English was a bit rusty the day you arrived. It's perfect now. Better than mine."

"It's fine when I'm with you. But sometimes the words come out wrong. I told you how I buckled and spoke German that first night on the beach. Dick was furious with George, but it was me who blew our cover. Dick's incredibly anxious. When George didn't show up yesterday, he swore at me and said if George didn't turn up by tonight, he and Henry were moving ahead without him. I'm supposed to meet them later at Grand Central."

Grete nestled closer. Every bone in her body wanted to warn him about Agent Lanman, but she wasn't prepared to risk her parents' safety. "Peter," she said instead, "What's Track 61?"

He tensed. "Where did you hear that?"

"I didn't hear it. I read it." She tipped her head back to look up at him. "I found a slip of paper hidden inside George's book. It has a diagram labeled Track 61."

"What?" He seemed genuinely puzzled. "Do you have it?"

"Not with me."

"Where is it?"

"In the book. I left it at home. I thought that's why you gave it to me, so it would be safe." Peter frowned, and she resented his unspoken reprimand. He had left her with a stash of damning evidence and she had no idea what to do with it all. "What's Track 61?" she asked again.

Peter looked around, lowered his voice. "Track 61 is a secret rail tunnel under Grand Central. We learned about it at Quenz Farm."

"A secret rail tunnel for troops? Or . . ." Her mind scrambled, "ammunition?" Grete recalled the ornate drawing of the passenger car and the name etched on the side. "Who's Ferdinand Magellan?" She knew he was a historical figure. Beyond that, she couldn't say.

"He was a Portuguese explorer. It's also the name of the presidential rail car which pulls into Grand Central on Track 61."

"Presidential rail car? You mean Roosevelt's private train?"

"Track 61 is for Roosevelt's exclusive use. There's a private platform and a freight elevator big enough to hold his limousine. The elevator goes up to the Waldorf Astoria Hotel so FDR can get there without going through the station or being in the public eye, or in danger."

"But your orders are to destroy the power convertors," she stammered, remembering what she had told Lanman. "Is there more?" she asked, growing alarmed. "Is the target Track 61?"

Peter snatched her hand and raced to the elevator, furiously pressing the button. "We've got to find George."

CHAPTER 12

THE ELEVATOR HURTLED BACK DOWN TO THE LOBBY. On fifty, Grete was convinced Peter had not known about the diagram of Track 61. His supposed comrades were hiding secrets from him and now, she was too. She looked ahead, watching the numbers above the doors count down, unsure if she would ever be able to look Peter in the eye again. On thirty, Peter touched her elbow and her stomach did a somersault. Deep down, she believed Peter was a good person in terrible trouble. She wished she thought less of him. Answering to Lanman would be easier if she suspected Peter of wrongdoing. She had a sudden vision of George at FBI headquarters. He was sitting under a bare light bulb at a card table with an overflowing ashtray. Betraying Peter and incriminating her. Her hopes plummeted for ten more flights. Stopping on fifteen, she reassured herself that she had dumped the bag full of sand. If George steered the FBI to the baggage claim office, there would be nothing there. No evidence linking Peter, or her, to any plot. She sorted through other ways George might entrap her. There was the book, of course, but as far as George knew the book was lost. The elevator set down on the ground floor, the doors parted, and Grete stiffened, fully expecting the FBI to whisk them away.

On the street, she had a sudden burst of clarity.

"What about those waiters?" she said. "The ones who recognized George. One asked about his wife so they must know him pretty well. That coffee shop is only a few blocks from here. Let's go see if they have some idea where George might be."

Peter turned toward her with a steady, penetrating expression. It was the same look that had drawn her to him at the parade; the one that made her feel like a woman instead of a girl.

"Good idea." He laced his fingers through hers and led her toward the coffee shop with the quiet, commanding ease she found so attractive. *Oh, Peter*, she wanted to say, *runaway now. Go to Chile or Argentina.* The words were on the tip of her tongue, but she could not bring herself to say them out loud. Lanman could be watching.

Mayer's Coffee House looked just as they had left it. The same waiter sat exactly where he had the last time they were here, on his haunches, enjoying a cigarette in the sunshine. He wore a white jacket, unbuttoned and splattered with grease. Grete waited for Peter to say something. He had been quiet since they left the Chrysler Building and she wondered if he sensed a change in her. When it was clear Peter was not going to speak up, she tentatively approached the waiter.

"Excuse me," she said.

The fellow took a drag and looked up, squinting into the sunlight.

"We passed by the other day." She paused, unsure. "With a man named George." Another pause as she considered if George would have used the name Davis or Dasch. "I think you used to wait tables with him?"

The waiter exhaled a plume of smoke. "What about him?" He sounded nearly as reluctant as Grete to admit his association with George.

"We're looking for him. It's important."

"He owe you money?"

"What? No. Nothing like that."

The waiter tapped ash off his cigarette and nodded over his shoulder toward the coffee shop door.

Grete hesitated. Could it really be this easy? She turned to Peter, expecting relief or gratitude. But he remained mute, twisting his mouth as if he were trying to staunch the anger welling inside.

"He's here?" she asked.

"Look in back."

Grete and Peter made their way past a cash register and long counter with a row of red-topped stools. The only natural light came from the front window and quickly faded toward the back. The coffee shop was narrow with scratched wood-paneled walls. It smelled of coffee and grease, stale but comforting. She scanned the place for men in dark suits, Dick or Henry, anyone with shifty eyes. Linoleum tiles squeaked underfoot as they proceeded. Several customers sat at the counter with heaping plates of eggs and pancakes. A few wore waiter's jackets. Grete picked up stray comments about the stifling summer heat, the Allied offensive, and baseball.

"Two on base and no outs," one grumbled. "Calling that game in the bottom of the ninth was a crime!"

"La Guardia and his damn blackout laws."

"It was rigged."

"Giants had it in the bag!"

"Whadd'ya talking 'bout. Dodgers were up by three!"

"La Guardia's a Yankee man," the cook weighed in. He was a stooped, gray-haired man, flipping eggs on the griddle, who addressed the newcomers without turning. "Booths in back. Waitress be with you in a minute."

The kitchen doors swung open as a harried waitress passed through balancing a full tray.

"Take any seat."

"We are looking for someone . . . in back?" Grete said.

The waitress sighed. "Keep going."

Grete peered beyond a payphone and down a narrow hall. The restrooms were on the left and the back door was propped open with a mop. Shy of that was another door that she had missed in the dim light. Peter lifted his head, indicating she should stand aside, and pushed open the door. Silent for the last half hour, his words burst out.

"George, where in hell have you been?"

Around Peter's shoulder, Grete saw George at a flimsy table with two full ashtrays under a light bulb exactly as she had imagined the FBI headquarters to look, but the similarities ended there. Three men with loose ties and razor stubble were also clustered around the table. Their heads were lowered as if in prayer, except rather than a bible each studied a hand of cards. Windowless, the room reeked of cigarettes and unwashed men. Boxes were piled along the walls. On a tack next to a refrigerator, a calendar turned to January featured a snowy mountain range. Grete had the uncanny feeling that time stood still here. Cards were spread across the table. A mound of cash sat dead center.

George looked up. His jaw dropped and a cigarette fell from his lips. He breasted his cards as if Peter might spoil his hand. "Pete and . . . Opal," he said, recovering quickly. Grete had nearly forgotten the phony name, but she did not regret it. The less George knew about her the better. "This is my pal Fritz," George said, nodding across the table. His jacket and tie were off, his sleeves rolled up. "And Malloy and this boy's Tom." The men mumbled hellos, eyes trained on their cards.

Peter ignored them. "George, I've been looking all over for you. We need to talk."

George waved him away. "Let me finish this hand."

Peter grabbed George's cards and slapped them faceup on the table. Eight of hearts, nine of diamonds, two spades, and another suit whose name Grete had forgotten. She felt a thrill at the way Peter wordlessly took command. He swept George's jacket off the back of his chair and ushered Grete out the door, through the coffee shop and onto the street. A moment later, George joined them, blinking in the sunlight. He brushed lank hair out of his eyes, drawing attention to the silver streak.

"Hey," he said, snatching his jacket and shrugging it on. "What was that all about?"

The waiter, still outside, dropped his cigarette and left.

Peter looked down the street. When he spoke, his voice was slow and measured. "I've been waiting two days for you. Did you forget about meeting the boys?"

"I didn't forget."

"Where were you?"

George pointed back over his shoulder towards Mayer's unlit sign.

"You've been here since Tuesday?" Grete asked. Peter placed a warning hand on her wrist, and she reminded herself to calm down and not do anything that might jeopardize the help Lanman was offering.

George blew air into his gaunt cheeks, momentarily inflating them. "Since sometime Monday." He tapped a nicotine stained finger against the side of his nose.

Grete froze as it occurred to her that the irritating habit might be some kind of signal. She looked across the street and into nearby doorways. A deliveryman unloaded boxes. Someone else hosed the sidewalk. A cab flew down the street. An apartment window opened then slammed shut. She could not see Agent Lanman, but sensed he was close by.

"Doing what?" Peter spat.

"Playing Pinochle," George said as if the answer were obvious. He fumbled in his pocket. "Must have left my smokes." He turned to walk back inside, but Peter seized him by the arm. George pulled away. "Look, Pete, I'm not monkeying around. Cards relax me. I don't have to tell you I'm a nervous wreck. I'm trying to force myself to go through with something I hate. The idea of squealing on those boys." He looked warily at Grete. "I'm no stool pigeon."

"George." Peter sounded incredulous. "We made it this far. This is our chance. Why are you throwing it away?"

"It's not how it seems. Playing cards takes my mind off things. I can't eat or sleep, or face those other boys." A flush of something very like guilt washed over George's face. Grete understood that in his own convoluted way, George was saying the same thing Peter had said. It was rotten to turn the others in without giving them the opportunity to come forward on their own. George reached into his jacket pocket for a cigarette before seeming to remember that he had left the pack inside. "I'm all tied up about what I got to do."

Peter exhaled slowly. "What was I supposed to tell Dick and Henry when you didn't show?"

"The truth. You didn't know where I was. You didn't, right? Then again, you managed to track me down. You're a resourceful fellow, aren't you Pete?" He yawned. "I knew you were perfectly capable of keeping those boys in line. It's better for you to see those poor suckers alone. Tell them I had to leave New York for a couple days to meet some important contacts."

Grete had heard more than enough. "You've got to get to the FBI before they find you." Lanman had told her to urge Peter to move ahead with the plan. If Peter was waiting on George, she had no choice but to push George too.

Two women left the coffee shop, pinning hats and pulling on gloves. George waited until they reached the end of the block to speak again. "I've got a couple new suits at the tailor. I'll pick them up, get a bit of shut-eye, and be on my way first thing tomorrow. Take it easy Pete, everything is going as planned."

Grete was happy to see Peter reach his boiling point. "You're joking, right?" He stepped forward forcing George back. "Are you telling me you've been waiting all this time for new suits?"

George raised his hands. "*Fidelity, Bravery, and Integrity.* It's the FBI motto. Look, Pete, I know G-men. It's important to present the right image. This is make-or-break time."

Grete's thoughts shot to Agent Lanman and his dark suit, white shirt, polished shoes. "What happens if they don't believe you?" she asked. George could not convince the FBI over the telephone and she imagined he would have less credibility face-to-face.

"Why shouldn't they believe me?" George asked. "I'm not asking for anything. We'll help them and that'll be proof enough."

Grete had expected Peter to question George about the book and the diagram of Track 61, but she was beginning to understand why he didn't. Peter was playing his hand too.

"Listen, Pete," George said, "I'm dead tired. I'll be on the train to Washington first thing tomorrow. I promise I'll do everything in my power to verify my identity and yours and explain what we're up against. Everything's going as planned," he said again. "All you got to do is keep those other boys quiet. Calm their nerves. Look out that Henry doesn't drink too much and make sure Dick doesn't get any crazy ideas."

WITH TIME TO KILL BEFORE PETER was to meet Dick and Henry, Grete suggested a movie. She had assured Agent Lanman that she would stay with Peter. Two hours in a dark, air-cooled theatre seemed like the best way to pass the time. She could avoid talking.

For the second time that morning, Peter rewarded her with an appreciative, if slightly diminished, smile. Ounce by ounce, the pressure was draining him. He took her hand and gave it a weak squeeze then brought it to his lips and kissed it.

Grete put her hand over his. "Why didn't you tell George that Dick already has a crazy idea? It might have made him move faster."

"George takes a lot of pride in being the group leader. I don't know what he'd do if he found out the others were going around him."

"Bit of a double standard."

"That's George."

"Most people only see what they want to," she said with an unpleasant sense that she was suffering from the same affliction.

They turned the corner onto Broadway. Times Square had become a wartime hub. Men outnumbered women and GIs outnumbered everyone else, jamming the streets, making the most of their leave. Grete heard southern drawls mingled with Aussie twang, indecipherable to her ears. Some men slurred in the universal language of drunkenness. More than a few looked as if they had been up all night. A crowd milled around Forty-seventh Street where Pepsi-Cola had a center for troops to shower and shave. Marquees advertising *Porgy and Bess* and *Oklahoma!* vied for attention with billboards for defense bonds and cigarettes.

Though Times Square's famous lights were dim, the signs still shone with mosaics made of mirrored squares, which caught sunlight during the day and headlights at night. Grete and Peter threaded through the frivolity. Peter kept his eyes lowered. Grete's pace slowed as they approached the Paramount where Alfred Hitchcock's *Saboteur* was playing. The movie poster showed a frightened woman clinging to a handsome man surrounded by images of destruction: a dam under surveillance, an airplane factory on fire, the shadow of a man lurking outside a crowded party, gun in hand.

"Oh," she said. Her head shot toward Peter.

A sad smile played across his lips as he looked up at the sunlit marquee. "I never believed in . . . How do you say *omen*?"

"Omen. It's the same in English," she said—which seemed like one. She expected sirens to blare or the sky to light up as they walked under the marquee.

"Grete!"

Grete spun around, colliding into Rose.

"Rose?"

Another omen, one which Grete did not know how to interpret.

Dressed in a form-fitting shirtwaist, Rose peered at Peter with open curiosity. "Are you seeing *Nazi Agent*?" The accusation ricocheted into the street and, Grete imagined, into the ears of each and every GI.

"Why would I see a Nazi agent?" she croaked.

Rose waved a gloved finger to the Rialto marquee where *Nazi Agent* was spelled out in towering letters. "The movie *Nazi Agent*." Her gaze swept from Grete to Peter then back to Grete. "Are you feeling better?" She peered past Grete's hemline. "How's your knee?"

Peter took Grete's elbow. "Grete's just overwarm."

Grete flinched. Was *overwarm* even a word?

"It's hot out," Rose agreed cheerfully. She turned to Grete, and when no introduction was forthcoming, she plowed ahead. "I'm Rose," she said, extending a hand to Peter.

Peter shook it and offered a handsome grin that made Grete blush with pride. "Peter."

"Grete and I work together," Rose said, "on the home front." She lifted her chin and smiled, seeming to expect a reciprocal explanation, but Grete had become as withdrawn as Peter was earlier.

"Really?" Peter looked at Grete as if she were the one with a cache of secrets. Grete flushed as it dawned on her that he was not entirely wrong. "What do you do?" he asked Rose.

Rose leaned toward him. "We're spies." She winked. "You know, like Mata Hari."

"Funny," Grete said. Was Mata Hari a double-agent? Grete was pretty sure she had been shot by a firing squad. "Rose and I volunteer together at a salvage depot," she clarified, "cutting up old rubber."

"We destroy top secret brassieres and classified girdles." Rose held a finger to her lips. "It's all very hush-hush."

"That's the opposite of lending support," Peter joked. His eyes alight with mischief.

Rose laughed and Grete marveled at his sangfroid.

Across the street, a group of "Star and Garter" chorus girls had set up a booth on which caricatures of Hitler, Mussolini, and Hirohito were mounted. "Records for our fighting men!" a platinum blonde called as three others invited people to hurl disks into the Axis leaders' gaping mouths. "Open your trap, Jap!" a man shouted, knocking a bucktooth loose as he tossed a phonograph record at Hirohito.

"Are you going in?" Rose asked. "My brother saw it last night and said Conrad Veidt is terrific. He plays twins. One is a loyal American, the other . . ." She lifted a delicately arched eyebrow and lowered her voice, "an evil Nazi."

"Sounds interesting," Peter said.

"I thought your brother was younger," Grete said. It occurred to her that she was now suspicious of everyone.

Rose's mouth twisted as she considered Grete. "I have two. The older one is the critic, and a Freudian to boot. He says Veidt's twins represent the conflict so many Germans feel about their homeland. You're German, Grete. What do you think?"

"I'm American," Grete said. "I haven't an ounce of sympathy for the Germans." She felt Peter tense beside her.

"Yes, of course," Rose apologized. She studied Peter. "How about you, Peter?"

"I'll let Grete decide what we see," he said.

Grete caught his eye. It was difficult to know whether he had intentionally misunderstood or was simply baffled by Rose's chatter.

"*This is the Army* with Ronald Reagan is playing a few blocks down. It's very romantic," Rose was saying. "There's also *The Invaders* with Laurence Olivier and Leslie Howard which I haven't seen but heard is top-notch."

"No," Grete snapped more harshly than she intended. She had already seen the movie about a German U-boat sunk by Canadian bombers that leaves six crewmen stranded on enemy territory. Watching the film, she hadn't been all that interested in the military plot. But that was before she met Peter. She shuddered, recalling the U-boat surfacing in icy Canadian waters. "We were thinking about something lighter," she said, steadying her voice.

"*Yankee Doodle Dandy*?" Rose suggested. "Jimmy Cagney isn't much of a singer, but boy can he dance! I see too many movies," she tittered. "Ma says it's a waste of time and money, but I love them. Everything always turns out okay in the movies."

Grete nodded, surprised again by how much she genuinely liked Rose.

"Don't blow my cover," Rose said with a conspiratorial wink. "Promise not to mention you saw me here."

"What?" Grete asked, eyes widening. On the lookout for Agent Lanman, she had seen no sign of him.

"On Friday. When you come for Shabbos." Rose put her hands on her hips. "Remember?"

"Oh—of course," Grete said, fanning herself. "The heat's made me scatterbrained."

"You ran off the other day before I could give you my address."

Rose pulled pen and paper from her purse and jotted something down. "Here." She passed the slip to Grete. "Take the Westchester Avenue El to Elder Avenue and walk down the hill to Wheeler. We're at 1175. You can meet both my brothers!" Rose's smile faded. "The older one has been called up and will only be home a few more weeks."

Grete blanched. Peter looked as young and fit as all the GIs in uniform. She thought to make some excuse, flat feet or asthma, but could not muster such a bold-faced lie. "I didn't know that. I wouldn't want to intrude."

"It's no intrusion," Rose said. "At times like this it's better to be with friends. Peter, you should come too."

"That's very kind." Peter's voice quivered. "I hope I can be there." He turned away, but not before Grete saw a flicker of regret in his eyes.

CHAPTER 13

PETER WAS WHISTLING "OVER THERE," his steps falling in time, as he and Grete entered Grand Central. The tune did not sound nearly as upbeat as it had during *Yankee Doodle Dandy*.

Grete had imagined that the movie would be a good way to pass a few hours, but by the time the troops were marching in front of the White House, she realized it was far more than a sentimental distraction. It was the most patriotic display she had ever witnessed. In one scene, a newborn clasped the flag on the Fourth of July. In another, Negro sharecroppers sang the "Battle Hymn of the Republic" in front of the Lincoln Memorial. And then there were the headlines stretched across the screen in ten-foot letters: SUB SINKS LUSITANIA, WAR IS DECLARED! The theatre was packed with troops whooping and applauding. When the soldiers on screen began singing "Over There," the crowd sang along in a collective, teary-eyed, baritone.

> Send the word, send the word over there—
> That the Yanks are coming. The Yanks are coming . . .
> And we won't come back till it's over
> Over there.

Grete sank into her seat, the velvet scratchy, not comforting. Peter was stock still beside her. *Nazi Agent* might have been easier to bear.

"What a hoot," he said afterwards.

"Hoot?" she asked, thinking that he, or she, misunderstood the meaning.

"George thinks he's going to school Americans on propaganda, but no one's better at it than Hollywood. What a load of sentimental slush!"

"I suppose," Grete said, feeling deflated. They walked the next few blocks, Grete trailing slightly behind, silently seething. She had fallen for it all: Roosevelt's weekly chats, the endless flags, victory gardens, and pins. She considered the barrage of swastikas and slogans Germans faced daily. Schoolchildren were taught with anti-Jewish primers. She had seen one called *Der Giftpilz*, *The Poisonous Mushroom*, which accused Jews of kidnapping Christian children to use their blood in matzos. Older students were required to join the Hitler Youth or the League of German Girls. With some shame, Grete could recall envying the girls' smart scouting uniforms and badges. The *Volksempfänger*, an affordable radio, only played approved broadcasts and folk music. Small wonder most Germans had become indoctrinated. Those who were not interested in ostracizing Jews simply because they were Jewish changed colors as food grew scarce and they were promised sustenance in exchange for compliance. The Nazis had created a culture of wickedness and desperate people fell under its spell. Some were gullible; others greedy or cruel.

After Kristallnacht, Mama had asked the widow downstairs with the parrot to store some of their most cherished possessions for safekeeping. When Grete was leaving for New York, she had knocked on the widow's door, hoping to recover a small etching of a mother and daughter with sentimental value. "I don't have it," the widow had said. The door was cracked open just far enough for Grete to see the etching hanging on the wall inside.

GRAND CENTRAL WAS AUSTERE AFTER THE RAUCOUSNESS of Times Square. Instead of rowdy GIs, there were only solemn ones. Grete searched shoe shine chairs and newsstands for FBI agents and found any number of men who could fit the bill. The idea that the

FBI was protecting the nation's safety should have been reassuring. But her footsteps were heavy and her conscience was low; she was leading Peter into a terrible trap.

"Dick said he'd be downstairs by the Oyster Bar," Peter said. He directed her to the center of the concourse next to the information booth. "Wait here. Henry's probably tight and won't recognize you, but Dick might."

"Peter," Grete began. Anyone could be watching and she did not know how to warn him. "Be careful." Peter reached forward to stroke her cheek, and then he was gone.

Grete looked up at the opal clock. It was nearly seven. She would have to invent yet another excuse for her poor uncle. There was a steady stream to and from the USO lounge. The sound of piano and ping-pong drifted downstairs. Lonely, pensive looking GIs sat on the stairs. The more disheveled ones leaned against the marble banister. Others were hugging their loved ones. Grete assumed they were saying goodbye; for some, a final goodbye. A dozen men stood in a circle, hands clasped and heads lowered as a preacher led them in prayer. There were more troops than there had been on Sunday night, and more security. Guards stood at attention in the corners of the hall. Her eyes darted back up to the clock. She could have sworn it had been seven, now it was a minute to. Popcorn growled in her belly. Peter was meeting Dick and Henry downstairs, discussing who knows what. She looked up the entrance ramps then down the stairs toward the tracks. Dick and Henry were there, so were the power convertors and Track 61. She swallowed her fear. She had told Lanman she would stay with Peter and could not be lax at this critical moment.

Before she knew it, she was on the lower level. Several doors along the wall were open through which she could see ramps leading down to the tracks. Numbers above the doors were listed in pairs: 14-16, 24-26. The numbers climbed to 42, no 61. There was a distant sputter and a gust of fetid air as an engine came to life. Grete proceeded carefully. She had become quite adept at blending into the crowd. Her pace slowed as she approached the

Oyster Bar

Uncle Jacques had taken her to dine at the vaulted underground restaurant when he had introduced her to New York three years earlier. Jacques had been visibly delighted as trains rumbled into nearby tunnels and their table vibrated, calling the meal a *quintessential* New York experience. Grete had never eaten an oyster. She could not stomach the slimy mollusk, but her uncle had been so pleased to be there that she had been content too, her whirling brain silent for once. After dinner, and a fat slice of chocolate cake that made up for the meal, Uncle Jacques had led her outside the restaurant doors, positioned her in a corner, facing the wall, and told her to wait.

"For what?" she called as he strode toward the opposite corner. In response, he had waved over his shoulder, urging patience.

All at once she heard a soft voice that seemed to radiate from the corner beside her. "*Kindela?*" Grete's heart thrummed; *kindela* was Papa's pet name for her. If she closed her eyes, it was as if Papa were murmuring into her ear, *kindela, kindela*. She rested her hand on the wall and kept her head turned, hiding her sadness, as Uncle Jacques returned, explaining the angles and curves that made the Whispering Walls possible. Her uncle tried so hard to please her, but especially in those early days, his efforts had only made her more homesick.

NOW SHE EYED THE ARCHWAY OUTSIDE THE OYSTER BAR, on alert for Peter, Dick, and Henry. It was dinnertime and the place was bustling. A handful of children were racing from corner to corner, testing the famous Whispering Walls. The principle seemed lost on them as they pressed their mouths against the cold stone and shouted, "Can you hear me?!"

Grete saw Peter and the others exactly where Peter said they would be. Huddled together, the men ignored the ruckus. She slipped behind a pillar. The acoustics allowed her to hear their conversation with surprising clarity.

"I had a hunch all along George would give us up and now he's disappeared," Dick seethed. "How are we supposed to . . ." The children's cries obscured his words.

Grete recognized Peter's slow, deliberate manner. It was the one he employed when trying to be most convincing. "George is making important connections on behalf of the group. His orders are to do nothing until he returns."

"Where'd George go?" Henry asked, his voice as loud and innocent as the children playing beside him.

"New Jersey. There's a priest there . . ." Peter's explanation was drowned out by the children's laughter. Henry began pacing, stumbling over the giggling children who were growing louder and more rambunctious, their mothers shouting over them.

Dick's angry words were easy to hear. "Who put you in charge?" he asked. "I don't have any more confidence in you than I did him. Everyone knows you were in a camp."

The reference to a camp made Grete grow stiff. She looked over her shoulder, wondering if anyone else had overheard. No one seemed bothered. She sidled closer to hear Peter's response.

"The Gestapo and Germany aren't the same thing," he said.

"Tell that to the FBI," Dick scoffed. "Or . . ." Grete read his lips: "Hitler."

A group of soldiers exited the restaurant, talking loudly, stumbling, and clasping each other on the shoulder. Grete could no longer hear the men, but Dick's sour expression was clear enough. He pointed toward the luggage office. Peter raised his hands in protest. Grete snapped back behind the pillar as Dick took off with Henry in tow. They thundered past her without a second glance. She steadied her nerves before peering out again. Peter had caught up and put a restraining hand on Dick's shoulder. Dick shrugged him off and argued while Peter kept still, seeming to listen. His shoulders sagged as Dick broke into a smirk. Her heart began to race again as the trio stormed toward the luggage office. She knew the bag of sand was gone. She couldn't say how Dick would react.

Grete recognized the attendant, Ophelia, behind the counter.

Dick waited, increasingly impatient, while Peter made a show of checking his wallet, patting his pockets and turning them inside out before seeming to admit he had lost the claim check ticket. Dick's face flushed angry red. Turning his back to Peter, he addressed Ophelia directly, indicating shape and size of the bag with his hands. She nodded in recognition and looked at the cubbies then back toward the men, shaking her head. She held up her hand to roughly Grete's height and motioned by her ears, wavy hair.

Grete shrank farther back. The moments stretched interminably as she deliberated. Footsteps approached and she braced for confrontation. The steps grew closer, pounding harder. She scrambled for an excuse, her mind frantically blank. She should never have come downstairs. She should not be with Peter at all. A child ran past her, stumbled and fell, and she thoughtlessly reached out to help him to his feet. His mother rushed over to thank Grete and pacify the boy. When Grete looked up, she met Henry's eye. His gaze seemed shy and apologetic. While the others argued, he tilted his head as if trying to place her. It took all her willpower to turn calmly and walk away. At the bottom of the stairs, she glanced back. The men were gone. Her eyes shot to the open track doors and she was gripped with fresh terror. Even if Dick did not have a bag of sand, there were plenty of means of destruction. Her eyes scanned the concourse for Agent Lanman or a security guard.

She made her way up to the Great Hall, debating what to do, and was on the verge of approaching a guard when someone snatched her by the arm and wheeled her around. Peter's features were contorted and angry. Was his anger directed at her? Did Dick know Lanman had spoken with her? Had he told Peter?

"What is it? What happened?" She looked past him for Dick, Henry, or Lanman.

"There's no talking sense into Dick," Peter fumed. He marched through the Great Hall. Grete took one last look for Lanman then followed. Peter walked so furiously she found it difficult to keep up. He strode up a ramp and out onto the street as if he were try-ing to shake her. Blocks passed before she thought to ask where they were going.

MORE THAN MODESTY WAS AT STAKE, Grete reminded herself as she questioned the wisdom of going to Peter's hotel room. The pomp-ous clerk with the mustache was on duty, overseeing his tiniest of fiefdoms. He snickered as Peter collected his room key. She felt his eyes follow her as they crossed the lobby to the elevator. Upstairs, her concern about propriety was replaced by apprehension. Peter was distracted and fumbled with the lock. The key turned and he touched her arm, alerting her to danger. He pushed the door open and reached inside to flick a light switch.

"Stay here."

Grete peered inside. The room was bathed in waxy light. The closet door was open. Peter walked cautiously toward it. Motioning at her to stay back, he flung it open so that the flimsy door bounced on its hinges.

"What is it?" she asked. Hangers clanged as Peter rummaged through.

"The maid must have let George in," he said glumly. "His stuff's here." He pushed a suit aside, releasing the stench of stale ciga-rettes. Peter stooped and retrieved the Gladstone bag, setting it down at the foot of the bed and raking inside. She knew without him saying a word that the money was gone.

Grete searched for something encouraging to say. The room was cramped and ugly. Her fear abated and her sympathy for Peter returned as she imagined him laying his head down on the vis-ibly lumpy pillow. The bedspread was a putrid shade of green, the carpet topped with balls of lint as if someone had vacuumed too hard in an attempt to mask stains. The shabby hotel room clari-fied Peter's reliance on her, which she had sensed since their first meeting. She could not guarantee George would be true to his word nor could she shield Peter from deceit or danger. All she could do was provide a dose of sorely needed companionship. She went to the window, pulling back the dusty curtains to see the view Peter had spoken of, and saw rooftops and water towers and, off in the distance, a barely recognizable glimpse of the Chrysler's needle. She turned back to see Peter staring at an envelope with the Governor Clinton Hotel crest printed in the corner. The white envelope stood out against the dark wood of the desk. Peter picked it up between thumb and forefinger as if it were toxic then ripped it open and pulled out the letter. His eyes grazed the page before he collapsed at the foot of the bed, head in hands.

"George is on his way to Washington." He did not sound as relieved as Grete would have expected.

"Good!" She forced her voice to convey a sense of optimism she did not feel. She could only hope George would confess to the FBI and that he would clear both himself and Peter. She waited for Peter to tell her what had happened at Grand Central. She had assumed he brought her to his room so that they could talk privately. But now that they were here, he was distant and distracted. "What did Dick say?" Goosebumps prickled her arms as she braced herself for the answer.

"Dick said he was done waiting for George. He wanted to find the subbasement where the convertors are stored and destroy them."

"Did you?"

Peter shook his head. "There are miles of tracks down there and the subbasement is ten stories underground. Dick thinks the basement with the power convertors is near Track 61, which is under the Waldorf. He had a compass so we tried to walk toward the northernmost tracks."

"Were there guards?" *Was the FBI lying in wait?*

"It was pitch-black and we didn't see anyone." Bed springs squeaked as Peter shifted his weight. "The police are already guarding highways, bridges, and defense factories. Their manpower is stretched thin."

"So what made you turn back?"

"I told Dick there was no point moving forward and risking detection if we didn't have the means to destroy the convertors."

"The sand," she said, secretly proud that she had managed to forestall one disaster. She resisted the urge to smile.

Peter sighed. "I can't take much more of this."

Grete dropped down on the bed beside him. She put a hand on his shoulder and felt him tremble. "You're exhausted." She remembered how peacefully he had slept on the train to Amagansett. "Let me stay here while you rest."

Peter squeezed his eyes shut. "I couldn't sleep if I wanted to."

Grete pulled her legs up onto the bed, laid her head back on a pillow, and patted the mattress. She told herself she was being kind, not simply staying with Peter because Lanman had threatened her. She would wait for Peter to drift off and then sneak out. George had promised to be in Washington tomorrow. She prayed he would keep his word, go to the FBI, and confess.

Peter stretched out beside her. She felt his body soften. He rested his hand over hers. "I'm sorry for involving you in this. I never should have spoken to you at the parade."

Grete stared up at the ceiling. In her heart, she did not regret the last week. Peter had changed her in a fundamental way, allowing her to understand that people were not necessarily good or bad. Most were victims of circumstance. More importantly, he had shown her that she was still capable of emotions.

"Peter," she said, on the verge of confessing. The mattress creaked as he turned toward her. Her thoughts whirled. She had a vision of her family reuniting one day. She could not risk that. "You didn't involve me. I chose to help." It was important he understood that. She propped her head on the crook of his arm and curled closer. Fatigue settled over her. She yawned. Peter's lips brushed her forehead. It was not at all like the kiss on the beach, which had sizzled with passion born of desperation. This was tender and brotherly. Peter was saying goodbye.

CHAPTER 14

GRETE WOKE TO THE SOUND OF running water. Someone was humming in the shower . . . *And we won't come back till it's over . . . Over there.* Peter's slightly off-pitch voice made her tingle with warmth. Her sleepy mind lumbered and she yawned into the pillow. Consciousness came slowly. Her nose wrinkled at the stale hotel room smell. An itchy bedspread tickled the tips of her toes. Her eyes fluttered open. Light filtered through a gap in the curtains. *Sunlight.* She bolted upright. It was morning. Her uncle would be frantic if he discovered she had not slept at home. She sprang out of bed and snapped up the telephone, furiously dialing.

Jacques picked up on the first ring. "Where are you?" His tone shifted from fear to relief to anger.

"I'm so sorry. I'm at my friend . . . Rose's. I must have dozed off and slept right through the night."

"Rose?"

"She works with me at the salvage depot. I'm sorry," she said again before deciding she should stop talking. She wondered how many white lies one could tell before white turned to gray.

Moments stretched as Jacques seemed to accept her explanation. "Thank God you're safe. Your parents would never forgive me if something happened to you." Tears filled her eyes as she mumbled another guilt-ridden apology. "I'll see you tonight at dinner," Jacques said as firm as she had ever heard him.

Grete set the phone down. She was lying to Jacques, lying to

Peter. And she had a sinking sense she was also lying to herself. Her eyes fell on the letter Peter had left open on the desk.

> *My Dear Friend Pete,*
> *Sorry for not having been able to see you before I left. I have gone to Washington to finish what we started. I'm leaving you, believing that you will take good care of yourself and the other boys. Rest assured I shall try to straighten every-thing out to the very best. My bag and clothes I put into your room. Your hotel bill is paid by me, including this day. If anything extraordinary should happen, I'll get in touch with you directly. Until later, I'm your sincere friend, George.*

Grete latched onto the vague words *straighten everything out* and recalled Peter telling her that the salutation *My Dear Friend* meant the situation was under control. She took a harder look, admiring George's looping script. It was nothing like the spiky scrawl she had seen in the diagram of Track 61.

Someone rapped on the door. It started to rattle and shake until Grete thought it would splinter. The door flew open. Dick's eyes lit on Grete. He was on her in an instant, backing her toward the bed. His nose looked even more bent and fleshy from this close angle. His nostrils flared. Henry followed on Dick's heels. He slammed the door closed with a bang that made all three of them jump.

"Where's Pete?" Dick demanded.

Grete considered how to slip past him. Her shoes were at the end of the bed, but she would happily forego them to get out. Henry blocked the door, arms folded, awaiting orders.

Dick listened to the trickle of running water. "Pete in the shower?" He looked her up and down. "You must have worn him out." Before Grete had time to be offended, he grabbed George's Gladstone bag and began rummaging through. He pulled out the lining, shook it, and slammed the bottom as though he could force it to cough up the missing money. Grains of sand sprinkled to the bed. *"Wo ist das Geld?"* he cursed under his breath.

Grete had a vision of George traveling to Washington on a packed train with $80,000 stuffed in a paper bag, on the lookout for an SS man or an everyday thief.

Dick's attention shot to the desk. He dropped the Gladstone and snatched up George's letter. Quickly glancing down the page, he frowned and handed it to Henry. Henry held the letter too close to his face, his lips moving in a way that made Grete think he could not read English.

The sound of running water dwindled to a steady drip as Peter turned off the taps.

"Hungry?" he called. "Should we get breakfast?"

Dick held a finger to his mouth, cautioning Grete.

"Grete?"

Dick nodded, indicating she should answer.

"Ich bin am Verhungern," she said. The German scorched her lips, but she was sure Peter would understand why she used it.

The bathroom door sprang open and Peter leapt out from a cloud of steam. He raised his fists and took in the scene: Dick uncomfortably close to Grete, Henry by the door, letter in hand. There was a smudge of shaving cream on his jaw, beyond that he was naked except for a towel with the name Governor Clinton Hotel running from hip to thigh. Beads of water glistened on his shoulders. His chest heaved as he stormed toward Dick.

"How dare you barge in here!"

"Wo ist George?" Dick demanded. Between the humidity and tension, the room felt suffocating. Sweat gathered on Dick's brow. Henry loosened his tie and Grete could see a dark stain ringing his collar.

"Keep your voice down," Peter cautioned, "And speak English like Kappe told us to."

"Since when do you listen to Kappe?" Dick's English was halting and heavily accented, but he was using it, which seemed like a good sign.

"Let her go and we'll talk."

Dick laughed meanly. "You've had plenty of time to talk and you haven't given a single straight answer." His eyes roved over Grete, making her cringe. "Maybe she'll be more cooperative."

"She's just a girl," Peter said. "She doesn't know anything."

Grete wanted to believe that Peter was bluffing to protect her, but he sounded almost too convincing. His face gave nothing away. Either he was telling the truth or he was an accomplished liar. She realized, with sinking clarity, that both could be true.

Dick and Henry exchanged looks as Dick took another step toward her. Grete stumbled backward and dropped onto the edge of the flimsy mattress. Dick edged closer until all she could see was his stomach and belt.

She looked around for something to grab. A lamp was within reach.

Peter shoved Dick away, his voice slow and precise. "Take a seat and calm down." He nodded toward the chair. "I'm going to get dressed and we'll go downstairs and discuss this."

"I'm not going anywhere with you." Dick brushed his shoulder where Peter had touched it. There was a radio on the desk and he turned it on. Big band blared incongruously through the room. Dick dragged the desk chair between the bed where Grete sat and the doorway where Henry was fidgeting. "We are going to have this out here and now." He sat down.

Peter sighed in resignation. He bent over and picked up Grete's shoes, passing them to her and letting his fingers brush hers. That, at least, felt reassuring. Grete slipped the shoes on while Peter pulled clothing from the bureau. "Let me get dressed." He stepped into the bathroom, leaving the door open so that Grete could see his face in the steam-streaked mirror. She tried to catch his eye, but his features remained indistinct. A trumpet boomed from the cheap radio.

"Where is the money?" Dick asked again.

"What money?" she said.

"Did George Dasch run off?"

She offered a bland smile. "I know a George Davis. Is that who you mean?"

Dick's brow knit together in an angry line. "*Ja*. Him."

Peter reappeared barefoot in beltless trousers and a white undershirt. Wet hair fell across his forehead and his eyes blazed with anger. "I told you, she doesn't know anything. Let her go," he said again. "Then we'll talk."

"She's been glued to your side for a week. She must have heard something."

His words hit like a slap. Dick had been aware of her all along. He was a spy, after all. It was naïve to think she had been incognito. She had been frightened when Peter told her about the SS man, petrified when Agent Lanman suggested deporting her to Germany, but she had never considered what Dick or Henry might do to her. The room seemed to shrink around her yet the door seemed farther away than ever. She counted the steps—six, seven? She could reach for the lamp, toss it at Dick, and spring past him, but Henry was guarding the door. She wasn't sure how she'd get by him.

"We've been going around town," Peter said with a shrug. "Enjoying ourselves. George was busy and . . ." He steadfastly ignored Grete. "I was lonely." Grete tensed, troubled by his callous tone. She could hear the truth in his voice: Peter was lonely and she was a distraction. Nothing more.

Henry perked up. "Dick and I went to the Swing Club last night. You should have been there Pete. The girls were so pretty." He met Grete's eye and blushed.

Dick glared at Peter. "I never trusted you and I've got no confidence in George. Where is he?"

"I told you, he went to Washington to meet a contact."

"You said he went to New Jersey."

"That's what I thought until I got his letter."

Dick pressed his fingers into a steeple. "When'd it come?"

"It was here when I got back yesterday. George must have got in because his clothes were here too, and the bag." He nodded toward the empty Gladstone, the sight of which seemed to newly infuriate Dick.

The phone rang, the shrill noise piercing the room. No one moved.

"Pick it up," Dick said.

Peter answered. There was a brief pause while he listened. "No. 1421." He hung up.

Dick sat taller. "What was that about?"

"Wrong room."

"You sure it wasn't *Herr Strich*?"

Peter offered a tight smile. "George would never be so brief."

"If it wasn't him, then it was someone checking up on us."

The smile vanished from Peter's face as he turned back to the phone.

"Who was it?" Henry asked, always a step behind the others. His gaze bounced from Dick to Peter. Grete felt a pang of sympathy. Henry had a child's mind in a man's body.

"Kappe or the FBI," Dick said. "J. Edgar Hoover could be listening in the room next door for all I know." Silence infiltrated the room. Henry lifted his chin as if he might be able to hear Hoover and his team of G-men on the other side of the flimsy wall. Grete eyed the door, hopeful Agent Lanman would spring inside and rescue her.

"With Hoover's men after us," Henry whispered loudly, "we'll wind up like Dillinger."

"Kappe's here?" Peter said. His voice lost its usual steadiness. He sounded more afraid of Kappe than Hoover.

"Could be. No one tells me nothing," Dick said with obvious resentment. "All I know is I intend to follow orders. Anyone who squeals has got to be removed." He cracked his knuckles, sizing Peter up. Grete shrank back.

Henry picked up on the threat, reciting words like a pledge. "And anyone who kills another of the boys because he squeals doesn't have to be afraid because he'll be treated like a hero."

"*Halt die Klappe*," Dick snarled. Henry was instantly quiet. Dick turned back to Peter. "If George really is in Washington, what's he doing there?" He pointed at the letter in Henry's hand.

"What's he mean by 'finishing what you started.'"

"Do you really want me to answer that in front of her?" Peter asked. He was still going out of his way to avoid looking at Grete.

"I'll decide what to do about her later," Dick said.

Grete stiffened. Dick seemed like a man without scruples. From what Peter had said, he had been eager to kill the Coast Guardsman on the beach. She watched as Peter dug his fingernails into his pant leg. As furious as he seemed, he seemed equally determined to keep the focus off of her. "Who can understand George?" he said. "I suppose he means finish the operation."

"Yeah? And what about this—" Dick snatched the letter from Henry and waved it in front of Peter. "'Straighten everything out?' What's there to straighten out and who's he straightening it out with?"

Calmly yet somehow seeming in control, Peter turned to Henry. "Come on, Henry, why are we standing around here? Open the door and the three of us can go get something to eat."

"Let's go, Dick," Henry griped. "I'm hungry."

"We're going," Dick assured him. "But there's a couple things to straighten out here first."

Peter went to the nightstand and pulled a manila envelope from its drawer. There were food stains on the corner and Grete recognized it as the same one he had tried to give to Hannelore and Robert. It seemed like ages ago since they had dined with Peter's sister.

Peter removed a fistful of bills. "You and Henry take what's here and get away. Go to Argentina or Chile while there's still time." He sounded sincere and Grete understood that he was urging them to flee before George could give them up. He thrust the money forward. "Take my share and let her go." Grete choked back tears of guilt and fear. Lanman knew about her. Dick had known all along. It seemed the only one she had been fooling was herself.

Dick pocketed the money without letting Grete go. "You're a military man, Pete. You know I can't just run. What kind of soldier would that make me?" The question sounded almost rhetorical.

"Like it or not, I got to see this thing through."

"You don't owe them anything!" Peter exclaimed, suddenly unable to disguise his true feelings. "Kappe doesn't give a damn about us. If we're caught they'll just send another bunch of chumps."

Dick pulled his chair forward and sat down, knee to knee with Grete. She felt the heat of his breath and smelled his sourness. "Tell me what George is doing in Washington." Grete looked past Dick toward Peter. Deceiving him to help her parents was one thing. She would not betray him to Dick. Dick's tone grew more pointed. "Pete and you had plenty of time to get acquainted, huh? Did he tell you he was in prison?" She raised her chin, confident she knew Peter at least as well as Dick. "Back in the *Vaterland,* he picked the wrong team." Dick turned to Peter. "But you learned from your mistakes, didn't you, Pete? It's better to play both sides. If the Gestapo catch up with George, you're with us and if he gets away, you had his back all along."

A vein in Peter's neck bulged and for an instant Grete thought he might give in to Dick's goading. Her knees trembled. Some of what Dick was saying rang true. How many times had she encouraged Peter to go to the FBI on his own? With sickening clarity, she saw that he could have let George go to Washington to protect himself. If George succeeded, he was safe—and if the plan fell through, he could claim George acted on his own.

"No one blames you for looking out for yourself," Dick said evenly, turning back to Grete. "Pete tell you how he joined the storm troopers back when that fairy Röhm was Hitler's right-hand man. You met the Fuehrer, didn't you, Pete? Shook his hand?"

"What?" she burst out. Her fingers tightened on the bedspread as she recalled the times Peter had taken her hand in his and the dizzying effect it had had on her. She rubbed her palms on her thighs as if to remove the taint.

Dick beamed with satisfaction. "Ah—didn't tell your Jewess that, did you?"

Outrage stoked her courage. "I don't know what's going on

here," Grete said, working hard to steady her voice. "Why are you wasting your time with me? If I were you, I would be more concerned about what your so-called leader is doing in Washington."

Peter gave her a straight warning stare, which she returned with an angry scowl. She no longer had the slightest regret about speaking with Agent Lanman.

Dick clenched his fists. "We're getting there. For now, I want to make sure you know all about our friend Pete so you're perfectly clear who you're in bed with." He laughed at his pun. "Did Pete tell you how he managed to escape when Hitler murdered Röhm and his men?" Dick looked over his shoulder. "You're a lucky fellow, Pete. Resourceful."

Grete remembered George saying the same thing about Peter. She had always considered resourcefulness an admirable quality, but in Dick's mouth it sounded slick, resourceful at someone else's expense. Had Peter used her as a decoy? Her thoughts grew barbed. It wasn't resourceful to use other people; it was cunning. Some would say ruthless.

"Grete." Peter looked at her for the first time since the men had come barging in. "I told you all this. I was fighting communists."

"Judeo–Bolshevism," Dick swore, glaring at Grete with undisguised disgust.

"Grete," Peter said again, "I hate Hitler every bit as much as you do. All I wanted was a way out so my family wouldn't suffer."

It was reassuring to hear Peter confess his hatred for Hitler openly in front of the others. But she still felt uneasy. She strained to remember what he had told her earlier. Just as she had brushed aside the mention of fuses and timing devices, she had willfully disregarded Peter's ever-evolving story. She had become so accustomed to not thinking about her past in Germany or a future without her parents, she had focused solely on the moment they were in. Peter had listened to her as if she had something valuable to contribute, and he had held her as if she were precious. Now she questioned both his behavior and her feelings for him. Shame coursed through her. But she wouldn't give Dick the satisfaction of admitting it in front of him.

"Convenient, huh?" Dick sneered. "Pete's got an excuse for everything. He makes it sound like it was dumb luck he stumbled on this means of escape. But Kappe knows what he's doing. He picked Pete because Pete's a soldier with an inside knowledge of how things work. Not too many men can say they lived through Hitler's purge and a Gestapo prison. Pete's a survivor. He knows how to navigate danger."

"Kappe picked me because he had something to hold over me," Peter spat. "My choice was to join you misfits or get sent back to a concentration camp. My entire family was threatened."

"*Ja.*" Dick nodded too enthusiastically. "We heard about that." His eyes fixed on Grete, the corners of his lips curled up into a smirk. "Pushed your poor wife right over the edge, didn't it, Pete?"

Grete's head snapped toward Peter, whose ashen face left no room for doubt. Peter was married.

"*Rede nicht* über *meine Frau!*" Peter sprang at Dick and lifted him out of his chair.

His words blared like a bullhorn blasting in Grete's ear: *Meine Frau!*

Dick kicked free. "I heard she had some kind of breakdown."

Peter lunged again. There was a thud as Dick slammed into the wall. Dick touched the back of his head then looked down at his hand in disbelief. His fingers were sticky with plaster and blood.

Henry rushed toward him. "Dick! You're bleeding!" He rummaged in his pocket and pulled out a handkerchief, holding it out for Dick. Grete watched as a scrap of paper fluttered to the floor.

Dick plunged forward, fists raised, but Peter gripped him by the collar and shoved him back. *Thwack*, the wall split and plaster rained down. Dick covered his head but Peter kept punching with slow, sharp blows. Henry peeled Peter off Dick and drove his fist into his stomach. Peter doubled over, gasping. Henry took another—harder—swing. Peter ducked and punched. Dick charged, and the three fell wrestling to the floor. The bedside table wobbled and the lamp crashed down. The room spun. Grete found her footing. Her eyes lit on the paper that had fallen from Henry's pocket. She could make out the number 61, which was enough to make her snatch it up. Then her hand was on the doorknob. She flung the door open and ran.

CHAPTER 15

MERCIFULLY, THE APARTMENT WAS EMPTY when Grete got back
from Peter's hotel. Vagabond greeted her in his usual languid
way. Jacques had left a note in their spot by the phone, explaining
that he had gone to work and expected to see her at dinner. Grete
did not want to think about the worry she had caused him. She
bolted the door and went straight to her bedroom, locking that
door as well. Vagabond watched, tail twitching, as she opened the
steamer trunk. The shell Peter had given her in Amagansett was
carefully rolled inside the handkerchief he had sent with the invisible ink. George's ragged ten-cent notebook was there, too. She
was debating whether the stash would protect her, or make her
more vulnerable, when Vagabond leapt into the open trunk, scattering everything across the floor.

Decision made.

She retrieved Jacques's lighter from his humidor and brought
the incriminating evidence to the bathroom, intending to burn
everything and flush it down the toilet. As she unfolded the handkerchief, the shell fell to the floor. She got on her knees to look
behind the sink and found only jagged remains. She picked up each
piece, memorizing the swirls of color, before tipping them into the
basin and turning the tap on all the way. The shell was gone in an
instant, washed into sewage pipes then dumped back into the sea.
If only it were as easy to forget Peter. She reached for the handkerchief and dangled it over the toilet. When she struck the lighter,
the fabric ignited in an ammonia-fueled whoosh that stopped just

short of scorching her. She dropped it into the toilet where it simmered, staining the bowl in dark soot. Shaken, she turned to the
notebook, paging through descriptions and sketches. Peter had
said it was important evidence and she couldn't quite bring herself
to destroy it. She found the diagram of Track 61 folded inside.

The spiky handwriting and the number 61 sent her mind reeling back to the violent encounter in Peter's hotel room and the
paper she had scooped from the floor while fleeing. Back in her
bedroom, she turned her purse upside down. Out fell her keys,
wallet, and loose coins. She shook harder and the torn slip feath-
ered to the bed. The paper was discolored and deeply creased, as
if it, too, had been tucked away for some time. She flattened it out
and laid the diagram of Track 61 beside it, confirming what she
had already guessed. The handwriting matched. Henry or, more
likely, Dick, had drawn the diagram. George must have filched
it to add to his stockpile of evidence against them. Grete looked
from one page to the other. The tattered slip was a fraction of the
size of the original diagram and contained no words, only the
number 61 and a mysterious sequence: 1961900.

She sank to the bed, adding, subtracting, and shuffling 1961900
until her eyes watered. She assumed the number 61 referred to
Track 61, but could not make heads or tails of anything else.
Frustrated, she flopped back onto her pillow and her thoughts
roamed to the previous night, Peter's tender kiss, and Dick's tirade.
Peter was married. She shook with anger and embarrassment,
though she was not sure either emotion was warranted. Peter
hadn't exactly lied. She had deluded herself, acting impulsively
and convincing herself she was being useful, aiding a righteous
fight. When doubts crept in, she had brushed them aside. She had
fled before she could fully grasp what it meant that Peter was married, and did not know if he had divorced. The more she thought
about it, the more she understood Peter's reticence. He was facing
obstacles far more pressing than romance. She pushed the papers
away then, thinking better of it, refolded them and pressed them
inside George's book. Remembering Peter's reprimand, she put

the book in her purse. Better to keep everything close. Exhausted, she closed her eyes. Eventually, she heard a key in the front door. Uncle Jacques called her name and she rose to greet him.

"What do you say we go out to eat tonight," Jacques said. Grete detected a note of false enthusiasm as if he were the one who owed her an apology.

"That would be nice," she agreed too readily. "I'm so sorry about last night. I fell asleep and it was morning before I knew it."

"How about we go down to the Automat?" he suggested. "I know it's your favorite."

"What?" She stammered. "No."

Jacques forehead creased with concern. "Are you feeling all right? You look pale. Look, Gretel, I know how hard it's been being separated from your parents. I'm no substitution for them, and I spend too much time at work."

"No," she protested. Hearing Jacques apologize for her transgressions was unbearable. "You've been wonderful." She brushed away tears.

"Come sit with me a minute," he said, going to the sofa and patting the cushion by his side. Even that seemed conciliatory. It was the first time she had seen him seated anywhere in the living room other than his favorite chair. She sat down beside him. "I've left you on your own too much," Jacques said. "I should spend more time with you and talk more." She tried not to think about the hours she had passed with Peter and the lies she had told her uncle. "I just didn't want to get your hopes up."

"About what?" She was immediately alert. "What happened?"

Jacques shook his head in disbelief. "After months of badgering State Department officials, someone finally called my name. I met with a man who was familiar with the fate of Jews from Mannheim. It seems most were deported to the same French camp. This man believes your parents are probably still there, which is good. I gave him the names and addresses of our relatives in France who may be able to petition on their behalf and he said he would contact the French consulate."

Grete exhaled. "What's the name of the man you spoke with?" she asked, anticipating Lanman's name. Then again, Lanman would never be so obvious.

The crease on Jacques's forehead deepened. "Duane Traynor. Why?"

Grete leaned back into the sofa, trying to absorb Jacques's words. Calling it good news felt like bad luck and going out to dinner seemed too much like a celebration. "Would you mind if we had dinner another night?" She waved her hand vaguely over her belly.

"Of course," Jacques said. He looked confused. Worse, he sounded concerned.

GRETE THOUGHT THE NIGHT WOULD NEVER END, yet somehow it was morning. She curled into a ball, reluctant to start the day. Her sheets were a warm tangle, her thoughts a jumble. She could not bring herself to face Peter and did not want to think about what Agent Lanman would do when he discovered she wasn't holding up her end of their bargain.

The day stretched ahead, excruciatingly long. The heat had broken, giving way to overcast skies and drizzle. She roused Vagabond from his mid-morning nap and was rewarded with a hiss and a scratch. A siren blared outside and she was relieved to see it was only a fire engine, as if a blazing fire were less menacing than her own personal drama. The telephone trilled, startling her. They didn't get many calls. She snapped it up. "Hello." Silence filtered over the line along with some garbled background noise. "Uncle Jacques?" She heard the low hum of a busy place. Her fist tightened around the receiver. The cord stretched as she peered into the entranceway. She stepped away from the window with an uneasy feeling she was being watched. The line went dead. Her heart dropped and she slammed the receiver back in its cradle.

Uncle Jacques had gone to work and left behind a newsstand worth of periodicals, which lay scattered across the breakfast table. The front page of the *Times* announced that secrecy had been imposed as Churchill arrived in Washington. By now, George should be blocks from the White House, within arms' reach of the world's most powerful allies. She did not think George was the least bit competent, but even the most bungling criminal could wreak havoc. Would Churchill and Roosevelt visit Hyde Park? Would they travel via Track 61?

She turned to Walter Winchell's column in *The Daily Mirror*. Though he was controversial for his outspoken views and poison-pen, Grete had a soft spot for Winchell who called Nazis *Rat-zis* and regularly denounced Hitler. His breakneck staccato, familiar because of his radio program, rang through every word.

. . . It's a baby boy for the Fortune Peter Ryans of the Doctors Hospital, New York City. She is the former Anne Worall of New York and Mount Kisco and the New York Social Register . . .

. . . The lowest form of petty thief is being hunted by the New York Police and the Army Intelligence. He may show up in your city with his lowly racket. He preys upon the mothers, the wives or sweethearts of enlisted men by saying that he is from the soldier-relative unit of the Army and that the son or husband or the brother needs $25, he says, to make a last visit home before sailing overseas. Several families have been taken in by this swindler and he is still at large. Always remember the ABC's in this war, especially in this case. The ABC's—Always Be Careful . . .

A small item hidden under a coffee ring caught her interest, *FBI agents are swarming through the Florida swamps because of stories that Nazi submarine crews in civilian clothes are at large in that state . . .*

Her hand flew to her mouth. Each morning brought a barrage of false alarms and rumors, "L.A. Area Raided!" "Hitler Dead!" The Winchell piece could be another false report. Except, she knew it was true. Had Agent Lanman pursued her lead? Her thoughts raced in farfetched, but not completely illogical, ways. Winchell and Hoover were known to share a table and swap information at the Stork Club. Had George already confessed? Perhaps he had gone to the press instead of the FBI? Peter said he was preoccupied with propaganda, and Winchell was the ultimate mouthpiece. It would be exactly like George to seek him out.

She was pushing aside a newspaper when she noticed the date: Friday, June 19th. It was Shabbos. Rose had not specified a time, but she was hardly the type to stand on ceremony. Grete liked the idea of arriving early and making herself useful. Chopping vegetables or setting a table was far better than twiddling her thumbs at home, and it was infinitely more sensible than clandestine assignations at the Chrysler Building. What better time to pray for her parents and collect her thoughts than Shabbos? In the absence of her own family, there seemed no better place to be.

CHAPTER 16

MORNING PUDDLES HAD FADED TO STEAM by the time Grete stepped off the El train at Elder Avenue. Only twenty minutes away, the Bronx was a world apart from Manhattan. Rose had said her street was down the hill from the station and Grete started down the sloping sidewalk. She passed a barbershop with a red and white pole spiraling outside and a deli with an open grill of hot dogs and a sign advertising a lunch special of Romanian strip steaks, French fries, and baked beans for $1.35. There was a flurry of activity as shoppers, mostly women and children, came and went from a large open-air market. The stand fronting the street showcased fruit and vegetables stacked in gravity-defying pyramids. The yeasty scent of fresh bread beckoned her down an aisle. The floor was coated in sawdust, which stuck to her shoes. Grete followed the stream of shoppers whose bags grew bulkier with every stop.

There was a dull thud and she turned to see a butcher in a blood-splattered apron submerge a headless chicken into steaming water before deftly plucking its feathers. A downy carpet collected at his feet and he spiked the bare carcass on a metal hook. Her stomach flipped. The meat shop she frequented displayed ribs and roasts under glass counters, garnished with parsley and paper bows. The butcher reached for his next squawking victim and she spun around, straight into Agent Lanman.

"Grete." Lanman did not bother with pleasantries. "I told you to stay with Peter."

His appearance was hardly a surprise and she had an excuse

at the ready. "I saw Walter Winchell's column this morning and assumed you found the Florida group and didn't need me."

Lanman folded his arms. "I'm surprised you're willing to jeopardize your parent's welfare."

"I'm not!" People turned at the sound of her raised voice and one matronly woman stepped closer.

"You okay, dear?" she asked, eyeing Lanman. His dark suit made him stand out in a market full of merchants and housewives.

Grete forced herself to smile and nod, "Fine, thank you." She could not afford to lose her wits. She lowered her voice and addressed Lanman, "Peter got a note from George yesterday saying he'd gone to Washington to meet with the . . . with your associates."

Lanman appeared neither surprised nor interested in her disclosure. "The Germans have started deporting Jews from France to Poland," he said evenly. "Your parents are still in Camp de Gurs, but it's only a matter of time before they're sent east."

Grete staggered backwards. Uncle Jacques's news about the State Department official had sparked an ember of hope inside her, which Lanman had tamped down. She should not have been surprised that Lanman was as heartless as everyone else. Still, she could not draw a breath. Despite everything, she had always believed she would see her parents again. She started to tremble. Unable to speak, she dug through her purse until her fingers found George's notebook. She was on the verge of handing it over when she remembered the papers she had folded inside. Maybe it was wiser not to cede everything at once. She fingered through the book until she located the diagram of Track 61 and wordlessly thrust it forward.

Lanman unfolded the paper, studying it. "Why are you only giving this to me now?"

"I didn't have it before," she said, which was more or less true. "And I wasn't sure how to find you." Lanman frowned as if he didn't fully buy the explanation, but the tug of the diagram was too great to ignore. He turned the page over and over again as if to gage its authenticity.

"Where'd you get it?"

She had not anticipated the question. She reached back into her purse and was about to handover George's book and explain that the diagram had been hidden inside when an idea occurred to her. "It was with George's things. He left some belongings in Peter's hotel room when he went to Washington."

"Why would he leave this behind?"

Grete shrugged to indicate that she could not possibly begin to explain George; true enough. She kept her hand on her purse, prepared to surrender the notebook if the diagram did not suffice. But Lanman readily accepted her ignorance. She was just a girl after all, and a refugee to boot. If the situation were not so terrifying, Grete might have laughed. It was rare that being underestimated worked in her favor.

Lanman refolded the diagram and tucked it in his inside pocket. "Look, Grete, I'm not going to tell you again. Find Peter, stay with him, and if something else comes up contact me at FBI headquarters in Foley Square. Give my name to the guard at the door. He'll know how to reach me. If you can't manage that, light a lamp in your bedroom window." He turned on his heels, leaving Grete to shudder at the thought of Lanman or anyone else watching her bedroom window.

THE SKY OPENED UP AS GRETE WATCHED LANMAN turn the corner out of the market. Shoppers scrambled for shelter and merchants covered their wares with tarps. Grete had forgotten an umbrella and was quickly soaked. She stood in the downpour brushing raindrops and tears off her cheeks. She had no choice but to follow Lanman's instructions and find Peter.

She started toward the El with renewed purpose, her shoes squishing with every step. She stopped to wipe sawdust off her heels and found a wet chicken feather stuck to her ankle. Peter would know something was wrong if she showed up like this. Rose had said her apartment was nearby. She decided to go there first to borrow some dry clothing and an umbrella before going to

Peter's hotel. She had not wanted to go back there, ever, but she didn't have much choice.

The buildings along Wheeler Avenue were less than a dozen stories, their stoops occupied by pots of geraniums which glistened in the rain. Number 1175 had double doors and a tiled vestibule with rows of mailboxes. Inside smelled of simmering roasts and baking bread. Grete skimmed the names on the boxes. The cooking odors intensified as she reached the second floor, the scents warm and soothing. Rose's apartment was at the end of the hall and she paused in front to admire a pretty gold mezuzah. She was reaching up to touch it when the door flew open.

"Grete!" Rose said as if she had been awaiting her arrival.

"I'm early."

Rose engulfed her in a warm embrace. "You're soaking wet," she said, stepping back.

"I forgot an umbrella."

Rose tilted her head, assessing Grete with a twisted frown. "Come in and dry off. I'll lend you something to wear. If we can find anything that fits." She sounded doubtful.

Grete allowed herself to be ushered inside where a narrow hall opened into a tidy living room. The apartment smelled of furniture polish, but that scent was quickly eclipsed by whatever was wafting from the kitchen. There, pots rattled on the stovetop, one bubbling with broth, another overflowing with onions. The table had its leafs extended and an embroidered tablecloth was laid out. Silver candlesticks stood in the center and a challah was partially hidden under a decorative cloth. Two windows were open in a valiant effort to stir a breeze in the oppressively hot room. They faced a courtyard from which a smattering of rain, but little fresh air, blew inside. A woman stood at the sink.

"Ma," Rose said. "This is Grete. The girl from the salvage depot I told you about."

Rose's mother turned, wiping her chafed hands on a dishtowel. There was a plucked chicken, seasoned and splayed on the cutting board. Grete could almost hear the squawking birds. She swallowed, pasting a smile on her face.

"It's a pleasure to meet you Mrs. Weiss. Thanks for having me," she said, suddenly aware she had shown up empty-handed. It seemed impossible that she had walked the entire length of the market without buying even one small gift. Mama would have been mortified.

Mrs. Weiss offered a weary smile. "Rose said you could use a home-cooked meal."

"That's Ma's way of saying welcome," Rose translated.

Rose had inherited her mother's figure and ivory skin. Beyond that, they seemed nothing alike. Rose was the most effervescent person Grete had met in this country of bubbly people. Mrs. Weiss was subdued and serious. Her family was still in Europe, and now her son was leaving for boot camp. It was a small wonder she managed to muster a smile at all.

"We'll help in a minute," Rose said. "I'm just going to get Grete something dry to wear. She was caught in the downpour!" She put her hands on her hips and shook her head as if Grete were a hair shy of wild.

Getting caught in the rain is the most ordinary thing that has happened to me in days, Grete thought. Though she admired Rose's ability to turn mishap into adventure. Her breath steadied as she followed Rose into a crowded bedroom with two single beds, one meticulously made, the other untucked. There were two dressers, too: a tall one topped with cufflinks and loose change and a squat one holding an assortment of bobby pins, a jar of cold cream, and a soft pink lipstick.

Rose paused, seeming to consider the small space. "I share the room with my brothers, but Phil, the older one, sleeps on the living room sofa. I'd give up the bed if it meant he didn't have to go. Of course, I know it's a worthy cause." Her words tumbled out as if she were conducting a conversation she'd had many times. "I'm being selfish. It's just, having escaped all that, I can't imagine going back."

Grete tried to put herself in Rose's shoes—or Phil's. "He can repay the Germans for their atrocities. Fight back!"

Rose shrugged. "GIs all seem so brave, but my brother is just my brother, silly Philly, not some stranger in uniform. He doesn't complain, but I know he's scared. I can't imagine holding a gun let alone firing it and killing someone."

Grete's hand twitched, grasping an imaginary gun. She focused on her target and was neither surprised nor disappointed to see it was the Nazi brute who had thrown her in the Rhine. She took aim and squeezed the trigger.

Rose opened the closet and began rummaging through. "How's this?" She held up a slightly worn floral print and frowned. "No. This one's better." She exchanged the floral print for a navy blue tea dress with cap sleeves and oversized buttons.

Grete accepted gratefully. Now that she was inside, she realized how uncomfortably wet she was. Rose drew the shades and turned on a light, bathing the room in a dim yellow glow. Grete turned her back, self-consciously stepping out of her dress and shimmying into Rose's, cinching the belt as tight as it would go. Rose plopped onto the messy bed. Grete flushed with fondness for her. She had assumed the disorderly bed belonged to the little boy, but it made perfect sense that Rose was the sloppy one.

Rose offered her now familiar slightly dubious expression. "The sleeves are a bit wide but it'll do."

Grete let the belt out a notch and bloused the fabric, hoping that would help. "It's lovely. Thank you." She shook out her wet dress. "Where should I hang this?"

Rose took the discarded dress and tossed it at the foot of the bed. "You seem distracted." It looked as if she were about to add *again*. Rose was being kind. When Grete looked back on her mad dash up Broadway with the box of salvaged rubber, her tumble into the gutter, and the strained meeting outside the Rialto, she was horrified by her behavior. Now she had shown up on Rose's doorstep sopping wet. Small wonder Rose hadn't slammed the door in her face.

"Grete, what's going on?"

Denial seemed useless. Rose was smart and, even if she wasn't, it was wrong to keep deceiving her. Still, Peter's secret was not hers to tell, and it would only make Rose complicit as well.

Rose kicked off her shoes and tucked her bare legs under herself. "Sometimes it helps to talk."

"I'm so used to holding it in." Tears welled in Grete's eyes and spilled over. "I'm sorry," she choked out between sobs, collapsing onto the bed beside Rose. She had been stoic for so long, crying was a tremendous relief. She was grateful to Rose, and her softly lit room, which somehow gave her permission to let her guard down. Rose passed her a tissue and waited out the torrent. Grete's sobs decelerated into hiccups. "Everyone says I'm lucky and I tell myself that," she lowered her voice, confessing what felt like sacrilege. "But most of the time, I'm just lonely."

"What about Peter?" Rose asked. "You two seemed close."

"Really?" she asked, annoyed that she sounded so hopeful. Peter was a secret she had held close to her chest. It was strange to hear Rose say his name out loud. Stranger still, to think that she sensed something between them.

"Some couples are just meant to be. Did you know each other in Germany?"

She wondered how Rose would react if she told her that Peter was married. She could not begin to fathom what Rose would say if she knew he was a German spy.

"No. We met here. At the war parade."

"Last Saturday?"

"His family is in Europe." Grete spoke softly. Peter had always referred to the people he left behind as family, not his wife. "He has a sister here, but he doesn't get along with her husband."

"So you understand each other. I mean, you both know what it's like to worry about loved ones left behind." Rose brightened. "And he's so handsome!"

"You think so?" Grete was annoyed to hear herself trilling like a love struck girl.

"Not in a conventional way, there's something about him,

strength and vulnerability mixed together. It's hard to put one's finger on exactly."

That's for sure, Grete thought. "The thing is, he's mixed up with some shady men and it has put him in a difficult spot." The confessions tumbled out—all true, but not the whole story, either.

"Does he play the horses?" Rose jumped to conclusions.

If only Peter's problems were so mundane. "No, nothing like that. Peter's a good person." Despite everything, she believed that to be true.

"Is he coming?"

"Here?" Grete came back to reality. Confiding in Rose, even obliquely, was not in either of their best interest. It might even put Rose in harm's way. Lanman had told Grete to find Peter and it was high time to make up an excuse and leave. Grete hesitated. Her abrupt departure was sure to make Rose even more concerned. "Gosh, I apologize, I completely forgot that I promised to meet Peter."

"So, he's not coming for dinner?" Rose sounded rightfully confused. "Did you not want me to invite him? It just seemed like the polite thing to do because you two were together and he seemed so sad."

Grete nodded. Interesting that Rose had picked up on Peter's distress. "No, it was very thoughtful of you, but Peter's work—"

"He works on Friday evening? Doing what?"

Grete sighed at the enormity of the hole she had dug herself into.

Someone tapped on the door. "Rose?" Mrs. Weiss called. "Your other guest is here."

Grete shrank back into the shelter of Rose's room while Rose went to greet her guest at the door. There was some unintelligible conversation and Rose returned with Peter by her side.

Her eyes landed squarely on Grete. "He made it after all."

Peter offered a tentative smile as if he were happy to see her, and unsure how she would react. He was wearing a dark navy suit she had not seen before which made his shoulders look even broader, his waist trim. Grete's chest felt as if it might burst. Secretly pleased that Peter had tracked her down, she wanted to tell him to run.

Candles sparkled as Rose's mother waved her arms over them, closed her eyes, and chanted the prayer to welcome Shabbos. Her voice conjured centuries-old traditions, transforming the kitchen from everyday workstation to sacred space. The overhead lights were off and shadows danced on the walls. The evening breeze came through the open windows and the curtains fluttered. Grete glanced sideways at Peter whose head was bowed in prayer. She could not muster a single *Amen*. What Agent Lanman was asking of her went against the ethics of any faith. More blessings were recited over the wine then the challah. Rose's father tore the bread into pieces and dipped them in golden honey before passing them around the table. The honey was meant to usher in a sweet week. Grete savored the sticky sweetness. Her family had always salted their challah to symbolize sacrifice or tears or both, and she preferred the sweet version.

Dinner was strained. Grete pushed food around her plate while trying to avoid Peter who was seated too close on her right. His elbow brushed hers as he sliced his chicken and praised the meal. Mrs. Weiss sat at one end of the table, her chair mostly empty as she jumped up and down, serving everyone. At the opposite end, Mr. Weiss was a man of few words. Rose sat between her brothers across from Grete and Peter. She tried to catch Grete's eye and when Grete did not respond she kicked her under the table. Grete kept her head down. Rose was the least of her problems.

Phil narrowed his eyes at Peter. "How do you know my sister?" Phil was small and dark like his parents and, like them, he seemed tired and slightly suspicious.

"Grete introduced us." Rose offered the tiniest of headshakes to indicate Peter should not mention Times Square, which Peter immediately picked up on. A lull fell over the table.

Little Heshie provided the only relief. He spoke without a trace of an accent and had loose blond curls and an eager expression that struck Grete as entirely American. Everything about Mrs. Weiss softened as she spooned a heaping serving of potatoes onto Heshie's plate, and she beamed as he described his day, which consisted of visiting his father at work, unloading cherries, and petting a puppy. The adults seemed to rely on the boy for lighthearted conversation and another silence ensued after he exhausted his repertoire.

Rose turned to Peter. "So," she said. Grete had the sense she had been biding her time, awaiting this moment. "Grete told me you couldn't make dinner." She looked at Grete for confirmation.

"Yes, what happened?" Grete asked. "Shouldn't you be working?" There were a hundred things Peter should have been doing, none of which Grete could convey in front of Rose and her family.

"I had another letter from George." Peter's arm rested against hers and she shifted away as guilt threatened to consume her. "He's in Washington, so work was put on hold."

Grete breathed a sigh of relief. "That's good."

"Is George a friend of yours?" Rose asked, raising a brow at Grete.

"A colleague," Peter said.

Grete recalled the first time she had heard Peter describe George as his *Kollege*. A week later, his inflection had softened and his pronunciation sounded nearly as American as Heshie's. *Peter is a liar and a spy,* she told herself, hoping that if she said it often enough it would be easier to betray him.

CHAPTER 17

GRETE HAD NOT BEEN ABLE TO IMAGINE a situation more awkward than dinner at the Weisses until she found herself alone on the sidewalk with Peter. She could not find it within herself to be angry with him, only sad and confused. Soft light tumbled from open windows along with muffled voices and the clatter of pots. She pictured the women she had seen at the market sitting down to dinner with their families. And she could not shake the sense that she was on the wrong side of things: outside when she should have been in. Rain clouds were rebuilding in the night sky and Wheeler Avenue felt confining.

"Why'd you come here?" As relieved as she was that Peter wanted to explain himself, she could not understand why he would show up at Rose's and expose the Weisses. Had he been following her? Did he see her with Lanman? More troubling was the realization that he may have committed Rose's address to memory.

Peter hung his head like a boy. "The nets closing in. I don't have much time."

She resisted the urge to turn and call out Lanman's name. "You said George was in Washington, confessing." George's phrase, *straighten everything out*, came to mind, but she refused to use it. "That's good! This will be over soon and the FBI will know that you tried to prevent a disaster."

"George is in protective custody."

She breathed a sigh of relief. "So he reached the right people and they're protecting him." *And they'll protect you*, she thought.

George and Peter were helping the Americans and the Americans would free her parents.

"Custody," Peter repeated. "George was arrested."

"No . . ." She could hear her tone dip. "How could he be arrested if he turned himself in?"

"Funny, huh?" Peter did not sound remotely amused. "George expected a warm welcome from J. Edgar Hoover, a cigar and a pat on the back. Instead, he's locked up."

"Well," she stammered, "the FBI's not shy. If they were planning to arrest you, they would have."

"It's not that simple. It's better for the FBI to keep me in play. They'd rather follow me and find out what I'm up to before alerting Abwehr." Grete missed a step and a sharp pain flared as her ankle rolled. Peter offered his arm for balance. Refusing help, she shook the ache away and forged ahead. "It's safe for now," he assured her. "I gave them the slip."

"Safe?" She resisted the urge to laugh out loud. Lanman was lurking in the shadows. Soon, Abwehr would be tracing their steps. Peter either didn't pick up on or chose to ignore her sarcasm. "Once the group is arrested, the operation will be public knowledge and German intelligence will close down all U.S. sabotage. The FBI wants to keep it quiet for now so they can glean more information. They're waiting for me to lead them to Dick and Henry."

"Why? George must have said where to find them."

"George doesn't know where they are. Dick made me promise not to tell."

"You don't owe Dick anything." She had some sympathy for Henry, a man-child in the wrong place at the wrong time, but none whatsoever for Dick. "Take the FBI to Dick and you'll be a hero like William Sebold."

Peter pounded a fist into his hand, making her jump. "There aren't any heroes in war, only victims. Sebold signed his own death warrant. Either he's floating in the East River or starving to death in some German camp."

"No," Grete said, trying to fend off images of her parents

ravenous in a labor camp. She had to convince Peter to turn himself in, every moment mattered. "That won't happen to you here. The FBI will value the information you provide. They'll protect you."

"Like they're protecting George?" She could think of a million reasons why George could have rubbed the FBI the wrong way, but Peter did not let her begin. "Besides," he said, "it's not my safety that worries me."

"You're worried about your wife?" Now that the tables were turned and she was the one lying to protect her loved ones, it was hard to muster much indignation over Peter's omission. "Did you think I wouldn't help if I knew about her?" Even as she posed the question Grete wondered whether she had been motivated by a noble cause, or the potent aphrodisiac of romance and risk.

"I should have told you about Ursula," Peter said. Grete's heart fluttered. It was one thing to know Peter had a wife, another to hear her name on his lips. She found herself wondering all sorts of things she had previously blocked out. Was Ursula tall? Thin? Dark or fair? Did she love Peter, and did Peter love her?

"It's a lot more complicated than what Dick said." Peter's voice dropped to a melancholy low she had never heard from him. "Those bastards killed our child."

Grete stopped walking, too stunned to respond or even move. Peter kept talking.

"I met Ursula while I was studying in Berlin. She was a nursing student. We were married only a few weeks before I was sent to Poland. We hadn't known each other long, but war draws people together." Grete nodded slowly. He might just as easily be explaining their bond. "When I got the orders to go to Quenz Farm, I burned them. A few days later, the Gestapo showed up. They came every day after that. Neighbors stopped talking to us. The grocer refused to serve us. Worst of all, Ursula's family disowned her. One day when I was out, the Gestapo brought Ursula down to headquarters and told her I had stolen money while I was in Vienna and that I would receive eight years on a chain gang. It didn't matter that I'd never been to Vienna in my life. They insisted she divorce me."

For the second time in as many hours, tears welled in Grete's eyes. Her grief proved her feelings for Peter. She wanted to spare him more pain. "I'm not angry." The words left her mouth along with any trace of resentment. "You don't have to say anymore."

He rubbed his eyes. "I told Ursula to divorce me, but she was already in . . ." He sighed. "In a family way. She was frightened to have a baby on her own. She had no money, no means of support, and was very sick, vomiting from morning to night. Of course, the Nazis didn't care. They tormented her until she had a breakdown and they took her to the hospital. They had to operate and she had this . . . I think you call it a miscarriage."

A sour taste rose in Grete's throat. She thought she might be sick.

"I know he was not really a baby, not yet. He was not due for months, but I had held my hand on her stomach and felt him kick. We had a crib. While Ursula was in the hospital, they forced me to write a farewell letter to her. I could have resisted, but what was the point? With the baby gone, she was better off without me. I wrote the letter and went to Quenz Farm the same day. We never even said goodbye." Peter exhaled slowly. "I hated the Gestapo before, but it was political. After that, it became personal. I want revenge, not only for me but for Ursula and our baby."

Grete cupped her hand over her mouth. She felt simultaneously sick and ashamed. Peter had not told her about his wife because he did not want to relive his grief. What she was doing, setting him up to save her parents, was far worse. For a moment she wondered if Mama would want her to be so duplicitous. Peter reached for her hand and she pinned it to her side. Of course, Mama wanted to live. Ideals were one thing; reality another.

"Finding you at the parade was like a gift. I kept telling myself it wasn't fair to drag you into this, but I wasn't thinking logically— not about you." Peter drew her toward him. Her willpower shriveled and she succumbed. "I intend to do the right thing. I'll face the FBI. But I couldn't leave things between us the way they were. Maybe I'm being selfish. I needed to be with you one more time. I needed this." He kissed her.

Grete collapsed into him. She thought she could smell the ocean in his hair. He wrapped his arms around her and she could almost feel the sun on her shoulders. Though it defied all logic, she felt safe. A car horn jolted her back to present: a wet street corner in the Bronx.

"Peter." She pulled him into the recessed entranceway of a nearby shop. The shop was closed, its windows dark, and she could whisper in the shadows. There had to be a way to help her parents and protect Peter. Together, they could come up with one. Tears spilled from her eyes as she explained how Lanman had approached her. "He threatened me. He said boats go two ways, and then he said the United States would help my parents if I did what he said." She buried her head in his chest. Apologizing seemed useless.

Peter held her close and she could feel his heart beat fast against hers. "You didn't have a choice." He had said the same thing about himself and his friend Herbie. Was it possible they were all choiceless?

"What now?" she asked. She looked into the shop's darkened windows, wishing the door could open into a parallel world where she, Peter, her parents, and Jacques could live in peace.

"I'll go to the FBI. George—"

"George!" she said, too loudly. "I gave Agent Lanman the diagram of Track 61, but I still have George's book. Take it to the FBI." She dug into her purse, her fingers lighting on the warped book. As she began to pull it out, the paper that had fallen from Henry's pocket came loose in her hand. "I also have this. Henry dropped it at the hotel." She passed the crumpled slip to Peter.

"Henry's no good at remembering things. Dick was always leaving him notes to remind him of stuff."

"It says 61 and some other numbers." She recited the sequence from memory, "1961900."

"That's today's date," Peter said simply. "And a time, seven o'clock."

Grete frowned. She had become so accustomed to the American way of doing things she had not thought to flip the month and day. Military time hadn't even occurred to her. She pieced the information together: Track 61, tonight at seven.

CHAPTER 18

GRAND CENTRAL WAS BUZZING with daily commuters and week-end tourists as Grete and Peter entered the Great Hall. The yellow light from the chandeliers bounced off the marble, creating tawny shadows. Grete watched Peter stride away, painfully aware that this was one of the last times she would see him. They had parted many times before, only for him to reappear. This time felt different; permanent.

A choral group was performing on the East Balcony and Grete found a place among the spectators. Peter seemed to understand that there was no point arguing when she had insisted on coming along. Still, he had made her promise to wait upstairs, and his tone left no room for objections. The ensemble broke into a rendition of "Rock of Ages" and Grete eyed the opalescent clock: 6:45. As passengers hurried toward trains, she was conscious of men in dark suits, white shirts, and snappy hats scattered among them. She counted four; one perusing papers at a newsstand, one standing by the main entrance, and two more pacing among the crowd. Two others may or may not have been FBI. There were so many men in dark suits, Grete felt as if her eyes were playing tricks. She raised her shoulders, retracting her head like a turtle, as an agent she recognized as Lanman began discretely showing sketches to befuddled travelers. No doubt George had provided detailed descriptions of the other men. She would not have expected less. Lanman also had the drawing of Track 61 she had given him, which explained why he was here. She looked toward the stairs

Peter had descended, wondering how he had managed to skirt by unnoticed. No doubt about it; Peter was resourceful.

Grete watched as Lanman approached a group of GIs. The measured way in which he questioned each individual made her believe he was unaware of the urgency. Of course, the diagram she had given him did not include the date and time. Grete eyed the clock: 6:50. Nineteen hundred hours or seven o'clock was fast approaching. She had no way of knowing what would happen then. Peter had been adamant about wanting to stop Dick and Henry on his own, and she hadn't bothered to disagree. Peter had his ways. She had hers. She kept her eyes and ears primed for disturbance, prepared to alert Lanman if the situation grew dire. The challenge was recognizing trouble.

Grete watched as Lanman shared the sketches with another group of bystanders. This time one man scratched his head before taking a sketch out of Lanman's hands to examine it more closely. The man said something Grete could not make out and pointed downstairs. Lanman waved his arm high in the air and snapped his fingers to signal to the other agents just as a group of drunken GIs ambled into the station, creating a distraction. As Lanman tried to alert his men, Grete recalled the words he had used when he first spoke to her: *Our case will be stronger if we catch all the saboteurs red-handed.* Peter was right; the FBI had wanted to keep him in play. Lanman had been biding his time, waiting for this precise moment.

The choral group broke into "Chattanooga Choo Choo" and the soldiers found partners and began twirling them around the floor. Grete didn't stay to watch. She had to warn Peter. She tipped her hat forward, as if that one small alteration might disguise her. The stairway to the lower level was no more than fifty meters away, the length of a swimming pool. She took a deep breath. How many times had she glided through the water, swimming countless laps? She could do this. Moving as calmly as possible, she cut through the crowd and descended the stairs slowly at first, then two at a time, until she reached the lower level. Stopping shy of the last step, she peered into the concourse, which was also, thankfully, busy. A guard patrolled the floor. Another sat with his back against a wall, playing cards with a few GIs. The Oyster Bar was hopping and a line snaked out of the luggage office. Along the wall to her left, open doors led down to the tracks. Commuters flocked toward one. The numbers over the door read 24-26. A conductor shouted a list of destinations: Sputen Duyvel, Hastings . . . A man dragged a large suitcase. Another, who she feared was FBI, stood to the side, watching. Grete locked arms with a woman and gabbed about the weather until they passed safely through the entrance to the tracks.

She stepped out onto a ramp in a vast underground tunnel. It was one of many ramps leading away from the station. Each sloped down to a platform, running between a pair of tracks. A well-lit train rumbled to the right of the platform and the commuters flocked toward its open doors. More trains idled on platforms to the left. Grete looked behind her. Rather than descending the ramp, she walked in the shadows along the top of the platform until she reached the far side of the lit train. The bright lights threw the remaining space into darkness. The air was dank. The enormous tunnel strangely oppressive. Peter was not exaggerating when he said there were miles of tracks down here. He had also said that the basement that stored the power convertors was ten stories underground and that Track 61 was somewhere nearby. As her eyes adjusted to the darkness, Grete could see more tracks leading away from the station. All empty, except for the final one where a dark train was parked. The sketch of Track 61 had shown a freight elevator leading to the Waldorf Astoria—north, or so she thought. She struggled to get her bearings.

Grete rushed toward the parked train. Its nose pointed toward the station, its body stretched into darkness. The platform running between the train and the wall was no more than an arm's length wide; meant for service crews, not passengers. Grete took in the cavernous expanse. Bare bulbs were set high on bedrock walls. Most were dark, but a few threw off sparse shadows. Dizzy with fear, she began treading down the narrow ledge. She thought she could hear footsteps behind her, but when she paused to listen she realized it was the sound of her pulse clamoring in her ears. She closed her eyes and held her breath as she passed one railcar then another.

She was three cars down the line when a whistle blew and the commuter train pulled away from the station. Another train groaned to life and Grete could see more travelers descending a distant platform toward it. Grateful for the commotion, she tried to catch her breath. Something, pigeon or bat, fluttered above her head. Her eyes adjusted to the darkness. She teetered down the ledge and had passed two more cars when a door at the head of the track banged open and light streamed toward her. Someone shouted, "This way." Hidden on the far side of the dark train, Grete could not see faces, only bouncing beams of light. A rat scurried in an oily puddle. She jumped backwards and covered her mouth so as not to scream. Her back scraped against the stone wall. She turned, groping with her hands to feel what she could not see. There had to be a door here somewhere—one leading to Track 61. She moved quickly, running her hands along the coarse wall. She had almost lost hope when the surface suddenly grew smooth, metal not rock. She pressed harder. The wall shifted. She applied her full weight and a panel cracked open. She eased it wide enough to squeeze through and closed it softly behind her.

She found herself on top of a vibrating metal landing and heard a distant hum. The structure was more zigzagging ladder than stairway. Beneath her was a long, dark pit. Grete's teeth chattered and she was hit by a gust of foul air. There were no whistles, only a hiss as a train pulled into the station far below her feet. She remembered the headline announcing Churchill's arrival in the United States. Were Roosevelt and Churchill aboard the Magellan pulling in on Track 61?

Grete started down the stairs. The steps were steep and narrow, the footing slippery. She considered kicking off her shoes, but was anxious it would make a sound. Two flights down, she turned, descending with her back to the basement as if she were on an actual ladder. She was halfway down when the panel leading into the main tunnel screeched open. The agents' voices rang out. "Follow me," one called. "Hurry." Feet clambered, moving fast, and she quickened her pace. A loud bang ricocheted below. The stairs shook as the Magellan drew closer. She lost her balance and nearly fell. Her hands chafed against the metal rail. The temperature dropped as she scampered down one flight after another. She leapt the last few feet, falling onto her back and landing in another pitch-black tunnel.

This one was smaller, a passageway wide enough for a single—presidential—rail car. She looked up expecting to find Peter, Dick, and Henry standing over her, but her fall was overshadowed by the Magellan pulling into the station. Its headlight gleamed down the tunnel. Three figures were silhouetted in the light with their backs toward her. She recognized Peter's broad shoulders, Henry's slack ones, and Dick's military stance. Footsteps rumbled above her. She had come to warn Peter, but now that she was here she could do nothing more than crawl into a corner and curl into a ball. She was hiding behind the stairs when she felt a cool rush of air. The G-men came shimmying down, vaulting past her toward the incoming train. They raced toward the Magellan, clicking flashlights on and off and shouting. Someone must have pulled a lever because an overhead light snapped on and the train came to a loud, grinding halt.

Grete cowered in the corner, her back pressed against rough rock. She was trembling so badly she feared the motion would give her away. She heard movement, but did not dare peer out. The train idled in the distance. Its headlight blinding to look at. The agents swarmed toward it.

"Spread out," one called. "Careful. It could be a trap."

"Richard Quirin. Heinrich Heinck. There's nowhere to run. You're surrounded," a voice she recognized as Lanman's shouted. "Dick, Henry, come out with your hands up."

Her thoughts rocketed. Lanman had not called Peter's name. Was it possible he didn't know Peter was here?

"Dick!" Henry cried. He sounded scared and more childlike

than ever. "It's no use. They got us."

"Richard Quirin. Heinrich Heinck. We're United States Government Officers, Federal Bureau of Investigation. You are wanted in connection with violations of United States espionage law. Come out or we'll shoot."

"Don't shoot," Henry sobbed. Feet shuffled across the floor as he gave himself up.

Dick did not respond. Grete heard the unmistakable sound of a gun cocking and braced herself for shots. Dick swore. There was more commotion as he surrendered.

"Cuff them," Lanman said, "and take them up the elevator."

Grete allowed herself a fleeting breath as agents marched Dick and Henry away on the far side of the track toward, what she assumed, was the freight elevator.

"Where are you taking us?" Dick demanded.

"Foley Square."

"FBI headquarters?" Dick said pointedly.

Grete had the sense he was relaying a message to Peter. Was George correct when he said the Gestapo had agents posted in the New York office? Was there an undercover Nazi who could help them escape? It would explain why Dick wasn't giving Peter up now.

Metal clanged against metal and cables whined as the elevator came to life. A gate squeaked open and the men filed inside. Grete's heart leapt as the gate slammed closed. The elevator rose.

Lanman and two remaining agents scoured the platform. The overhead light did not illuminate much and the agents used flashlights to search dark corners. She gulped back tears, expecting Lanman to flash his beam on her, pull her to her feet, and declare that she had blown her last chance to save her parents. She could almost feel their blood on her hands.

"Fan out," Lanman said. "Start at the top and reconvene back here."

Numb with fear, she listened to their receding steps. Far down the platform, the idling train hissed. She heard machinery grind and shift. The basement quaked as the engine whined and the train began slowly accelerating in the opposite direction. Grete hugged her shoulders, willing herself to become invisible. Afraid to move, she knew it might be her only opportunity to escape.

Someone reached out, dragging her out of her hiding place. She struggled and would have screamed but a hand clamped her mouth.

"Grete." Peter's lips nuzzled her ear. "It's me."

She threw her arms around him and buried her head into his chest. Peter did not hug her back. Instead, he picked her up off her feet and swung her down into the track. Voices echoed down the tunnel as the agents turned back toward them. She sank to her belly and squirmed under a ledge scarcely wide enough to conceal her slim frame. The agents had already combed this length of track. If she wedged herself under the lip, flat on the ground, she was hidden; given they did not search this way again. She remained perfectly still, waiting for Peter to jump down beside her and hide. But Peter never did what was the expected. When she looked, he was gone.

Backlit as he was, she could see nothing more than his shadow as his hands rose in the air. "I'm Ernest Peter Burger," he called. His voice booming down the tunnel. "I surrender."

CHAPTER 19

PETER SWORE THAT NO ONE WOULD ever discover his true identity, but so much of what he had said proved to be wrong. For a week, there was no word: nothing in the newspapers, no sign from Lanman. Grete eyed her bedroom window, wondering if an agent was posted on the street below. She lit the lamp and switched it off again so often she worried she might start a fire. One minute she wanted to hear from Lanman to ask about her parents and Peter, the next she preferred to remain in the dark. More than once, she donned hat and gloves to go down to FBI headquarters. Twice, she made it as far as the elevator. But she always turned back. She did not want to have her hopes dashed. Still reeling after Peter's arrest, she spent her days reliving her narrow escape.

That night, ten stories below Grand Central on Track 61, she had lain stiff as a corpse, listening with her heart in her throat as Lanman cuffed Peter and recited the same damning words he had spoken to Dick and Henry, "Ernest Peter Burger you are wanted in connection with violations of United States espionage law." There was no mention of George, nothing seemed to be *going as planned.* Under the platform shelf as far from the open track as she could squirm, she hardly dared to breathe as the freight elevator came to life and Lanman ushered Peter away. Not trusting her legs to carry her, she had waited for what felt like hours. Eventually, the overhead light switched off and the tunnel grew eerily quiet. As her nerves slowed and exhaustion caught up with her, she may even have dozed. The next thing she knew, trains far above her head were whining and whistling. By the time she climbed cautiously back up the stairs and crept into the terminal, early morning travelers were making their way through the station.

THE NEWS, IF YOU COULD CALL IT THAT, broke a week and a day later.

Grete woke to Jacques's familiar knock. It was Sunday: park day. She sighed. She had slept the better part of the week and was still groggy. She sat up to look outside, hoping for rain and an excuse to stay in bed. Bright sunshine. She groaned. After declining Jacques's invitation to the Automat, she was in no position to put him off again.

"Gretel," Jacques called, "it's getting late."

"I'm up." Maybe blue skies and fresh air would do her good. She splashed water on her face, brushed teeth and hair, threw on a dress.

Jacques was waiting in the entranceway. The Sunday *Times* lodged under his arm. "Interesting reading." He tapped the paper.

Grete was suddenly wide awake. Interesting reading was not good reading during wartime. Her gut knew it had to do with Peter. "What is it?" she whispered, dreading the answer.

"Let's get to the park."

"No." She snatched the paper away from Jacques who looked too surprised to object. A banner headline stretched across the front page: "FBI SEIZES 8 SABOTEURS LANDED BY U-BOATS HERE AND IN FLORIDA TO BLOW UP WAR PLANTS." *Oh.* She staggered backwards.

"Disgusting," Jacques said. "It's one thing to terrorize Europe, but these monsters won't get away blasting and burning here."

Grete dropped the paper and might have fallen along with it if Jacques had not held her up. "Gretel?" Clearly concerned he led her to the sofa.

"I'm just a bit under the weather."

Jacques went to the kitchen to get her a glass of water and she did her best to pull herself together.

"Thank you," she said, sipping the water and offering a false smile. "I haven't been myself this week."

"It's hot out today," Jacques said. "We can skip our walk. But," he said in his firmest parental voice, "if this keeps up, I'm calling the doctor."

Grete bit her lip to keep from crying. "Uncle Jacques," She put her hand on his. "Please don't worry. I had a little bug and it left me drained. I promise it's nothing."

"I'll go get some chicken soup, and maybe a bar of chocolate?" He winked. "Back in a jiffy." As kind as Jacques was, he was not the nurturing type. Grete could tell he was relieved to go. She finished her water and summoned her courage, picking up the newspaper with trembling hands and spreading it out across the table.

Under the headline was a grainy photograph showing four boxes of explosives hidden on a Florida beach. "Boxes containing TNT," the caption read, "which was to have been used to destroy war plants and railroads." The article listed deadly targets along with biographies of each man. Grete quickly found Peter's.

Ernest Peter Burger was a naturalized citizen of the United States. In the same year he was naturalized, his family urged him to return to Germany. He did so and became a writer and propagandist. Early in 1942, he *volunteered* for sabotage work. He had a wife living in Germany.

Frustrated by the lack of information, she turned to the paragraph on George. George was born at Speyer on the Rhine. Leaving home in 1922, he went from Hamburg to Philadelphia as a stowaway. In 1930, he married an American girl, Rose Marie Guille. *Snooks*.

Along with the boxes of TNT, photographs showed Nazi caps and mugshots of each man. George, Dick, Henry, and men from the Florida group, Edward John Kerling, Werner Theil, and a sketch of a man with a Clark Gable mustache named Herman Neubauer. Each looked guiltier than the next. And there was Peter. Grete trembled and tears spilled down her cheeks. He looked like a middle-aged stranger whose features were vaguely familiar. Her despair plummeted to panic as she read: "All to Face the Death Penalty."

It was impossible to say how much time passed as she clutched the table fighting to make sense of the words. She had the same gasping-for-air sensation as when the Nazi at the swim club had thrown her into the Rhine. Dizzy with disbelief, she closed her eyes to steady her breath and saw the word *death* dangling in front of her like a noose.

How had she been so naïve? She had pretended she was on an adventure, Nora Charles solving the latest caper, and had gone along with Peter until she was in too deep to turn back. Worse, she had urged Peter to return to Amagansett, sure he would be hailed a hero. She had cooperated with Lanman though there was no proof he was ever going to help her parents. She didn't even know if he could. She brushed away tears. Peter had given himself up to distract the FBI agents away from her. If she had not followed him to Track 61 would he have escaped?

She staggered to the bathroom, scarcely reaching the toilet before retching. She was on the bathroom floor with her forehead pressed against the cold tiles when she heard someone at the front door. "Grete!" It was easy to recognize Rose's impassioned voice. Her tone suggested she knew Grete was home, and Grete knew she would ring the doorbell until she alerted the whole neighborhood. Grete heaved herself up onto shaky legs. When she cracked open the front door, Rose burst inside, waving the *Daily News*.

The paper featured a front-page photograph of George. His hair was brushed back emphasizing the silver streak. He was clinging to a letter board that read "FBI-NYC" as if it were a life preserver and he was lost at sea. Though she had never liked George, the image filled her with sadness. George had expected Hoover to welcome him with open arms. *Fidelity, Bravery, and Integrity*, he had spouted the FBI motto as if he were an honorary agent. She looked at the photo of George in baggy prison fatigues recalling how he had insisted on wearing a new suit that would make just the right impression. He had been stripped of everything. There was no mention that he had turned himself in and all he had risked was reduced to three words: CAPTURED NAZI SPY.

"George," Rose growled, "This is Peter's colleague?" She opened the paper, revealing the same sorry photograph of Peter that had appeared in the *New York Times*. "Did you know?"

Grete pulled her further inside, locking the door behind them. She took the paper, her eyes perusing the page . . . *Despite their training, the two gangs of four men each fell afoul of special agents of the Federal Bureau of Investigation almost immediately . . . before the men could begin to carry out their orders the FBI was on their trail and the roundup began. One after another they fell into the special agents' net.*

Rose stormed into the living room, plopping down on Uncle Jacques's favorite chair, which she seemed to fill despite her diminutive size. "Grete, what is going on?" Grete eyed the door, grateful that Jacques was not home to witness the scene. "Grete!" Rose snapped.

Grete looked back at the article, growing increasingly outraged at the distortion of truth. If not for George and Peter, the authorities would never have known the saboteurs existed. "It's not true."

"They have the wrong man." Rose's shoulders relaxed as she sat back and exhaled. "It's a case of mistaken identity." She sounded as if she were referring to some slapstick Charlie Chaplin movie.

More than anything, Grete wished she could tell Rose she was right and that the FBI had confused Peter with someone else. She considered lying, but if the papers showed Peter's photo today it might very well show hers tomorrow. Sweat gathered on her brow.

"No." She sighed. "It's Peter, but . . ." She reached for the *Times* and opened it to a tiny paragraph buried inside. "Did you see this? It says the men were drafted against their will. Peter didn't volunteer and he never intended to go through with it. Planning something is different than doing it." She repeated Peter's skewed explanation, "Say you planned to push someone in front of a train—"

Rose stumbled to her feet. "Have you lost your mind?"

"Sit." Grete practically shoved her back into the chair. She had had no desire to unburden herself, but now that Rose was here, she wanted to explain, if only to justify her own actions.

"Is Peter a Nazi spy or not?" Rose demanded.

"Shush," Grete pleaded. "My uncle will be back soon." Rose bit her lip, looking furious and Grete swallowed and began again. "Try to understand, Peter didn't sign up for this. He had to go along with it to protect his family. What would you do? What would any of us do?" When Rose remained quiet she went on. "Peter spent seventeen months in a Gestapo prison. He endured it all, except he couldn't take it any longer when the Gestapo started to threaten his family." She decided it was best not to muddy the waters by mentioning Peter's wife. "He was forced to come here to save his family." Void of details, the explanation did not sound particularly convincing. After all, it had taken several tries for Peter to persuade her. "Don't you see? Peter didn't do anything."

"He came here!"

"We all came here to escape the Nazis."

"He came in the middle of the night on a U-boat, carrying explosives. And," Rose gasped, "he came to dinner at my home!" she shouted as if that were the ultimate atrocity. "I had to destroy every newspaper in the Bronx so my parents wouldn't get wind of this." She sat back in Jacques's chair, folded her arms, and waited. "How could you?"

"The story in the paper is . . . misleading," Grete said, tripping over her words.

Rose's eyes grew wide. "Is Peter a double-agent?" The color drained from her face. "Are you?"

"No," Grete said, "Of course not." She considered telling Rose about Agent Lanman and his offer to help her parents, but was superstitious about expressing her secret hopes out loud. "The paper doesn't have the story straight," she said instead, pointing to a particularly egregious paragraph. "Look. This says the group leader was arrested in New York, which is wrong. George wasn't arrested, he turned himself in. And it wasn't in New York, it was in Washington."

If possible, Rose looked even more alarmed. "How do you know that?"

"Because I was there when Peter and George called the FBI."

"You met the leader of a Nazi spy ring?"

"You're missing the point."

"Why would the paper report something that isn't true?"

"The FBI must have got to them," Grete said, aware of how paranoid she sounded.

"So the FBI's lying?" Rose's brow knitted together. She clearly did not believe a word Grete was saying, but was willing to humor her a bit longer.

"Peter and George alerted the FBI because they were trying to stop the others. They were trying to prevent a disaster here in the United States."

"So why doesn't it say that?"

"I don't know," Grete admitted, crestfallen. She looked down at the paper, hoping it might offer an answer. *Every American must be proud of the brilliant work the FBI did in rounding up these Nazi agents before they could explode so much as a fountainpen . . .* "I suppose the FBI wants credit for capturing them." The explanation gained plausibility as it left her lips. "If the FBI admits Peter and George turned themselves in, it would make them seem less competent and if it looks like the operation might have worked, Germany might send another group."

Rose twisted her mouth, scrutinizing Grete's face as if she had never fully seen her before. "How'd you get mixed up in all this?"

Of all the questions Rose had posed, this one was the most difficult to answer. "Look, you met Peter. I'm sure once he explains . . ." She was hit by the absurdity of her words. Rose would never see Peter again. In all likelihood, she would never see Peter again. Another wave roiled inside her and she rushed to the bathroom, fell to her knees, and heaved into the toilet until she was wrung out and empty. When she picked her head up, Rose was standing in the doorway.

"Here," Rose said, passing her a towel.

Grete took her time swilling her mouth out and splashing cold water on her face. When she came out of the bathroom she found Rose seated at the end of her bed. She flopped down beside her and, while Rose was unable to offer any consoling words, she scooted closer and patted Grete's knee over and over again.

EACH DAY BROUGHT NEW SCATHING REPORTS. Peter and the others were labeled *Dynamiters and Vermin*. Their capture was portrayed as a massive achievement by Hoover's G-men, who were in the process of hunting down co-conspirators, referred to as *spy aids*. Grete barricaded herself in the apartment on alert for footfall or sirens. One minute she was convinced she had done nothing wrong, the next she questioned every moment she and Peter had spent together. Who was she to have singlehandedly determined Peter's innocence? Why had she inserted herself in his troubles? Was she a *spy aid*?

Her soft spot for Walter Winchell turned to stone as she tuned into his weekly radio broadcast. "The apprehension of the spies by the G-men, based on the slightest of tips, will take your breath away," Winchell pronounced with authority. His rapid-fire delivery lingered on one tiny word: *tips*. When she had first read his column about the Florida saboteurs, Grete had wondered at the source. Now she had little doubt Winchell was being spoon-fed information by Hoover himself. Small wonder George idolized Hoover. He too was a blowhard, one who had mastered the art of trumpeting his own horn.

Rumors abounded. One disturbing report cited a motorist in Bridgehampton, a town a few miles west of Amagansett, claiming that a man who fit the FBI description of Lieutenant Kappe flagged down his car and asked for a ride to the train station. The authorities converged on the sleepy village and a nine-state alarm was raised. Another story quoted two women who said they had met a man matching Kappe's description in a Bronx park. A nationwide search was launched. Grete didn't know what Kappe looked like, yet she saw him everywhere.

Days passed. There was no word from Agent Lanman and Grete lost hope that he had ever intended to help her parents. She retreated to her bedroom and hid under the covers, fending off Jacques's insistence on summoning a doctor by referencing vague "female" problems. She was lying in bed one afternoon when there was a thud on her door. Vagabond's tail twitched.

"Grete!"

It took her several seconds to recognize her uncle's voice, and a moment longer to understand why it sounded so strange. She had never heard him shout before. What's more, Uncle Jacques had used her proper name, not her fairytale nickname. Alert with fear, she tossed back the blanket and went to the door. Vagabond fled as her uncle burst into the room, brandishing a letter.

Oh no.

Jacques fanned the page in front of her face, creating a windstorm. The stationery was pale blue, tissue thin, and battered along the edges. Grete's heart skipped.

"It's from your parents!" he cried. "They're alive!" Jacques's words drowned out all the other nonsense in her head. "Your mother and father are safe!" He hugged her, rocking back and forth, and dancing a little jig. "It's a miracle!" She had never seen him so lighthearted and only now realized how weighed down he had been all these years.

"What does it say? How are they? Where are they?" Her questions tumbled out faster than her thoughts.

"Portugal." Uncle Jacques clutched the paper to his heart. "They're in a resort town near Lisbon. No one is on holiday because of the war and the hotels are filled with refugees, trying to escape."

Grete snatched the letter, reading feverishly. Her parents were alive! First and foremost the letter confirmed that. It was written by her father in carefully scripted English. Though his penmanship looked different without the umlauts and ligatures of his German, the sight of his signature made her heart swell. Nothing was blacked out or censored, but it may as well have been. Papa neglected to say when or how they had left Camp de Gurs, nor did he say how they had reached Portugal. He and Mama were in good health. They had submitted birth certificates, which they had been savvy enough to pack and keep all this time, and were awaiting visas. Grete searched for a date, but that part of the letter was smeared and she could only speculate. Had Lanman kept his word? Were her parents safe because of him? It was impossible to say and Grete was not sure it mattered so long as they were alive. She sank onto the bed. Tears streamed down her cheeks and she wiped them away and burst into laughter as if every emotion she had been suppressing was suddenly set free.

"I'm going to the State Department office now," Jacques said, holding his hand out for the letter.

She looked up, only then noticing he was wearing his best suit. His attaché case was in his hand. No doubt it was stuffed with every last bit of tax information and documentation to support her parents' cause.

"I'll go with you," she said.

"No. This won't be easy," he said carefully. "The German quota is full. Getting a visa is tricky even with a sponsor. I don't know how long it will take, but I promise I'll get them out." He patted his heart—or perhaps it was his wallet. She sensed he seemed to want to spare her the callous notion of graft.

If only he knew what she had done.

ON THE FOURTH OF JULY, a date surely chosen for maximum effect, the government released a list of charges against Peter and the other men. All eight were labeled *Agents of the German Reich and Enemies of the United States.* They were accused of sabotage, espionage, and conspiracy to commit those acts. According to the newspaper, a death sentence could be imposed under any one of those charges. The men were being held at FBI headquarters in New York until the government decided on a place and time for their trial. Grete's mood swung from disbelief to despair. There was no mention that

George had ever gone to Washington to confess, there was nothing about Peter giving himself up—and now both were locked inside a New York prison.

That afternoon, Grete found herself climbing the subway stairs into the towering, gray world of lower Manhattan. Narrow streets meandered like rivers surrounded by tall buildings that blocked sun and sky. A rank harbor breeze tunneled through unfamiliar thoroughfares as she walked east toward the city's municipal buildings. There were no children here, only grim-faced office workers in dull suits. In Foley Square, she discovered not a public park so much as a teardrop-shaped clearing of concrete pathways and trampled greenery. A soft drizzle began to fall and people ducked under umbrellas. Buildings bordered the park like headstones. Grete did not know which tomb housed FBI headquarters.

She came back the next day. There was sunshine instead of clouds, but the buildings looked just as drab. Newsboys stood two to a block, shouting harrowing headlines, "Nazi Saboteurs Face Stern Army Justice!" "The Eight Nazi Saboteurs Should Be Put to Death!" She made her way to a cluster of onlookers gathered at the base of the stairs to an imposing Federal building. UNITED STATES COURTHOUSE was etched into the granite frieze supported by massive Corinthian columns. Squinting into the sunlight, Grete could see a modern-day skyscraper sprouting incongruously from the building's core.

The woman beside her was looking up as well. "Why'd they put them here? Why not the Tombs?" she asked the man next to her.

Grete turned her head to listen. These buildings were tombs, she was not the only one who thought so. She waited for the man to say something about Peter, even though she knew it would only be about what a traitor he was.

"FBI headquarters are on the thirteenth floor. The Tombs might be a notorious prison, but these rats are safer here. If the Nazis get hold of them, there's no telling what they'll do."

"Nazis killing Nazis?"

The man nodded knowingly. "So they can't squeal."

A half dozen motorcycles rumbled up the street followed by two armored police wagons and more motorcycles. The procession pulled to the curb and the mob closed in. Eight soldiers wearing helmets and wielding machine guns stepped out of the paddy wagons. More emerged from the building.

Someone pushed past Grete. "They're bringing them out now!"

"Where are they taking them?" the woman beside her asked.

"To Washington and, from there, the gallows," said the man who seemed to believe he had all the answers.

"They got to have a trial first. That's the American way. If they don't, it makes us as bad as the Krauts and Japs."

"So give them their day in court. Sign me up for the firing squad when it's over."

The prisoners were herded onto the sidewalk and toward the waiting vans. Grete edged closer and caught sight of Dick, a defiant sneer plastered on his face. Henry trudged on his heels looking stunned and confused. The others followed. They did not look like Nazi masterminds, just ordinary men in wrinkled suits and handcuffs that were pinching their wrists. The Florida group was there too. Grete recognized a scruffy boy as Peter's friend Herbie. Peter had said he was twenty-one, but he looked younger, anxiously chewing gum. George came after Herbie, dragging his feet and muttering as a soldier prodded him with the butt of a rifle.

"George," a man with rolled up shirtsleeves, holding a pad and pencil, called out. "Did you sing for Hoover?" George flinched as a camera flash exploded.

Peter was last. Shoulder to shoulder with strangers in the hot sun, Grete's thoughts returned to the day when she and Peter first met. Their time together was as brief as a dream. One that was quickly fading in the light of day. She pushed forward. She did not dare whisper in German, but she found herself mouthing the word *Ruhig*. Peter glanced up for an instant before his eyes lowered with the air of a man resigned to his fate. The guards placed him in the wagon, slammed the doors, and the motorcade zoomed away.

CHAPTER 20

GRETE HAD ALWAYS ADMIRED ROOSEVELT, who surrounded himself with informed advisors, and whose wife Eleanor was unexpectedly open-minded given her privileged pedigree. Not surprisingly, Roosevelt's magnanimity did not extend to German spies. A hardline was to be expected. Still, Grete was struck dumb when he ordered Peter's case to be turned over to the War Department—because of the men's clothing.

She read countless news articles, repeating names and memorizing protocol as if it would allow her to make sense of it all. When they came ashore, Peter and the others were wearing military uniforms, which would make them soldiers to be treated as prisoners of war. They were wearing regular suits when they were arrested, which could make them civilians to be tried in civil court or spies who deserved fewer rights than prisoners of war. Conspiracy to commit sabotage carried a two-year sentence which the New York Times deemed, rather unprofessionally Grete thought, as "ridiculous." Shooting was the penalty for soldiers; hanging for spies.

Roosevelt, evoking wartime powers, ordered a military tribunal. The sinister name made Grete sick with fear. According to the paper, military tribunals were known for swifter justice and harsher penalties. There would be no jury and a seven member military commission would serve in place of a judge. Most disturbingly, tribunals were held in secret. Grete pulled out an old history textbook trying to decipher terms and discovered that the only civilians to be tried by a military commission had been the seven men and one woman who were charged with conspiring with John Wilkes Booth to assassinate Lincoln. All got the hangman's noose.

A day later, she learned that the Justice Department would also play a role in the trial. Attorney General Francis Biddle would serve as prosecutor. Grete remembered seeing Biddle's name in the article about Japanese internment camps and again in George's ten-cent notebook. George had listed him as an aide; not an adversary. *Another glitch*, as Peter would say. The faith Grete had had in American justice was quickly fading. Two Army colonels, one who had worked in legal affairs for less than a month and a regular officer with little trial experience, were appointed to defend Peter and the other six men. George would be represented by a different Army colonel. She understood why George should receive separate council, but could not explain why Peter was being lumped in with Dick, Henry, and the other "Hitler agents."

THE MILITARY TRIBUNAL BEGAN WEDNESDAY, JULY 8th in, what the paper described as "grim secrecy." Just as the men had not been held in a proper prison, the trial would not be conducted in an official courtroom. Instead, the proceedings took place in an FBI assembly room on the fifth floor of the Department of Justice.

Very little was revealed to the public. Only Army photographers were allowed to take pictures. The few released were incriminating. One showed an FBI agent demonstrating how to set off an incendiary pencil. "This type," a caption in *PM Daily* explained, "can be started by tapping the apparently harmless eraser."

Grete scrutinized each photo. Except for the black crepe covering the windows, the tribunal room looked more like a classroom than a court of law. The seven member military commission presided from a long table on a raised dais at the front of the room. Before them were card tables stacked with evidence: the Nazi uniforms the men had worn ashore, shovels used to bury the crates, fuse pencils, and dynamite. An American flag hung over the dais. To Grete, the makeshift courtroom looked as staged as the patriotic scenes in *Yankee Doodle Dandy*.

The eight defendants sat in chairs lined up along the wall. They may as well have been awaiting the firing squad. In one photograph, George leaned forward, copiously taking notes on a pad balanced on his knee. Next to him was a member of the Florida group, his hands clasped in desperate prayer. Henry sat partially hidden by a pillar. Peter was not pictured. Rumor had it that J. Edgar Hoover attended every session, but he too did not appear in a single shot.

The hearings lasted eighteen days. Grete followed every word. As the trial proceeded, statements were released less and less often and the story moved from front-page news to the papers' inner folds. She could glean little more than what was revealed in the sparse coverage. Peter and the others plead not guilty, calling themselves refugees, not invaders. They said that they had made their submarine trip solely to escape Nazi prosecution and argued they were not spies because they had never sought military information. Their only defense was their written confessions, made after their arrests. George's was two hundred and fifty-four pages and took two days to read in court. Henry's was nine.

Attorney General Biddle dismissed the confessions as the self-serving ramblings of admitted Nazis who had been caught red-handed, exactly as Lanman had planned. The young Coast Guardsman who had stumbled upon the men that first night on the beach became a star witness. His name was actually John Cullen, and he had given a false name to George. Photos showed a tall, grinning boy next door in a Navy uniform, slouched in a chair with his legs sprawled confidently apart. In court, Cullen quickly identified George as the man he had encountered on the beach.

"The spies were not clever," Cullen was quoted as saying. "Otherwise I wouldn't be here."

Grete had questioned George's wits many times, but it was disturbing to hear him disparaged by a twenty-one-year-old who might not have survived were it not for George. In myriad articles touting his bravery, Cullen recounted a harrowing scene of a foggy night, salt air mingling with the smell of diesel fuel, and German-speaking strangers. The account was both remarkably similar to the one Peter had told and entirely different. After accepting George's bribe, Cullen said he ran to the Coast Guard Station to alert his superiors.

"I don't think they followed me," he said. "I ran too fast for that."

The FBI agents who had interviewed the men after their arrests also served as prosecution witnesses. Each stressed the pivotal role the FBI had played, tracking down and arresting the saboteurs. George's counsel interrupted, pointing out that George had called the FBI in New York a day after landing, and it was the FBI's failure that the call had not been pursued. According to him, everything George did was consistent with a premeditated plan to expose the operation. A plan that began long before the men landed in Amagansett. No one mentioned that Peter had been with George when the call was made nor was there any reference to George's black book or the evidence Peter had hidden on the beach.

In closing, Attorney General Biddle said that the only reason the saboteurs had been unsuccessful was because they had been captured before they could begin, which Grete knew was a lie. She suspected Biddle knew it too.

In his closing argument, the defense counsel seemed to have accepted that the saboteurs would be found guilty and focused solely on avoiding the death penalty. He singled out each man, describing them in terms meant to soften their character. Henry never grasped what he was doing or what he was supposed to do. Dick had a wife and twenty-month-old daughter in Germany whom he was trying to protect. Peter's friend Herbie was nothing more than a romantic kid from Chicago who ran away to Mexico because of difficulty with a girl and was roped in by a German agent. Peter was last. The defense counsel called him a victim of Nazi cruelty, who escaped Germany to save his life and spare his wife further harm. Peter's predicament, the defense argued, was impossible: He was considered a traitor both in Germany and the United States, and could be sentenced to death in either country.

AT HOME, AWAITING PETER'S FATE, Grete turned to George's note-book. She paged through start to finish, searching for some hidden meaning or sign: a covert communiqué that would tell her what to do—wishful thinking. Peter's intentions had never been straightforward. She ran her hand over the front and back covers and debated holding the book over ammonia, but knew the exercise would be futile. Realization hit. Peter was truly gone. Worse, he had sacrificed himself to save her. The permanence of her loss left her hollow. She had no one to rely on but herself. Grete picked up George's book, found the page with Hannelore's address, and tore it to shreds. Then, before she could second-guess herself, she emptied the petty cash drawer, stuffed the money and George's notebook in her purse, and left the apartment.

The New York Express to Washington was long and hot. She had no idea how she would explain the missing money or her absence to Uncle Jacques and consoled herself with the knowledge that this would be her final lie. The train sped under the Hudson River, through Jersey swampland, and across the Delaware, stopping at Philadelphia, Wilmington, and Baltimore. Unfamiliar names that made Grete feel increasingly alone. As the hours passed, she had too much time to think. The last time she had ridden on a train she had been with Peter. His absence stung. She reached into her purse, worrying the corners of George's notebook, praying she was not too late.

THE DISTRICT OF COLUMBIA JAIL was a hulking stone fortress with five massive chimneys and long windows with fat iron bars. A gravel drive led to the main entrance. A chain-link fence framed the prison yard, topped with rolls of barbed wire. Dozens of federal troops armed with machine guns were posted around the yard. More flanked the gate, still more guarded the entrance. Grete stopped dead in her tracks. She had bottled up her sadness and dread about her parents for so long she had become good at disguising her emotions. Still, with her parents, she had never lost hope. This was different. The prison was terrifying. She had made it to Washington's Union Station and the District Jail in a trance. Now her momentum stalled. Any romantic illusions she had harbored at her and Peter's clandestine affair were gone, replaced by helmeted soldiers, guns, and a bloodthirsty mob. The crowd's angry shouts turned to cries of approval as a car arrived with a pair of American flags jutting out over its headlights. The gate was opened and gravel churned as the car rolled to the main entrance, depositing a man in a priest's robe and another wearing a chaplain's collar. The clerics were accompanied by a third man who someone identified as the coroner. To Grete, the sight was strangely comforting. She had made it in time.

Taking advantage of the commotion, she summoned her courage and approached the open gate. Scattered among the guards were men in dark suits, whom she now understood to be G-men. She scanned the crowd, searching for trouble, frightened to tempt fate. She looked over her shoulder before inching forward and reaching into her purse. Her trembling fingers locked on George's flimsy notebook.

"Here," she said, pressing the book into an agent's hand. "This must go to Special Agent Lanman. It's urgent."

Lanman's name was enough to catch the G-man's attention. His eyes widened and he started to question her, but there was another disturbance as two Army ambulances entered the yard, and she was able to slip back into the crowd. The ambulances stopped in front of the main entrance. Grete's breath grew shallow as medics unloaded eight stretchers.

A steady rain began to fall. Grete remained, cold and shivering. Tears smarted her eyes and she used the heel of her hand to staunch them. Puddles formed in the gravel. A group of women huddled under a single umbrella. Reporters with press cards tucked into their hatbands stood vigil under a scrawny tree.

Shortly before five p.m., all the lights on the first floor of the jail were extinguished. People clasped hands and prayed. Others waved righteous fists. Reporters ran.

Grete's knees started to give way and she clutched the arm of the man beside her. "Where are they going?"

"To find phone booths and file stories."

"Why?" She eyed the dark windows. "What's happening?"

"Old Sparky."

"What?"

"The electric chair."

She let out a cry before remembering to cover her mouth and hide her emotions. She had imagined firing squads and gallows so many times she had almost reconciled herself to the horror. She had never considered this gruesome turn.

The prison lights flickered on and off. Grete grew woozy as the man beside her explained how each prisoner would be shaved bald for the electrodes then bound securely to the chair with straps around his waist, arms, and legs. Her knees quaked. She lost her footing and thought she might faint as he described the final indignity, a rubber mask each prisoner would be made to wear with slots for the nose and mouth. Blind with grief, Grete stumbled away.

The lights dimmed. She could not bear to think of Peter, so she thought of his friend Herbie instead. She imagined the hapless twenty-one-year-old, terrified and pale. She saw his body convulse as voltage ran through him and she imagined the other men shudder as they awaited their turn. She saw Henry bewildered, Dick furious, George disappointed and betrayed. The only person she could not make out was Peter.

The lights flickered on and off, on and off so many times Grete lost count. An unnatural cloud wafted over the prison along with a stench she was sure was burning flesh. Her tears dried as shock replaced horror. The jailhouse lights snapped on—and stayed lit.

She could not say how much time passed before someone upfront shouted, "Stretchers coming out." She raised her eyes. The soldiers formed two lines from the entrance to the waiting ambulances. Stillness fell over the crowd as the bodies were carried out one by one. Each corpse shrouded with a white sheet. Terrified she would recognize the shape of Peter's head or his broad shoulders, she could not bring herself to look away. Grete counted six stretchers before the cortege came to an abrupt halt. The ambulances rumbled to life. The crowd surged forward. She allowed the tide to carry her. Grete clutched the wire fence as the ambulances sped out of the yard. A siren keened through the city.

The crowd began to disperse. Grete leaned on the fence to stay upright. Too frightened to approach a guard, she turned to a reporter.

"Six?" she demanded, her voice shaky and shrill. Shock gave way to hope. She touched the empty place in her purse where George's notebook had been and her breathing began to slow.

The reporter understood her vague question. "At the very last moment, Roosevelt commuted two sentences. The ringleader George Dasch got thirty years and another guy . . ." He looked down at his pad and flipped a page. Grete wanted to wrest it away. "Peter Burger got life."

AUTHOR'S AFTERWORD:

When I wrote my first book, *City of Liars and Thieves*, I was a bit spooked to discover that the two-hundred-year-old murder that so fascinated me occurred steps away from where I once lived. On my way to work, run errands, or meet friends, I had unknowingly tread over a grave. The coincidences accumulated as my research continued, and I had the creeping sense that my discovery was not entirely chance. Was the victim reaching out, imploring me to share her story? For my second novel, I was determined to unearth another story that conjured that same eerie curiosity. I wasn't prepared to find more ghosts on my doorstep.

I began my search at Grand Central Terminal. Simply put, the station is beautiful. I have always been drawn to the celestial mural and New York's most romantic clock. Nearly a million people pass through Grand Central's doors each day. One can walk down the majestic staircase or across the Great Hall and traverse countless unknown tales. The first peculiarity to spark my interest was the existence of an abandoned railroad spur, Track 61, which was used to transport distinguished guests. Most notably, FDR used Track 61 when he came to New York, after which he took a private elevator (large enough to accommodate his Pierce-Arrow limousine) up to the Waldorf Astoria. This allowed him to remain safe during wartime and hide his disability from the public. In my mind, Track 61 became synonymous with the hidden secrets.

Grand Central also houses a secret subbasement known as

M-42. Located ten stories underground, it is the deepest basement in the city. M-42 does not appear on a single map or blueprint and its existence was only publicly acknowledged in the 1980s. Transformers that convert alternating current to direct current and power trains up and down the East Coast are stored there. Rumor has it that in 1942, M-42 was the target of Nazi saboteurs seeking to cripple troop transports and supplies. At the time, the transformers were more primitive rotary convertors and all it took to destroy them would have been a bucket—or bag—of sand. The claim has never been substantiated, but it was enough to inspire me. I had set out to write about Grand Central, but the reference to the Nazi saboteurs who landed on Long Island stirred a familiar haunting chill. The story I wanted to tell began to take shape.

I HAD SPENT EVERY SUMMER OF MY LIFE on the shores of Amagansett on Long Island's East End and thought I knew all about Operation Pastorius and the Nazi saboteurs who disembarked a U-boat carrying crates of explosives in the summer of 1942. As I started reading more about the landing, I began to understand that the beach where the saboteurs first stepped onto American shores was virtually in front of the house where I grew up. I had walked the strip from Napeague to the Coast Guard Station at Atlantic Beach hundreds of times and had little doubt I was treading the very same ground.

The saboteur story had always been presented to me as a comedy of sorts: bumbling spies arrived on U.S. shores and were quickly apprehended. There is a movie I watched as a child called, *The Russians are Coming, the Russians are Coming,* about a Soviet submarine stranded off the shore of Massachusetts which I always associated with the Nazi saboteurs landing in my hometown. I rewatched it recently and understood why I equated the two. The opening scene shows a periscope piercing gray waters. The New England fishing town is picturesque, and the movie, staring Alan Arkin and Carl Reiner, is belly-laugh funny.

As I began my research into the Nazi saboteur landing, the comic element was prevalent, too. The Coast Guardsman who stumbled on the men that fateful June night had described them as "not clever," which fed into that myth. A 2002 article in *The Atlantic,* "The Keystone Kommandos," depicts the four men who landed in Amagansett as buffoons and the mission as a spectacular failure. An editor's note in Louis Fisher's *Nazi Saboteurs on Trial* describes the men as an assortment of "die hard Nazis and longtime losers." An article in the German news magazine *Der Spiegel* called "The preparation bungling, the execution clownish." As recently as 2011 one news report stated that the saboteur plot was "blown by drunken blabbing (and) idiocy." The East Hampton Historical Society performs an annual reenactment of the saboteur landing that draws and amuses crowds. There is no denying that Operation Pastorius was a debacle but, unlike the movie about the Russian spies, there was no Hollywood ending. Six men died in the electric chair and two others had their lives destroyed. The story struck me as more tragic than comic.

I am not the only one to have been moved by the bizarre tale. An internet search led me to the 2,967 page trial transcript from the Nazi Saboteur Military Commission (edited by Joel Samaha, Sam Root, and Paul Sexton of the University of Minnesota). The military tribunal testimony had been declassified in the '60s and many historians have explored the subject. In researching my novel, I was privileged to read some of their work. Two were particularly helpful: *They Came to Kill: The Story of Eight Nazi Saboteurs* in America by Eugene Rachlis (1961) and *Saboteurs: The Nazi Raid on America* by Michael Dobbs (2004). Interestingly, but not surprisingly, George Dasch penned a rambling memoir, *Operation Pastorius: Eight Nazi Spies against America (1959).* Written in English, the memoir follows the same general premise as the two-hundred-and- fifty-four page confession Dasch submitted to the FBI. While biased, it contributed to my understanding. Dasch's vacillating moods, his use of slang, and passion for pinochle made him a rich character. I adopted his account of how he first fell in love with America and arrived in this country as a stowaway. To me, it epitomizes both his optimism and desperation, as well as his long-windedness. All these works proved invaluable to my understanding of the historical facts, but I wanted to delve deeper into the human side of the story.

The leap was not hard to make. I shared the Amagansett beach house with my sister, my parents, several dogs, and my maternal grandparents, German Jews who had escaped Europe during the Second World War. As a child, I was haunted by the notion of Nazi invaders infiltrating our home. As an adult, the irony that my Grandmother Grete watched my sister and me build sandcastles on the same stretch of sand where Nazis had once landed struck me as significant and I set about weaving the stories together.

The dates, while not a perfect match, were close. My Omi (German for grandmother) arrived in New York in 1933 when she was thirteen. She traveled here with her twin brother, Hansel (yes, my great-grandmother named her twins Hansel and Gretel). The twins lived with their bachelor uncle, Jacques, on the Upper West Side until their parents arrived in 1936. I am writing this on June 28th, 2021 and Omi died peacefully in her sleep last night at the ripe age of one-hundred-and-one. I feel honored to be able to include memories from my grandmother's life that make the story so much more meaningful. Born in Mannheim, Germany, her father owned an asbestos factory and she had a beloved dog named Stromer, whose tragic death was one I had heard about since childhood. Growing up, the story of a young girl sacrificing her beloved pet resonated with me. It was difficult to grasp the horrors of Kristallnacht and countless other wartime atrocities, yet I could relate to the personal anecdotes of a young girl. My Omi, who was a champion swimmer, often teared up as she recounted the day strangers overtook her swim club on the Rhine and threw her into the swirling waters. Another story that humanized the horror of her youth was that of the boy next door with polio who took his own life so that his parents could escape Germany.

Reflections from Jewish Survivors of Mannheim, a collection of memoirs by Jewish survivors of Nazi persecution in Mannheim, edited by Robert B. Kahn also provided firsthand accounts of the daily indignities suffered by Jews. I found the story of a father who suffered a heart attack at the visa office in Stuttgart particularly poignant and borrowed it to add authenticity to Grete's experience. While plotting Grete's story, I found myself repeatedly turning to Anne Frank's Diary. Anne's story is vastly different from my grandmother's and far more tragic. But it gave me insight into the thoughts a young woman might have amid the tragedy of war. In spite of everything, Anne experienced romance. And she relished nature, "I've found that there is always some beauty left in nature, in sunshine, in freedom, in yourself; these can all help you. Look at these things, then you find yourself again, and God as well, and then you regain your balance. And whoever is happy will make others happy too. He who has courage and faith will never perish in misery!"

THROUGH THE MAGIC OF HISTORICAL FICTION, I created a rendezvous for Grete to meet one of the Nazi saboteurs at New York City's war parade. The parade, the largest military parade in U.S. history, took place on June 13, 1942, the same day the saboteurs landed on Long Island. It seemed entirely plausible that a young Jewish refugee might encounter one of the saboteurs there and become entangled in his plight.

George Dasch, while intriguing, did not strike me as much of a romantic interest. Nor did the other two men who landed in Amagansett, Heinrich Heinck, a slow-witted alcoholic, and Richard Quirin, who toed the party line. Ernest Peter Burger was more of an enigma. Born in 1906 in Bavaria, Burger was an early member of the Nazi Party (I made him slightly younger and better looking). Burger joined the Party in 1923 at the age of seventeen and participated in the Beer Hall Putsch, which sent Hitler to prison. In 1927, he immigrated to the United States where he found work as a toolmaker in Wisconsin and, later, in Illinois. Burger was a member of the National Guard and, in 1933, became a U.S. citizen. That same year, he returned to Germany where he married and began work under Ernst Röhm. Röhm was a close friend and early ally of Hitler, but the pair had a falling out resulting in Röhm's murder. Hundreds of his men, known as Storm Troopers, were shot and killed during the purge. Burger managed to survive, but his background caused continual strife with the Gestapo. In 1940, he was arrested and held for seventeen months, first, in a Polish prison and, later, in a cellar of the Gestapo headquarters in Berlin. While he was in prison, his wife was harassed and suffered a miscarriage. In 1942, a year after being released, he was summoned to the sabotage school at Quenz Farm for "rehabilitation."

There is little denying that Peter was between a rock and a hard place. As the Defense Counsel stated during the trial, he could have been put to death as a traitor in Germany or the United States. We will probably never know what motivated him to establish ties with George Dasch and help convict his comrades, but hatred of the Gestapo was most certainly a motivating factor. While it is difficult to summon much sympathy for any member of the Nazi Party, I found myself believing there was more to Peter's story than meets the eye. He was a loyal German who despised what Hitler was doing to his homeland. Throughout the trial, he remained stoic, conducting himself with dignity. Whether his behavior was honorable or self-serving, he risked his life to benefit the U.S. and was rewarded with a prison sentence.

Several informative accounts such as *Nazi Saboteurs on Trial* by Louis Fisher (2005) and *Betrayal: The True Story of J. Edgar Hoover and the Nazi Saboteurs Captured during WWII* by David Alan Johnson (2007) conclude that the eighteen day saboteur trial was, at best, out of the ordinary, at worst, unconstitutional. More succinctly, the trial has been called a kangaroo court. There was legal precedent for the men to be tried by a military tribunal, but President Roosevelt overstepped by appointing members of the tribunal and serving as the final reviewing authority. In fact, the Defense Counsel had appealed to the Supreme Court, arguing the constitutionality of the closed military tribunal. The Court reconvened over summer recess to hold an unprecedented session. There, the defense cited the Articles of War, which stated that only espionage or assisting the enemy in an area of combat would warrant a military tribunal. Long Island and Florida, they argued, were not war zones and an encounter with an unarmed Coast Guard patrolman was not a military engagement. Attorney General Francis Biddle countered that the sinking of ships in the Atlantic and the landing of U-boats on U.S. shores had turned the East Coast into a war zone.

It took only a day for the Supreme Court to rule in favor of the prosecution. As Louis Fisher notes, the judiciary was largely shut out of the legal process. (The controversy raged anew in November 2001 when President George W. Bush, evoking wartime powers, issued an order authorizing a military commission to try those who aided the 9/11 terrorists.) Johnson takes Fisher's objections a step further, describing the trial as a travesty of justice spearheaded by J. Edgar Hoover for his own glory. In *Operation Pastorius: Eight Nazi Spies against America*, George Dasch says he had several face-to-face meetings with Hoover. One took place in the privacy of his cell. According to George, Hoover commended him for doing a "splendid job" and urged him "not to worry" about the outcome of the upcoming trial. When George next encountered Hoover at the conclusion of the trail, Hoover refused to look him in the eye. "Mr. Hoover," George claims to have cried, "Aren't you really ashamed of yourself . . .?" As George remarked in his biography, "I don't like to refer to the procedure that we had been put through as a trial. It was not a fair trial; it was not my idea of an honest American trial."

GHOSTS HAUNT ME AS I WALK THE BEACH in front of the Amagansett Coast Guard Station. The ghosts of men in limbo. Their pleas resound in the booming surf. Were the saboteurs innocent or guilty? Richard Quirin was most likely a diehard Nazi. Others, like the slow-witted Heinrich Heinck and the American Herbert Haupt, were trapped. Herbie's final letter to his parents has been published in various accounts. Its simplicity highlights his youth, making his execution particularly tragic.

> Dear Mother and Father,
> Whatever happens to me, always remember that I love you more than anything in the world. May God protect you, my loved ones, until we see each other again, wherever that may be.
>
> Love, your son,
Herbie

On August 6, 1942, six men, including Richard Quirin, Heinrich Heinck, Herbert Haupt, and three others from the Florida group, were executed in the electric chair. The men were electrocuted in alphabetical order. Each execution took roughly ten minutes and thirty seconds. To this day, the morning of August 8, 1942 remains the largest mass execution of prisoners in the U.S. as well as the fastest. The dead were buried in a paupers' grave on the southernmost edge of the District of Columbia near a sewage disposal facility.

Evidence suggests that because George Dasch and Peter Burger tried to foil the plot and turn themselves in, Roosevelt reduced their punishment. George Dasch was sentenced to thirty years hard labor. Peter for life. Both were to serve their time in the Federal Prison at Danbury, Connecticut. The FBI had promised them a presidential pardon in return for their cooperation—then reneged on its promise.

In 1948, President Truman commuted both sentences on the condition that Peter and George be deported back to Germany. From his memoir, I learned that George reunited with his wife and opened a store, by coincidence, in Mannheim. George claimed to have led a peaceful existence until an article about the failed mission appeared in a German magazine. He became an outcast again, chased from town to town. He blamed Peter for the leak, but as with everything else, no one could pin Peter Burger down.

It was reported that he had moved to Spain, or maybe Bavaria. Burger died in 1975, Dasch in 1992.

The Amagansett Coast Guard Station has been beautifully restored and, after a brief period as a private home, now occupies the same site that it did when the saboteurs landed in 1942. The building has a broad shingle roof that flows down over a wide wraparound porch. There is a single dormer window on each roofline slope and a tall lookout tower. Inside, one can find fascinating artifacts including a diorama of the Nazi U-boat and a translated excerpt from the logbook of the U-boat Captain Hans-Heinz Linder. I walk by the Amagansett Coast Guard Station nearly every day and never fail to think about the doomed men abandoned on this stretch of beach. In many ways, this is where their lives ended. Crossing the sand, I have a sense of stepping into their footprints. A windblown plaque outside reads, . . .ON THE NIGHT OF JUNE 12-13, 1942, IT WAS FROM THIS STATION THAT COAST GUARDSMAN JOHN CULLEN, ON BEACH PATROL, ENCOUNTERED A GROUP OF FOUR NAZI SABOTEURS WHO HAD JUST LANDED FROM A GERMAN U-BOAT.

EVE KARLIN IS THE AUTHOR OF *CITY OF LIARS AND THIEVES* a historical novel about New York City's first murder trial. She lives in East Hampton, New York with her husband and triplets where she works as a bookseller.